DENIM, DIAMONDS
AND DEATH

OTHER BOUCHERCON ANTHOLOGY TITLES

Florida Happens (2018)
Passport to Murder (2017)
Blood on the Bayou (2016)
Murder Under the Oaks (2015)
Murder at the Beach (2014)

To Tim —
The best looking man
at Bouchercon!

DENIM, DIAMONDS AND DEATH
Bouchercon Anthology 2019

EDITED BY
RICK OLLERMAN

DOWN&OUT
BOOKS

Down & Out Books
3959 Van Dyke Road, Suite 265
Lutz, FL 33558
DownAndOutBooks.com

Cover design by JT Lindroos

ISBN: 1-64396-065-2
ISBN-13: 978-1-64396-065-4

To Bill Crider and the Crider family

CONTENTS

INTRODUCTION

Bouchercon is 50! Fifty years old. That's a long time for anything short of a redwood. When I went to my first couple, it was a common thing to be asked, "How many is this for you?"

At first this question threw my over-literate mind into confusion and I'd say something articulate like, "How many whats is my what?" No more sure way of expressing one's lateness to the party could be found. We all have to start somewhere.

Bouchercon is, of course, named after a pseudonym of William Anthony Parker White, whom I had known (as a reader) as both a science fiction as well as a mystery writer under the name "Anthony Boucher." I'd always pronounced it the way a romantic young mind ought to pronounce it, *boo-shay*, and it was only when I was embarrassingly older that I heard someone say that "Boucher" actually rhymed with "couch" with an "er" on the end of it.

Much less glamorous, sure, but still better than another of White's pseudonyms, "H. H. Holmes," which he'd borrowed from the late Chicago World's Fair serial killer/house of horrors master, Herman Mudgett (subject of Erik Larson's *The Devil in the White City*).

After a couple of years, the formerly omnipresent question of "How many" seemed to disappear, or else my fashion sense, closely mirrored to that of ordinary hotel decor, allowed me to blend in enough that I wasn't asked anymore. Better, I wasn't tempted to act like I was one of the cool kids walking around asking, "Hey there, is this your first Boo*shay*con?"

This year, this fiftieth anniversary party, is hosted in Dallas, in everything's-bigger-in-Texas style. The conference is honoring many, including the late Texas native and much-loved author Bill Crider, a many times over veteran of these celebrations of writing and reading. I'm happy to say that his daughter, Angela, has a story in these pages, continuing the Crider presence in just one of many ways.

There are also stories from writers across the country, fifteen in all, presented to you here as a memento of sorts of this wonderful anniversary. After all, what better way to celebrate the world of mystery fiction than reading a collection of…mystery fiction?

Enjoy it, please.

Robb has a story in The Best American Mystery Stories 2019 *and is a fine short story writer. Here's a nifty little tale of using your best talents for the wrong reasons. Really, hard work has to pay off in the end, doesn't it? We've always been told that...*

IF I LET YOU GET ME
Robb White

"Five concussions since Pop Warner," I said. "That's four more than enough for me."

Football's a collision sport. The concussions were no lie. Anybody who plays the game nowadays would be a fool not to worry about lesions forming in your brain when you hang up the cleats.

That wasn't going to be my problem. The concussions were real—but they weren't the reason I walked out of the Cowboys' training camp in Frisco. But they gave me an out so I didn't have to explain the real reason, which was not enough size or talent to be an NFL running back. People in Round Rock who remembered me from high school would ask me what happened at camp to make me quit so I'd tell them that. No matter what answer I gave anyone, it didn't really satisfy them or me. I'd been asked the same thing a dozen times a dozen different ways since I walked away from football.

This time it was Billy Stoneman. He caught me as I came around the corner with a pallet full of cereal boxes and stopped me in the middle of the aisle.

"You was a walk-on, right, Duane?"

3

"Yep," I said. "Nobody drafted me."

"Too bad you wasn't black, dude," Billy said. "They'd a snapped your ass up in no time."

Billy's the one who ought to be worried about CTE. He played outside linebacker in our 4-3 defense like a kamikaze pilot. Helmet first, every play.

"I doubt that," I said.

A mother pushing a toddler in a cart with a basket full of Sugar Pops and Bold paper towels gave us the fisheye when she saw she couldn't get around us as I'd blocked too much of the aisle. Oh, well. She snorted through her nostrils like an angry bull and did a three-corner turn with the cart so hard her kid almost flew out.

Billy laughed.

"Look, Billy," I said, "let's catch up some other time."

"All them records, Duane, and lookit you now—stockin' shelves in a big-box store."

Billy never missed a good chance to shut up.

"You, me and the Buzzman ought to do some bass fishing this weekend. I got me a cabin out to Paloma Lake."

"Sounds good."

"Gimme your digits. I'll give you a holler about this weekend."

"I moved back in with my folks," I said.

"Uh-huh." The long look reminded me just how far I'd fallen.

I'm tired of all of it, the questions, the looks. Being a hotshot running back for a Class 5A team in high school and making first team my sophomore year for Texas A&I got my head all swole up with big dreams of playing in the NFL in Jerry Jones' billion-dollar stadium in front of the cameras. But running for 215 yards against Cisco Community College added up to all the weight of a snowflake. The running back coaches knew it before I did. But they did reward me with a clap on the back and an "attaboy" on my way out of the locker room.

My parents made it worse by throwing a big party before I left for camp. A Cowboys scout saw my senior year films and said I could have a real shot at making the special teams squad. My teammates from high school came, uncles and aunts from Waco, New Braunfels, and a married sister from Houston. My father got weepy-eyed after too many whiskey shots and told me how proud he was of me.

Billy walked up the aisle to the checkout. He wore the same buzz cut from high school but now there were fat rolls on his thick neck. The mealy-mouthed assistant manager barked at me and jolted me out of my reverie.

"What?"

"Why y'all standing there like some retard, Briscoe? Get that product up."

"You know what? Fuck you and your product. Put them up yourself, shithead."

I shoved the pallet jack toward him, spilling cereal boxes to both sides. One pallet fork clipped his ankle and he howled, flying backwards, thrashing like a man falling out of an airplane. He took down a display of Castle Barbecue Sauce on his way to the floor. Broken bottles, BBQ sauce everywhere.

Without a word to anyone, I walked out with a dozen customers' shocked stares booting me in the backside.

My father had arranged for the job—"until you get back on your feet," he'd said. My mother complained to him about me moping around the house watching TV all day. Their disappointment was worse for me than feeling like a zoo animal in that damn store.

"He ain't gonna press charges on you," my father mumbled over dinner that night. My mother never looked at me; she stayed laser-focused on rounding up all the peas to one side of her plate. The phone rang just then to break the tension. My father had the balls to get up to answer.

"For you," he said.

Billy. *Damn.* He called about going fishing. I agreed just so I had a reason to get out of the house.

When Billy swung by in his tricked-out Silverado the next

day, he had someone else instead of Buzz Manske in the truck. As soon as I recognized him, I tried to keep my face from showing surprise.

Cody Ceepo was no friend of Billy's; in fact, Billy had given him a rough time in high school. Cody's surname didn't help matters: *See*-po turned into *Cree*-po faster than a six-legged jackrabbit. Even Billy's weightlifting pals grew weary of bullying Creepo, but Billy never let go. I remembered him shoving Cody up against his locker while Cody had been engaged in a serious conversation with a girl and daring him to do something about it. "You're all gurgle and no guts, Creepo," Billy sneered, spit flecking Cody's face. When I asked Billy what that had been about, all he ever said was, "I hate rich pricks."

I figured money had to have something to do with these two being together.

"Hey, Briscoe, how's it hangin'?"

"Cody."

"You mind riding bitch?"

I wondered if he took the line from *No Country for Old Men*. He put too much spin on the last word.

"Throw your tackle in the back," Billy said. "Let's go, boys. Them sweet-tastin' widemouth are beggin' me to reel 'em in."

Turns out they weren't biting but the mosquitoes were. By noon, the sun was a broiling, reflective mirror sheen off the lake. Billy's pasty-white skin was burning.

I had moved off to avoid talking to either one of them. Eventually Billy stopped chattering and took his fishing seriously as the afternoon wore on. I think he was upset at the fish for not falling for his bullshit. Cody sidled over to me, untangling a snarl in his line.

"Goddam cheap Walmart reel," he said approaching where I stood on a pile of granite boulders, casting my line.

"Nice throw," he said. "What are you using?"

"Jitterbug," I replied.

"Big 'Stoney' Stoneman, number fifty-five, inside linebacker for your Fighting Roos," Cody mimicked the Friday night game announcer. "Billy swears by crawlers and minnows. So far he's hooked a single catfish and two bluegill."

"Sometimes they don't bite no matter what you toss at them," I said. I still couldn't gauge the nature of Billy's friendship with a guy he used to push around so much in high school.

"Look at the big lunk," Cody exclaimed, nodding in Billy's direction. "Like a Neanderthal jumping around on the rocks, hooting and hollering at the fish. I told him that redneck skin of his would turn hot pink by two o'clock, and he says to me, 'I don't give two shits, I'm here to fish.'"

He imitated Billy's twang: *Gawd-damn, boy! It's so quiet I can hear an ant pissing on cotton.*

"You're probably wondering how come your old teammate and I are hanging out like this. Guy used to call me 'Creepo' all four years in school. You remember that. Scared the shit out of me."

"The thought crossed my mind," I said.

Cody made a noise as if the comment deserved a laugh but he wasn't willing to commit.

"Good thing I didn't get my mother's family name. Bumcrot. I can imagine the torture with Stoneman and his muscleheads running the halls like lions looking for a limp."

"That's our Billy—one compassionate connoisseur of humanity."

"I always thought you were smarter than those other jocks, Duane."

"You thought wrong," I said. "I'm exactly the same."

"Naw. I don't think so," Cody replied. "That's why I arranged this little soiree by the lake."

"Billy said this was his idea."

"Ideas are like seeds. You plant them, you see what comes of it."

I looked at him harder this time. The familiar snobbery that used to drive Billy up a wall was still there, only Ceepo's face appeared older even with his expression half hidden by the shades. I remembered the silver Jaguar Spyder he drove when most of us were lucky to get a clapped-out Ford 150 to drive to school. Cody's father owned medical clinics, prime real estate, strip malls up and down Interstate 35. After football season, bored, we would cruise the streets Friday nights with a case of beer in the back seat. I remembered driving past a yellow brick manor house on Sam Bass Road with massive Greek columns and a wraparound front porch. Somebody said, "That's where Ceepo lives. Got servants quarters and a *Got-damn* infinity pool."

Daddy's money could get Cody into U. T. but it couldn't keep him there.

Billy took the string down to shoreline, whipped out his filleting knife and gutted, rinsed and set the fillets over a barbecue pit. Cody watched from the dock and smoked cigarettes.

After we ate, the booze came out along with some weed provided by Cody. I surprised Billy by taking my turn.

"Thought you was Miss Goody-Goody about dope," Billy said.

"I look like I'm in training, Billy?" It came out harsher than I intended.

By midnight, Billy was passed out inside the cabin. Cots were set up in the spare room off the living quarters. I wasn't happy about spending the night here but the notion of going home wasn't any more appealing.

"Now that he's shitfaced," Cody said, offering me a hit off a fresh joint he finished rolling with a lick, "us gents can have a decent conversation."

"What's to discuss?"

"Oh, the great themes of life and art."

"Bullshit."

"Then how's about we discuss your future, Duane?"

"What about my future? Doesn't have anything to do with you."

"Do you want to live your own life or do you want to stay poor as a shithouse rat, sponging off your parents, wearing out your eyeballs gazing at those dusty ol' trophies on the bedroom shelf?"

"You're talking about yourself, I take it," I replied.

He sucked in another lungful of smoke.

"My allowance from my parents is, shall we say, less than adequate for what I really need?" The joint flared like a burst of fireflies whenever either of us inhaled. He blew twin streams of smoke from both nostrils. "But I have come up with other means of supporting myself."

"Yeah, I can see."

"Not this, man. Strictly fun, not business. Do I look like some lowlife with his pants down to the crack of his ass hanging around high schools selling to kids?"

"What are you saying?"

"I'm talking about real money, boy. The kind that lets you live free and clear of other people and their stupid demands."

"I've heard about that kind of money," I said. "It don't exist."

"Oh yes, indeed, my friend, it certainly does exist. It's called fuck-you money and I know right where to find it."

Maybe it was the weed, the high. Maybe it was too much sun and Jack Daniels around the fire pit. But I didn't shut down when I heard what I took to be his usual brand of B.S. I listened. The night stirred with insect life after the brutal heat of the day. An occasional splash of water from a fish lunging to the surface, a loon's shriek from the far end of the lake, a coyote clan's yipping chorus. Three in the morning by the glow of my wristwatch. Some prof at A&I liked to call this time "the Dark Night of Soul."

An owl hooted from the cottonwood trees. A nocturnal field mouse coming out of its burrow, searching for food, would never hear the baffled wings of its swoop razor talons spread for the strike. Nature's a contact sport, too; it just doesn't have our rules.

Billy was up when I staggered out of the cabin, my bladder

about to burst. I gazed at him in the dawn light. He really did have a Neanderthal look squatting over the fire pit, shoving kindling around to make a teepee for the fire.

"*Shee-yit*, look at you, Duane Briscoe. Where's that other princess and why'd you two go on whispering all damn night like a pair of giggly bitches?"

"We had a long, deep talk about your piss-poor fishing skills. Besides, with all your snoring and farting, it was you keeping us awake. There was enough gas release to call the oil companies."

"You be careful I don't come over there and break your jaw for you, boy. I'm one bad hombre when I don't get my beauty rest."

Bantering with Billy, exchanging obscene cracks, used to be fun. Now it felt stupid, childish. Things seemed to be pressing me into smaller spaces, and I didn't like the feeling. I thought of those tiny brown scorpions encased in glass sold to tourists at Bergstrom International.

"Goddamned heat building up already," Billy complained. "Coyotes come up to the fire last night. See the scat yonder?"

I said nothing. I had a lot on my mind from last night's conversation with Cody. I felt better after coffee and a hot meal. Billy wanted to keep fishing, but I got him to compromise: a dozen bass by noon or we pack it in.

Cody came as far as the doorway and said he was staying in the cabin. "It's too hot to fish."

That provoked a fat wink from Billy to me. As soon as Cody went back inside, he capered about, doing his "famous" imitation of an effeminate homosexual. I'd seen it a hundred times. Political correctness had made it to our school before we graduated but it hadn't managed to penetrate the thick carapace William Stoneman carried his brain around in.

When Billy dropped me off, I had Cody's phone number and an address in Cedar Park on a piece of paper. Why I didn't rip it up when I got back, I don't know. I was digging myself a hole and couldn't put the shovel down; the only way out, I thought, was to go deeper in.

"You didn't say anything to Billy Boy?"

"You made it clear enough, Ceepo," I said.

"Easy, easy. Just checking. This is serious business."

We were standing outside a three-story house overlooking hill country north of Austin. No furniture, which told me it was vacant property owned by Cody's father. A pair of red-tailed hawks soared close enough to display the natural camber of their outspread wings as they banked. Even at their height, any snakes or lizards on the ground would be clearly visible.

"You can bird-watch later, Briscoe," Cody said, tugging at my triceps. "Let's discuss it."

It. The plan. Stealing two million worth of uncut diamonds.

"Probably twice that. Brenda's dumb. All tits and no brains."

I remembered Brenda Sue Gelber. She was as popular with the boys as she was despised by the girls. Her bra size was the topic of more locker room discussion than some of Coach Hosean's plays. Brenda dropped out her junior year to get married.

"That girl can play the angles when it comes to exchanging the goods for the gold. Brenda's leading this old guy around by his cock, but she's smart enough to know he's not going to play Sugar Daddy forever."

"Billy called it 'the angle of the dangle.'"

"Heck, I never thought old Billy and me would ever have something in common."

By that time, Cody had me by the short and curlies.

"He used to be a chip engineer for Dell. He quit to start his own tech company," Cody told me. "His patents made him a fortune. The *Austin Business Journal* reported his IPO offering at launch was issued a double down, once in a generation alert by Motley Fool."

"So what?"

"So my old man knows the guy, see."

Brenda, Cody, and me—a three-way split. Cody's third was based on the sole fact he claimed to be "the mastermind." Brenda would get me inside the house. I was the designated thief.

"Tell me about this…'Treasury room.' Seems like the risk is all on me."

"That's what he calls it, no shit," Cody said. "The Treasury room. She got him stoned on some of that excellent Mexican cannabis you sampled. He showed off what he has squirreled away in there."

Ceepo drew up a map of the house and grounds and one of the L-shaped room off the man's bedroom where he kept the valuables. Everything but the cash was secured behind illuminated glass cases canted at forty-five degrees so the owner could stroll past and admire his wealth. Besides the uncut diamonds, he had Brazilian Paraiba tourmalines.

"Brenda reckons he has a secret camera set up behind a two-way mirror facing the bed, which he thinks she doesn't know about. His first wife said he was a sicko. Liked to tie her up and urinate on her, all kinds of crazy shit. The guy's a collector, Duane. He keeps nude portraits of his women in another room off the bedroom. Brenda says that one's his Trophy room."

"Forget the other stones," Cody said. "Focus on the diamonds."

"You said he has Krugerrands, gold and silver bars, and rare coins," I mentioned.

"Leave all that alone, too. It's the fastest way to point the cops right at us. Diamonds can be passed anywhere, the rest is too risky. Texas Rangers might not know where to look but the insurers have their own investigators and they do."

"Cut or not, diamonds are no good to me," I said. "I don't know anything about them."

"You know about cash money, right? My guy in Amsterdam is handling the stones for me."

"So my cut will be—"

"Everything you can grab from the little chest of drawers in the middle of that room."

"No thanks."

"Look, you have the best part of this deal, come down to it. I can't go hawking the stones on the street like some Arab in a souk. I need a fence. He has to get a cut. The stones have to be cut to be worth much. I'll be lucky to clear twenty-five cents on the dollar for the whole lot."

"What if Brenda's wrong about what's in the drawers?"

"She isn't, trust me. The guy was bragging one night because he got whiskey limp so he takes Brenda in there to dazzle her with his gems and cash. He opens all the drawers in this small mahogany cabinet in the middle of the room, and she says it's stuffed to the gills with banded wads of hundreds and fifties. A couple hundred thousand, he said to her...And one more thing, buddy."

"What?"

"Keep your mitts off the high denomination bills in the bottom drawer. You see some bearded guy's name and mug you remember from American history class, don't get greedy. Those notes have been out of circulation for decades. Some it ain't even legal to own."

"But you can trust Brenda? She's the first one he'll think of when he discovers the loot's gone."

"Brenda's cool. She's got more to lose than you or me. That little honey plans to keep milking that cow until her boobs drop. You worry about you."

Brenda Gelber was going to call Cody within minutes of leaving the house. Cody put her up to nagging the old guy to take her to Savor Dallas on the following Friday. Cody'd also gave her a special powder to sprinkle on the keypad so I'd be able to see the impressions of the golden shower tycoon's fingerprints under black light.

"What's in the stuff?"

"A recipe of my own—some cocoa powder, baby talcum,

ardrox, and a dash of your basic yellow forty."

"How am I to know the right alarm sequence? What if he doesn't—"

"He went top down, right to left, Brenda said. Relax, Duane. You got this."

That's just what all my friends had told me when I'd left for the Cowboys' training camp.

The Friday of the heist, Cody had everything worked out in fifteen minute increments. I laid low in my Jeep between clumps of honey mesquite trees on the edge of the property line behind the house. Anybody was to get suspicious, I'd jump out in my neon-yellow vest holding a can of spray paint.

"What do I do with this?"

"Hell, Duane, find a manhole cover and spray a symbol on it, anything, do a damn smiley face—just look busy if anybody comes by walking their dog. If you have to, fire up a weed trimmer. Just don't let anybody get a good look at your face."

Between six and six-fifteen, I headed straight to the back of the house for the servants' quarters. The cook and her handy-man husband were away at a wedding in San Antonio. The two Doberman pinschers were to be locked in their kennel. Brenda said he lets them roam at night, hunting for possum and armadillo.

"You tell her to make sure about those dogs. I don't want to be running for my life with a Doberman clamped onto my nut sac."

While the owner was in the shower upstairs, Brenda would step outside to the deck and light a cigarette—my signal to make a beeline for the cook's room where I'd hide in the closet until they were gone.

"Wait an hour in case he forgets his Rolex or something and turns around," Cody insisted.

Once I'd cleaned out the stones and cash from the room, I'd head downstairs for the French doors off the veranda.

"That's why I chose you, football player. The house is armed with the best security money can buy. Once you crack that back door, you'll trip the alarms and it'll sound like hell's bells a-ringin', with cops on the way. People in his neighborhood don't play Twenty Questions from dispatchers. Every cruiser between Cedar Park and Austin will be coming fast and running dark. You'd better be in good shape for the sprint back."

"You worry about cracking a cuticle from biting your fingernails, Ceepo," I said. "I'll handle the running part just fine."

It felt good saying that. Cody was getting on my last nerve with his endless repetition of details. Truth is, I was more worried about Brenda getting me into the house without her aged lover boy becoming suspicious.

The mesquite trees were in bloom as I parked near them off the gravel roadway. The air was heavy, muggy, as though the atmosphere was ripe for a ripping. Thunderheads churned up from the Gulf Coast.

More monster houses sat beyond the woods but I was isolated where I was, sweating inside my work clothes and having second thoughts. The "swag bags" were folded and tucked inside my pants and itching like there were biting chiggers in there. The tangy fragrance from the cream-colored mesquite blooms triggered a bout of sneezing.

I had my hand in motion to put the gear shift in reverse when I stopped. Then—No. *No going back to stocking shelves and kissing asses in brown aprons...*

Six o'clock came and I made a beeline at a fast trot to the back of the big house. Five minutes later, I spotted a leggy blonde pacing on the flagstones of the deck, smoking. A thinner, more fashionably dressed Brenda than I recalled from school. She looked once in my direction and flicked her cigarette toward the in-ground pool.

She turned and went back inside. I ran toward the servants' door, one eye on the upper windows but there was only reflected glare. No shocked face looking out to see me bolting across his property like the thief I was.

Be open, door, be open—

Inside, my back pressed against the door, I let my eyes adjust. I wasn't winded and my mind was calm. I walked to the second room on the right-hand side of the hallway, opened the door, and sauntered in as if I lived there.

Two hours of stooping in the closet took a moment to shake off. But I'd heard nothing the entire time, no voices, no house sounds—just a distant air-conditioner hum.

Up the grand staircase, one hand on the smooth black walnut banister, I had a brief spell of giddiness. I imagined a troop of debutantes in customized ball dresses adorned with glittering necklaces and tiaras sweeping past me like models going down the stairs to the elegant marble foyer before the admiring gazes of well-bred males below. A rich Texan's meat market.

His bedroom occupied most of the second floor. The canopied bed was the size of a small yacht.

I spotted the keypad immediately, but I had all the time I needed now. I was in no rush. I wanted to check out his room of reclining nudes. No lock or keypad to deter neither visitor nor thief.

Six women, all tongue-out gorgeous, in huge canvas oils spaced around the room at eye level. Walls themselves painted black with a satin finish. Four blondes, two shaved, one with a tawny mohawk, a true redhead with a flaming red bush like Dragon's Breath opal. A raven-haired beauty with a clitoris like a baby's thumb peeking through her cleft rounded out the collection. Brenda had to be among these. The bosomy blonde at the end, I guessed.

The old-fashioned idiot, I thought. *He'd talked her into a cosmetic breast reduction.*

Seconds later, I was shining a black light on the keypad and pressing numbered buttons.

The door clicked several times like the ignition switch on a barbecue grill. I pushed it open with my fingertips. The lights were off. I was about to take my first step when all of it came together in my head in that one moment, and I needed every ounce of football agility to keep from falling headfirst into the room.

God damn it to hell—

The black rubber mat on the floor had to be a pressure alarm.

That stupid Brenda—

No. Not Brenda...

Don't ask me what clicked in to tell me that—maybe the male's lizard brain. That blonde on the deck had not been the Brenda on the wall because—

Because there was no Brenda Sue Gelber.

Oh shit on a stick...

The silent collision of two different planes of thought inside my head was a painless explosion: NOT BRENDA GELBER crashed into DUANE BRISCOE SET-UP.

All the shady, suspicious details meshed into a kaleidoscopic pattern in an eyeblink, from the time Cody jumped from Billy's truck to my last meeting at his place. I saw that weasel smirk on his face, secretly laughing at me, his patsy.

I returned to the L-shaped Treasury room. Without crossing the threshold, I flicked the light switch and saw all the empty, smashed glass cases, the empty drawers tossed onto the floor.

That's when I noticed the blinking lights of the keypad. Another lie—silent alarms—

I flew.

Friction burned the palm of my hand as I steadied my flight along curved banister rail taking steps six at a time; they blurred beneath my feet.

Skidding across the flooring, I came to a stop before slamming into the glass doors of the veranda.

If he'd set me up to this extent, there would be cops picknicking at my Jeep...

I exited that grand manor house by the front doors, zigzagging across the yard using one cluster of foliage to run interference, staying low as I used to when I hit an O-line stuffed backward by the defense.

And I kept running. I ran for days, walked, slept under overpasses and hitchhiked with truckers or begged a ride from anybody with a friendly face staggering out of a roadhouse bar.

I was in San Marcos before I found work off the books cutting trees. A guy hired me for a week in Yoakum to burn broken pallets. Half starved, I begged him for a small loan so I could eat. I delivered pizzas in Humble until somebody looked at me too long while I made their change.

I've been on the run for months. I check out progress on my case whenever I'm near a public library or an internet café. I moved from "person of interest" to "suspect." I found the real Brenda on Facebook. She's obese now, married with three kids and has a husband named Fidelio Garcia. Her once famous cleavage is lost within the belly fat in the selfies she posts.

The woman at the house had to be Tawny Blonde from the gallery of nudes. Same face and build. Breasts unlike Brenda's youthful, cannonball-sized ones. My brain had been too slow to make the connection in time. I'd fallen for the 65 power trap play we used to run where I'd take the fake handoff from the quarterback and draw in the safety for a deep pass to the wide receiver.

This time, it was me that fell for the basic deception play. Mr. Big Time, yet too small for the bigs.

My beard is longer, I'm thinner, and I wear scruffy Levi's. I keep a spare pair in my backpack with the rest of my earthly goods. After a stint for a construction company in Corpus Christi, I drifted down to the Rio Grande. I'm working on a cattle ranch near San Benito off Highway 281. A couple illegals helped me get a bunk in an abandoned trailer. I sleep under the stars when the heat's too much to bear. A hot wind blows yellow dust all day long; it gets into my pores, my mouth, and hair. I crave water the way I used to crave fans cheering me from the stands whenever I broke one and went long. I think about Cody

Ceepo a lot. I remember the last thing he said to me when I got into my Jeep:

Don't let those pre-game jitters get to you, Duane...

Not if I get to you first, Cody.

If anyone out there thought Carole only wrote crime fiction featuring characters of the feline persuasion, watch out. She can go dark. Really dark. Carole says she wrote this one for Bill Crider, thinking he would appreciate. I'm sure he would (with the lights on)...

LYIN' EYES
Carole Nelson Douglas

I'm tempted to close my eyes on the memory, but I can't. I can't even close my eyes on the dark.

Teen hothead. Yeah, I was. My homies called me Toro. Together we were the El Toros. We rocked just this side of a "gang." Banded together in self-defense at high school.

Other guys in school called me "wetback" and "greaser" and "spic." Those rich kids. Sons of Anglo bankers and lawyers and real estate bigwigs. Called themselves the Lancaster High Lions after the school football team.

But a few of them, a secret few, called themselves the Lions of Doom. They might have to play with black and brown team-mates, but if Manny Hernandez gave an Anglo Lion running back a too-hard slam-down in practice, he might find the family cat gutted and tied to their car steering wheel one morning. With the insignia of a diamond-studded lion's head ring impressed on the worn fabric seats in cat blood.

You never spotted that ring on guys in school, so you never knew when or where the Lions of Doom would take offense and strike.

Finally my day came. I was too strong, doin' too good. Champion wrestler. Might get a college scholarship. Not allowed my kind. My sin wasn't any show-boating feat at football practice, but from April Anderson stopping me in the high school hall.

"Luis," she said, "that was a good paper in English class."

Not good here and now. I tried to edge into the class-changing madhouse of bodies, mumbling, "Just some words. I'm not a words guy." The assignment had been to write about an admired person. I chose my grandma who immigrated from Mexico back in the sixties. She was one tough lady.

April Anderson wasn't. Her pale blue eyes fascinated me, and her skin was white under this kinda...well, veil...of faded freckles. I could write about that. Prom queen candidate. I hadda get away fast.

"Sorry. Next class." I bulled into the thronging kids heading helter skelter in opposite directions, ignoring complaints and push-backs.

Not fast enough.

Next day I was in the closest vet's office, two mittfuls of whimpering fur trembling in my big wrestler's hands.

"The dog is young," the vet said. "Bones heal, but thirteen breaks...someone used her for a football."

"In front of my nine-year-old sister, Yolanda, when she ran out early to feed her new puppy. She said the guy wore a big gold ring and kept kicking and kicking the dog while they both screamed."

The vet was shaking his head.

"Fix her," I said. "I'll pay. It will take a while."

"A twelve-week-old puppy. Whoever did this—" The vet was tall and Anglo and he studied my eyes. "You want to tell me?"

I shook my head "No, it'll be worse."

"She'll need a lot of physical rehabilitation."

"I'll work with her. Anything. Yolanda picked her out. This one looked kinda ugly in the pet shelter, with that black prune of a wrinkled muzzle and piss-yellow coat, but Yollie insisted on

her. Was afraid no one else would adopt an ugly dog like her."
My voice did not break, but for the last time in my sixteen-year-
old life, it wanted to. "How much?"

"A hundred dollars."

In the silence we could hear my sister sobbing in the waiting
room.

"It must cost a lot more. Mucho more." I wasn't asking a
question.

"You're a good brother, Luis." He put a hand on my shoulder.
"A hundred is a lot to you." He didn't wait for me to admit it.
"You step up on this, you'll see you can step up higher in life
than you think."

I nodded, heading for the waiting room. Everything I earned
on lawn cutting went for food. I'd cut more. I'd cut night and
day. I'd get Yollie her dog back and as good as new.

Or maybe not.

The high school guards were often Latino. They let the El Toros
into the football field at night sometimes. To practice, goof off,
left alone under the faint night lights. Then, that night, while I
was still thinking of Yollie and her battered puppy, my bros
were gone. Split.

A lot of Lions of Doom were the only ones here now. And
hunting a new football. You didn't interfere in their vengeful
acts. Fear turned my gut hard. I was a strong wrestler. I could
make them feel they'd picked on the wrong ugly dog.

I'm not such a big guy. Five-six, but I was built like a Rottweiler in high school. "El Toro." Wrestling used to be my sport,
but I later learned my mainframe was my brain. Who'd have
thunk it.

I spun low, into their calves, taking some off their feet. I bent
arms and twisted knees but there were six, seven, eight. Jed
Westlake, beefy wrestler, got me into a headlock and jammed
an elbow into my Adam's apple until I gagged and choked.

I was down and pinned. Brent Tyler, BMOC, was standing over me.

He leaned down, his pale face flushed red-rage purple in the greenish stadium lights. "You know what you did. April Anderson is mine. You know what we're gonna do. We're gonna take his balls, brothers!"

The Lions' tight kneeling circle growled as one, softly, so no one would hear.

Cold sweat. It owned me. My torso became an earthquake. Bucked off three of them. Blood thundered in my head and throat. Gasping for breath, my pulsing heartbeat swelled to make my ears pop.

Jesus, Mary, Joseph, no! Dios Mio.

He couldn't mean it. Even Brent Tyler couldn't get away with that.

A guy pinned each leg, each arm. My torso bucked one last powerful time. Brent's rabid face hung over mine like a rogue moon. Hot breath. His fist cocked before my eyes, the lion head ring glinting gold and diamond bright in the overhead light.

"You're never going to see April again."

The fist smashed into my face. I felt the Lion's head impact on my shattering cheekbone as someone grabbed my balls in the devil's own grip.

"Listen, spic," Brent spat out. "I am the King. The Lion King, the King of Doom, and you are rat dung. And I mean it. You are never going to see April Anderson again."

The heavy ring danced with my frantically dodging face, as his knuckles pressed hard on my cheekbones. Everything darkened, then exploded into unthinkable pain and arcing colors all over my body. Not the damned ring, His thumbs. *His thumbs.* Vomit flooded my throat. I blacked out, but not before I heard a mad bull's deep guttural rhythmic bellows echoing off the wooden bleachers and the trees and the asphalt near and far. Mine.

* * *

No one could hear that, hear me, and not call 9-1-1.

I only remember becoming conscious knowing I didn't want to do it ever again.

"*Jesus bloody Christ.*" The first EMT guy's voice whispered, like in church. "*Whoever did this...*" Seems I'd heard that line before.

"*God, what do we do? Who'd do this?*"

After that it was blood and darkness and motion and men muttering. "Steady, man. We've got you."

And sirens squealing and a choppy, reeling ride with a woman EMT murmuring, *Shhhh,* like my grandmother had. What was it about my grandmother? A school paper? School? That would all be history now.

No more teachers, no more books, no more Lions dirty looks.
No more teachers, no more books, no more Lions dirty
No more teachers, no more books, no more
No more teachers, no more
No more no more no more

After a lot of doctors and hospitals and a hush-hush lawsuit, I was told I'd won. But there was no trial, no jail time for anyone, everybody involved was underage with sealed files, all brushed off and arranged. Sympathetic murmurs surrounded me like polite whirlpools of unexpressed horror, heard but not seen. I was the guy whose eyes were gouged out, just something to pity and forget now.

What kept us sane, my family and me, was how good the little pup was doing. The vets at the university found her a "unique subject," and with the help of pins and braces she was growing straight and strong.

Now that we knew she would make it, I asked Yolanda what she wanted to name her.

We were in my bedroom, where I had mostly learned my way around, the dog lolling on the bed and Yollie sitting on the chair like my grandmother used to when I was sick as a kid. I wished I could see her.

"Name her something beautiful," Yollie said. "Her hair is sort of red-gold, like the lady on the poster above your bed."

"Poster. I don't…"

"But the lady in the poster has a lot more hair, like a lion, and her dress doesn't have much of a top."

Dios mio. I'd copped the cover from an old movie magazine I saw when I was what, twelve? My loss twisted my gut. I'd never see that sexy lady again, Rita Hayworth, my pre-teen crush.

"Can you put my hand on the poster, Yollie? And I'll tell you her story." I felt the tiny corner that had been turned up.

"Her name was Marga*rita* Cansino and her hair was really as black as yours."

"Mine?" I heard self-doubt.

"She was a beautiful, black-haired Latina, but nobody mentioned it after Hollywood dyed her hair red and renamed her Rita Hayworth. That was long ago. Latina ladies don't have to dye their hair red to be in movies now."

"But the poster calls her 'Gilda.'"

"That was the name of the part she played. She was very famous in the role."

"Gilda! We can call my dog Gilda."

A sissy name for the gangling, close-coated dog I ran my hands over now. I'd not feel macho calling it out. I was still good for playing chase and fetch in a vacant lot with a baseball, hurling it into the blind distance until the dog raced back to lay a slobbery ball at my feet. Until she got lighting quick and bigger and stronger. Mucho bigger. But *Gilda?*

I sensed Yollie throwing her arms around the dog's neck. "You are very beautiful, Gilda, and you are a Latina girl."

I was outa high school anyway so my family headed down to Waco where relatives lived and then I was to go to school in Houston for "rehabilitation." Yollie kept crying and crying when I left, and Gilda raced after the pickup carrying me away until I had to tell my father to turn around. The dog and I seemed to read each other's minds.

"Yollie," I told my sister, "I know she's your dog, but I need her now. And she still needs me. We'll both visit. That okay, huh?"

I could feel her tear-sticky cheeks nodding between my fingers.

It was against the rules, but in Houston they got the message that Gilda and I were already a team and they'd just have to teach her too. I was going to blind school, thanks to those Lions of Doom not letting me get away without taking one set of "balls." The EMTs desperately searching the dirt and grass to see if my eyes could be saved had made me want to cry for the last time in my life, but I no longer had the working equipment. So don't cry for me, Argentina or April. Prosthetic eyes are real sophisticated these days. They don't see, but people tell me I looked absolutely normal.

You think?

I wore dark glasses with strong black frames anyway. The nurses flirted and said the frames looked really distinguished with my black hair, *trust* them. At least I couldn't see their kindly lying eyes. The doctors found my case medically and psychologically unique and no expense was being spared. The attack made newspapers, but not when and where it had happened. I didn't mind wearing the dark glasses and sometimes carrying a cane, but mostly I liked having Gilda beside me, who, nursing staff claimed, looked "really chic" in her service harness.

There are places like that to teach people like me to "cope." And I learned. And they taught Gilda to be my guide and I was hers. And we went to law school together. People wanted to write features about me, about us, every once in a while. I refused. Time passed and Lancaster High graduated students who'd never heard of or feared the Lions of Doom, who had been disbanded, vanishing into their Jr. and Trey identities and their fathers' fine careers and social prominence.

So then I went home and set up shop.

"Luis?"

I had been positioned to gaze out my office window—I had to know, envision, everything about my surroundings. I turned my swivel chair just like a sighted person to face the client Yolanda had shown in, a woman wafting a crisp cologne scent. How many years had it been? Seven? In dog years, it was forever. Gilda sat beside me, her shoulder in reach of my seated hand. I put my hand on her neck and felt her muscles tighten beneath the silky fur.

"Yes. It's Luis. And it's April Tyler now, isn't it?"

"I saw your name online and wasn't sure it was you. And then Jorje, you remember, the skinny sophomore, he cuts lawns now, said you were back in town."

I heard her sit down to stay.

"Look at you. A lawyer. That's impressive. I'm sorry. Did you...was it in an accident?"

Of course no one at the school knew.

I fingered the scarred impression of a lion's head behind the left bow of my dark glasses.

"I guess you could say an accident had me. What can I do for you?"

"What a pair we make." Her laugh was forced. "So far removed from high school. I'm wearing dark glasses too. I can't afford to be seen. He might be having me followed."

"Who?" I knew.

Her next laugh didn't belong to a pale-blue-eyed girl who probably hated and covered her freckles, her delicate natural freckles.

"My husband. You remember Brent." She sighed. "He's the reason for the dark glasses. Sometimes the bastard uses my face for a ping-pong table. I want a divorce and I'm afraid he'd kill me first."

Her voice thickened. "I'm so ashamed. I don't want anyone in our circle to know, but...I'm *afraid*."

"Our circle?"

"Well, *my* circle is the same. The same old money and untouchable families as in high school. You might not believe this, Luis, but women married to powerful men can easily be framed for infidelity or mental problems. They'll brush us out of the way with no spousal support, nothing."

"Oh, I can believe it."

"I always liked you," she said, abruptly.

The pain came rushing back. The absurd high-schoolish "sin" of being "liked" by the wrong girl at the wrong school.

I had paid a devastating price. The case had made the news without naming names and had shocked many, but was finally left to be forgotten. Yolanda was playing summer secretary before she went on to Rice University. She couldn't take her dog to Houston. Besides, Gilda had healed along with me and grown to a hundred and twenty pounds, still no beauty. Her muzzle would always be a bit askew, but her bite could snap a cottonwood tree branch.

Was I ready to risk it again?

No.

"I'm sorry. I can't help you."

In the silence I heard her breathing stop.

"You don't understand. Every lawyer in this town thinks Brent is God. I could get killed and they'd find a way to absolve him."

I pushed the business card I'd extracted from the desk drawer, my fingers reading the embossed type, across the glass desktop.

"This woman. Out of Austin. Tylers have no pull there. She's a regular Gloria Allred on women's cases. She also uses some mucho tough private investigators."

The tips of April Anderson's longish fingernails brushed my knuckles as she swiped the card into her possession.

"You might want to move," I suggested. "Get a guard dog."

Her sigh was shaky. "Like yours? Thanks. *Mucho gracias,* Luis. I don't suppose I'll see you again."

"No, I won't see you again."

"For your own safety. I understand."

She didn't understand. It was for her safety.

Her clothes, some sort of slubbed silk, rustled as she stood. Silk is easy to hear. It hisses. She leaned forward and her chilly palm and wrist closed over mine. I felt a ridged scar. Like mine. My mind's eye pictured it. Her forearm raised in front of her face, the blue-veined soft wrist absorbing the ringed hand's blow, knocking her hand against her eye socket and the bridge of her nose. He always went for the eyes.

Fading steps said she was gone.

I couldn't close my eyes. The prosthetics looking good was no longer enough. I still couldn't see April, but I finally realized I didn't need to see her.

I needed to see him.

They say the night has a thousand eyes, but when you're blind it has a thousand ears.

Tonight, most of them are mine.

The birds have wrapped it up for the evening, but lizards and snakes skitter over the dry soil like autumn leaves, even though it's a humid, onion-soup heavy Texas summer evening.

Crickets chorus loud enough to beat the band, the old high school band.

A Gypsy-girl-skirt wind skirls in the tallest trees. Ninety degrees on the ground.

I once saw a tarantula the size of a softball rolling like a powder puff dusted in gunpowder across an entry road to a busy mall in broad daylight. Just another tumbleweed. Danger so often hides in things that aren't what they seem. Sometimes it's a puppy with a keen nose and a long memory.

Yes, I could see once. So what.

Now, I hear. I hear the almost computerized click of Gilda's nails on the invisible sidewalk's ribbon of concrete. By the feel of her, she's a solid, smooth-coated dog...Yollie describes short floppy ears like a goofy red-gold lab with a black wrinkled mean-business muzzle, mixed breeds like Rita Hayworth, who was Irish and Spanish. Gilda's 120-pound body is deep-chested and lean-flanked. And the legs on her...Like Rita. I think of her long, curved nail clicks as canine high heels. Gilda can't deny her big-breed strut, no more than I can muffle my regular, careful footsteps in the dark behind the old high school. We're moving even behind the bleachers where gang scuffles and drugs and unwary girls had gone down. Beyond that plunged a steep tangled ravine of underbrush and invasive trumpet vine and snakes and mosquitoes and wildflowers.

I can smell it, envision it, as though it were yesterday.

Gilda sniffs the same old shit by the bleachers. Butt ends of pot and regular smokes, sweat, and blood and semen. Like a Teen Hell bullring.

And El Toro is back.

Being blind makes you into the Coyote in the Roadrunner cartoons I loved as a kid. You have to act as if you don't see the yawning cliff, but walk right out over it, like Jesus on water skis, or like a coyote on an air mattress.

I've been used to doing that for seventeen years. Since my eyes was took.

That phrase sounds hick for a smooth Texas lawyer like me. They say you read for the law. I listened for it. I heard every weasel word, sensed every snarky coil of injustice writhing to nail the hapless and free the faithless back into their Daddy Warbucks's arms and dreams.

It matters who your daddy is in Texas. They don't call a son of a son of a shitass "Trey" for nothing. Rank runs very real, and often foul, here.

Gilda's small snuffle turns into the faintest growl and she

stops dead.

A scraping sound on the cracked asphalt behind the bleachers announces someone else is here. I stand in the feeble night lights I can imagine.

Man in Dark Glasses Walking Dog at Night.

Brent had called half an hour after his wife had left my office. She was right about being followed and I was right about him. He wanted a redo.

He started with a taunt.

"'You got the dog. I got the gun. Come on, boy, we're gonna have a little fun.'"

"Paraphrasing Hoyt Axton."

"'Paraphrasing.' Well, la-di-dah. Guess the wetback spic got himself some education after all."

"'Spic.' What they call a portmanteau word, Brent. 'Hispanic' crammed together into a cuss word you hear a lot here in Texas."

"Your stupid seeing-eye dog is shaking. What a coward, ready to scream again. Just like you when I gave you that eye job."

"She's not trembling from fear, Bigshot."

"Ugly puppy. Deserved a smash-up, just like you. You got too big for your greaser boots."

"And you liked to hurt girls' dogs and then you graduated to hurting the girls. Yeah, this is my baby sister's adopted baby dog you drop-kicked all over the block."

He spit toward Gilda. Her growl was soft and deep. My fist felt the vibration through her harness handle. It took all my weight to hold her back.

"Just a butt-ugly mutt whose face my boots did a favor."

"Not exactly, Brent. It's dangerous to take things at face value. Sometimes your eyes will fool you. Even the dog pound people didn't know what breeds she is. You're right. She's a mixed breed, but half Rhodesian ridgeback."

"Roadasian? Some kind of gook name. You can't fool me. That's no cop K9 dog."

"No. This breed can't be used for police work. Overkill, you might say. But if you're looking for personal protection, Brent, and I have a feeling you should be, the Rhodesian ridgeback is your animal. They used to be called African lion dogs. Rhodesia, as you remember from high school, is a country in south Africa. Gilda's ancestors cornered and took down *lions* in the old days. And that black pug-ugly muzzle? Some bull mastiff in there too. Bull is 'El Toro' in Spanish. You don't want to mix it up with them either.

"A dog can smell about a hundred thousand times better than we do. You think this dog will ever forget those stinky, kicking, bone-breaking feet of yours? She was just a puppy. A baby. But she was a baby shark, asshole. And I've been feeding her your scent as chew-toys ever since."

"You're full of shit, asshole."

His forward shuffle kept time with his hand groping the silk-blend side pocket of his suit for the advertised gun.

"Now you don't want to start sweating and move too fast, Brent. I gave Gilda some fresh mementos of you just yesterday. She's rarin' to go. Missing a sweaty tee from the gym, are you? Some Nike Air Zoom tennies?"

"You couldn't get into my private club. You can't even see."

"Everybody helps a poor blind man with a cane and a service dog, Brent. I'm not as harmless as I look."

"You can't make me afraid of a dog named Gilda, like that ugly chick on *Saturday Night Live*."

"No, not Gilda Radner. This dog's named after that super-star redhead in the old movies, Rita Hayworth."

"Yeah. Movie star, Rita Hayworth. Bitchin' looker. Had April all beat. You do remember April?"

"Appearances are deceiving. Rita's real name was Margarita Cansino. Spanish dancer chick. Latina. Gilda is her most famous role, that one made her a star."

"Your seeing-eye dog is still shaking."

"She's a *guard* dog, not a guide dog. And she's not trembling from fear, Bigshot. This Gilda is quivering to get on with the hunt. She's primed to take you down.

"For you, this is *Saturday Night Dead.*"

Brent's shoes scraped on loose grit. He was moving to our left, circling away.

I ducked left as my fist relaxed to loose Gilda, and I stumbled backwards when the pressure released. I just had time to grab the collapsible cane sheathed in Gilda's service vest before her hurtling body knocked Brent down.

Brent garbled out a grunt as something metallic spun on the sidewalk.

"No, get off me, you ugly mutt!"

Gilda's glamour girl nails frantically scraped cement in pursuit. He went crawling, rolling, crashing and scrabbling down the ravine to avoid her.

I shook the cane out full length and dragged it over the sidewalk to find the dropped gun. I knelt to slip it into my pants pocket. All the while, the soundtrack of Brent's moans and curses and groans as his body rocked and rolled against snapping saplings and whipping underbrush continued, then faded and stilled. There were rocks, big rocks down there and maybe rattlesnakes and rabid skunks. A guy could hope.

Finally, Brent and the ravine went silent. Crickets were screeching again. I called Gilda back. Not a scratch on her. She hadn't followed him beyond a few yards. Coward's panic had done the rest.

The newspapers reported Brent Tyler's death, a head injury against an upthrust boulder, as a tragedy and a reason for the city to clear out its remaining wild patches. Animal activists protested on behalf of disappearing wildlife in the face of urban sprawl. No one knew why Tyler had parked his beamer behind the high school's football field and gone into the ravine. His widow said he had always been sentimental about his gridiron glory days with the Lancaster Lions.

* * *

I felt like a movie private eye, a beautiful dame showing up at my office unannounced. Yollie was out at lunch.

She sat opposite me, her familiar scent as clean and confident as her name.

April acknowledged Gilda. "Hello, Office Dog. My, what big white teeth you have."

"So did my grandma," I said with a smile.

"I remember her from your English class paper. Wish I'd known her. I wish I'd known you better then."

I cleared my throat.

"Brent hadn't changed his will as he'd threatened. I'm starting by taking an around-the-world cruise. A couple of his buddies have been pestering me to give them the ring he always wore. Said it has some old sentimental meaning. I told them I buried him with it, and they seemed relieved."

I nodded.

"But I didn't."

I heard her lean forward as a hard object clanged to my glass desktop.

"I thought maybe you'd have some use for it. Or maybe your handsome dog could bury it."

"'Beautiful' dog. Gilda is a she. But she does like to bury things."

"Well." I heard April stand. "Then she and I have something in common."

Someday artificial eyes might see, and then Gilda and I might look up April. Brent Tyler won't be around to see that.

A scent of spring lingered.

Yeah, maybe this was one where I should have gotten the girl.

But I already had one.

April's footsteps faded down the hall.

"Ready for a run, Gilda?"

Mixing friends, the outdoors, fieldwork for grad school in a remote location in extreme weather…sounds idyllic. Until you add a touch of emotional instability, an inflammatory situation and a reptile. Then you have a party…

IN THE ROUGH
Julie Tollefson

Kari wiped sweat from her eyes and pulled a beer from the cooler. The first sip was always the best, when its icy cold bitterness hit the back of her throat and washed away the dust and grime of a day of field work.

She'd earned this beer. Temperatures that afternoon had hit triple digits with not a hint of breeze. She and Noah had spent the better part of it pounding pieces of rebar into the dry, compacted East Texas dirt and digging pits deep enough to hold five-gallon buckets. By quitting time, they'd woven two-foot-high strips of sheet metal between the rebar to construct a series of drift fences and pitfall traps across the biological field station where she and Noah and fellow herpetology grad students conducted research every summer.

She propped her feet on the cabin's porch rail and narrowed her eyes against the western sun. In the middle of the bayou, she could just pick out Al's scaly back and bulging eyes as the camp's informal mascot drifted atop the swampy waters.

"Storm's coming." Noah flicked icy water from the cooler at her then settled on the step below.

Humidity hung in the still air with a thickness that meant

thunderstorms brewed nearby. Normally she loved a summer rain and lord knew the parched ground could use it, but too much would destroy their chances of collecting good data.

"You remembered to drill holes in the buckets?"

Noah gave her a scathing look. "It's not my first rodeo. Or experience with pitfall trapping, I guess."

"I don't want to find any drowned specimens tomorrow." When a snake or lizard encountered the sheet-metal fence, it traveled beside it, looking for a way around. What it found most often, though, was a drop into one of the buckets they'd buried at either end. Drift fences and pitfall traps, a time-honored method of sampling an area's small animal population.

Noah finished his beer but didn't respond. He didn't need to. He would no more endanger their study than she would. They were all, including Devon and Brad, who should be arriving any minute, meticulous about protocol. They were on track to wrap up their study this summer and none of them wanted to sabotage their results at this point.

A gray Prius bumped over the gravel of the cabin's long driveway and stopped beside the Jeep. Brad leaped out of the driver's side and landed on the porch in two strides, grabbing a beer before he even uttered a hello.

"Best part of grad school." He took a long swallow before banging the can against Noah's. "Here's to field work, to the heat and sunburn and wind, to the bugs and poison ivy, and especially to the snakes and frogs and salamanders that make these two weeks together possible."

"You're sure in a jolly mood." Kari kept her eyes on the car, where Devon was taking his sweet time. Long legs in fashionably torn jeans appeared first, then he stood and flashed a quick smile of perfect white teeth as his blond hair caught the lowering sun. Kari's pulse quickened, a flicker of anticipation and desire. Like Brad, Kari's favorite part of grad school was field work. But her favorite part of field work now stretched his full six-foot-three frame after the two-hour drive from campus, his T-shirt the shade of red calculated to make her heart flutter.

Devon stooped to pull his bag from the back seat and emerged holding not his duffel but the hand of a woman.

Kari's beer soured in her throat. All the thoughts that had been circling since she'd arrived at the cabin—about Devon, about the tent she'd packed for privacy, about the not-so-secret pleasures of the week ahead—they all stopped, like a flock of birds torched by lightning. One by one, they fell to earth in a rain of charred yearning.

The woman, asymmetrical black hair cut short, nose and ears glittering with piercings, made a slow pirouette as she took in her surroundings. Her gauzy top, with its spaghetti straps and dropped shoulders and mix of floral and plaid fabrics, fluttered as she twirled. She looked delicate and fresh, a bohemian flower, decidedly out of place.

Kari, aware of her own sweaty tank top, mud-caked hiking boots, and the red East Texas dust clinging to her legs, felt a sudden urge to shower. It had never mattered to her before. Noah leaned across her to whisper to Brad. "Who's that?"

"That," Brad said, "is Willa. She's an artist. I have no freakin' idea where Devon found her, but she's been talking non-stop since we left College Station."

Willa made her way toward the bank of the bayou, her steps wobbly in dainty gladiator sandals not intended for the ruts and rocks of the cabin's yard. She knelt and traced fingers through the water. "It's so hot here. Let's take a dip in the pond."

"This should be good," Brad muttered.

Devon, finally, glanced toward the porch. "No swimming here, babe."

"Why not?"

"Alligators." He pointed to a spot a dozen yards from shore where Al's eyes and snout broke the water's surface, the rest of the big gator's body submerged. Willa stumbled back from the water's edge, and Devon pulled her close to nuzzle her neck. "But we can definitely paddle around. Canoe or kayak, your choice."

Willa flashed a flirty grin at him, brimming with promises, and pushed him away. "Aren't you going to introduce me?"

Devon pulled his duffel and a jacket from the back of the car, then took her hand. "Guys, this is Willa. Willa, this is everybody. You met Brad in the car. That's Noah with the caveman facial hair. Watch out for him. He's a real maniac. And Kari."

And Kari.

Wow. Just like that. Kari lowered her eyes to the duffel he'd dropped at his feet and the pristine, deep blue denim jacket he'd folded—folded!—over the top. She did not want him to see her anger. Devon had the uncanny knack of reading her feelings, and she did not want him to know her thoughts until she was ready. Which was to say she felt exactly the way he had expected her to feel when he'd brought another woman to "their" cabin.

In the kitchen, Kari heaped black beans and rice onto her plate. Noah's specialty, mainly because the only two skills involved were boiling water and using a can opener. She carried her plate to the porch to watch the sun set while she ate.

"Food's ready," she said to Willa.

Willa shrugged but didn't look up from her sketchpad. "I want to finish this while the light is right."

Kari peeked over her shoulder. Willa had captured the storm clouds to the southwest, a shaft of sunlight spilled across the bayou, even Al's bumpy eyes in the water. But her main focus was a quirky collection—cattle vertebra, twisted pieces of wood, a bobber pulled from the weeds along the bayou—all strung together and hung from the porch's rafters. Willa's pencil worked to capture Kari's favorite part of the sculpture, a mummified catfish head dangling at its tip.

Her first summer at the research station, Kari had discovered the macabre souvenir nailed to a tree. One afternoon, when rainy weather cut short their time in the field, she and Devon had drunk rum and Coke and strung their found treasures together.

Devon's fingers on hers as he took the mummified head, ran a large fishhook through its leathery skin and crimped the hook tightly closed. The way they laughed when he pierced his own finger with the hook, the blood dripping on the weathered planks of the porch. Another drink to numb the pain.

Kari fought the urge to rip the page from Willa's sketchbook and destroy it. The other woman had no right to what was so painfully, undeniably Kari's and Devon's. Her fingers tightened around her fork until her knuckles glowed white, then she forced herself to release her anger and refocus on its source: Devon.

The first drops of rain spattered the dust in front of the cabin. They were losing light rapidly, the last rays of sun swallowed whole by angry dark clouds that came close to matching Kari's mood.

When the storm broke, it announced itself with a flash of lightning so near Kari felt her hair lift. She leapt for the door, holding it open for Willa to scurry inside. A gust of wind threatened to shove the building off its foundation, and the last thing Kari saw as the door closed was the flathead sculpture swing parallel to the ground before its sun-rotted rope snapped and the pieces scattered on the wind.

The storm raged for nearly two hours, its ferocity driving even Brad and Noah inside. The cabin lost power in the first truly massive burst of wind, and they tapped every pot in the place to catch the worst of the ceiling's leaks. Brad brought out a deck of cards and by the light of a camp lantern had begun to deal a hand of Hold 'Em, when Devon rapped his beer can with a fork as if about to make a toast.

"This is as good a time as any to tell you, I guess," he began, eyes locked on Kari. "This is likely the last time we'll be together like this. Our study ends after this summer. And—" he looked at each of them in turn, "—I've taken a research position at the university."

41

Three sets of eyes found Brad, who looked stricken. "A&M?" Devon broke eye contact first. "They offered on Monday. I accepted this morning."

Brad pushed away from the table, his movements deliberate and restrained, but when the cabin door slammed behind him, it was as if all the oxygen went out with him.

Noah swept the abandoned cards into a pile. "That's low even for you, Dev."

Willa glanced, perplexed, from Devon to Noah to Kari and back again. "Isn't that good news? Aren't you happy for him?"

"Not now, Willa." Devon's response was as soft as Willa's question.

Kari found Brad at the water's edge, chucking pieces of gravel far out into the swamp with one hand and drinking a beer with the other. "Devon's a jerk," she said. She should feel more anger at Devon for stealing the job every one of them knew Brad deserved, but all she could think about was the way Devon had crafted his announcement to create the maximum amount of hurt not for Brad but for her. He'd cleared his throat, looked adoringly at Willa, then fixed his eyes on her, Kari, before speaking, a bit of theater designed to send daggers through her heart. And it had worked.

Brad crushed his empty can and dropped it at the base of a cypress. "You deserve so much better than him, you know."

Kari heard the wistful note in his voice, the one that had been there since the first summer when he'd returned to the cabin early one day and interrupted Devon and Kari together. She ignored it now as she had every other time. What else could she do?

"You're mad he got the job you wanted."

"And you're mad he brought Willa. The way he treats you? It's the same way he treats Willa and me and Noah. Everybody. He thinks we're all here to serve him, but we all know how he got that job. When he told them about our work here—" he waved a hand to take in the research station, "—how much credit do you think he gave you? Any of us? None. That's how much."

"You don't know that." A weak defense, because in her heart she knew Devon didn't deserve better. Already her brain was recognizing she'd known a day like this would come, a day when Devon's personality finally overrode the pure physical chemistry they'd always shared. Everything had always been about Devon. She wanted to punch herself for going along with it for so long. For helping him to actually be the Devon everyone but her seemed to think he was. *What an idiot.*

"I know him." Brad was well and truly wound up now. Every frustration and hurt he'd suppressed for the last three summers poured out in a bitter rush of angry words. "Kari, what are we going to do about Devon?"

They returned to the porch as the rain finally tapered to a sprinkle. Brad dug two cans of beer out of the ice chest and they settled side by side on the swing. He looked fragile and vulnerable, a side of him Kari hadn't seen before. Without thinking, she brushed rain-soaked hair from his face, her fingertips lingering on the curve of his ear.

He grasped her wrist. "Don't."

"I thought you wanted this."

"Not this way. I'm not interested in being another pawn in the sick game you and Devon are playing."

Kari sat, stunned, as the swing pitched forward and Brad lurched away from her. "The rain's almost stopped. Let's get the others and go to work."

A stifling silence met them inside, broken only by the plink of water still dripping into pots. Noah was first to his feet when Brad suggested they visit the frog pond, a low area about a mile from the cabin where they'd captured innumerable frogs after rains in past years. He held a flashlight under his chin and let a grin spread from one ear to the other. "To the frog pond," he said in his best radio voice.

Within minutes, they'd all gathered their gear, relieved to escape the confines of the cabin. Only Willa balked at the thought of chasing frogs in the rain in the dark, but when Devon gave her an ultimatum—"Come with us or stay here by yourself. Those are your choices."—she followed them to the Jeep.

Half an hour later, Brad parked beside the pond and cut the engine. Flickers of lightning streaked low on the horizon, far in the distance.

As the rumble of the Jeep died, another, louder roar took its place. Kari turned her face toward the sky, eyes closed, and let the calls of tens of thousands, maybe hundreds of thousands, of tree frogs and toads engulf her. Voices in the wilderness, each seeking a mate or validation or simply the solace that none of them were alone. She'd never encountered such an awesome display of nature. She pulled a field notebook, pencil and small digital recorder from her pack and put a couple dozen yards between herself and her friends and immersed herself in the work. The frogs called louder and louder, a song of hope awakened by rain after weeks of hot, dry days.

If only a summer storm could wash away the bitterness and anger Devon had brought with him this season.

As if she'd conjured him, Devon materialized beside her.

"I have nothing to say to you," she said. "No, wait. I do have something. How could you do that to Brad? You knew he wanted that job, and you know it's perfect for him."

"Come on, Kari. That's not what you're mad about. Did you think I'd wait forever? That once or twice a year was enough for either of us? I told you last year I wanted to be with you, but not in this sneaking around the cabin in the wilderness way. Not in the way you barely acknowledge me when we're on campus together. I want to be with you all the time."

She hated the way he could read her mind. "So you brought that girl here to make me jealous?"

"I brought her here because I like her. Because I've been seeing her for a couple of months and thought it was time to introduce her to my friends. And to make the point that I'm not on stand-by for you anymore."

Kari gripped her pencil harder. "Point made." She was about to add, "Now leave me alone," when Willa herself appeared, her inappropriate sandals sliding in the mud.

"Dev, how much longer?" Willa placed a proprietary hand on Devon's arm. He flinched, only a little, but enough to deepen her frown.

Kari almost felt sorry for her when Devon brushed her hand away and stalked off, but then Willa turned venom-filled eyes on her. The girl was beginning to suspect she may have been brought along as a prop, Kari thought, and she didn't like it.

Kari turned her face skyward again. The clouds separated to reveal a spray of stars shining as bright as diamonds in the black night sky. Though Devon would never believe her, the way he'd just treated Willa was Exhibit A in Kari's defense when it came to why she couldn't consider a relationship outside of their summer research trips. Devon could only care about himself. A few days together a couple of times a year, no matter how intense, were all Kari could take. She could admit that to herself now.

When Kari eventually returned to the Jeep, she found Noah on its hood playing the beam of his flashlight in a 360-degree arc across swamp and woodlands like a lighthouse on a rocky coast.

"What gives?" She hopped into the front passenger seat. Brad already sat behind the wheel and Willa sulked in back.

"Devon," Brad said, the name a curse.

Of course. The first drops of another band of rain fell, and thunder rumbled closer again. Typical of Devon to keep them waiting.

"I talked to him half an hour ago." Kari pointed her own light toward the grassy knoll where she and Devon had spoken.

"Last I saw, he was headed this way."

"He probably walked back to the cabin already." Brad had the sound of a man who'd stepped in cow dung past his knees. "But it won't hurt to walk down the road a little ways, just to be sure he didn't twist an ankle or something."

They split up, Noah and Willa taking the stretch of road between the Jeep and the knoll. Brad and Kari searched in the other direction. Fifteen minutes later, they reconvened at the Jeep, still without Devon.

The rain was picking up again and with it came more flashes of lightning. Kari counted slowly, one-two, before the thunder broke over them. Much too close for comfort. "I don't like this. Brad's right. He's probably at the cabin, warm and dry and laughing at us, and that's where we should be. If he's not there, we'll come back and find him after the rain stops. If he's avoiding us, serves him right to spend the night in this mess."

Lightning flared again, the crash of thunder following so close Kari's count didn't get past the "wuh" sound in "one." She jumped into the soaked passenger seat, and Willa curled her body against the rain in the back. Only Noah remained outside, still casting his flashlight around as if he hoped there was a way to make their group whole again. Wasted effort. They would never be whole again. Kari knew.

The cabin was still dark. They couldn't expect the electricity to be restored for at least a day, maybe several. During their second summer at the station, a violent storm had left them powerless for nearly a week. They'd returned from the field every night to a dark and airless cabin. Since then, they'd come prepared with protein bars, enough ice to keep their beer at least cool for a week, five-gallon containers of water, and everything they needed to cook over a campfire.

But the cabin wasn't just dark. It was empty, too. Devon had not returned. Outside, the full force of the storm's second wave hit, less ferocious than the first but still loud and furious enough to shake the walls after every flash of lightning.

Noah picked up the cards he'd left on the table and shuffled, then shuffled again. The *fllllllp* of the cards grated on Kari's nerves until finally she slapped his hands down flat on the table.

"Sorry," he mumbled.

Willa, red-eyed, stood in the middle of the room like a lost child. "What do we do? You said he'd be here."

Brad dropped into one of the wood-framed chairs. "We can't do anything until this storm passes and the sun comes up."

"We should call for help. We can do that, right?"

Kari recognized Willa's tone, a combination of helplessness and disbelief that Devon's friends weren't more concerned. She had a lot to learn about the meaning of friendship when it came to Devon.

Kari picked up Noah's abandoned cards and turned them over one by one. Seven of diamonds. Three of clubs. Jack of hearts. "No cell service here, and you saw how treacherous the road is. We barely made it back, and the stretch between here and the highway is even worse."

"So we just do nothing?"

"We wait," Brad said. "He's done this before. Disappeared without a word. And he always comes back. He lives to make the rest of us worry."

Kari remembered her first night at the cabin three years earlier. She and Devon had arrived a day before everyone else. While she started dinner, he'd left to set amphiuma traps in a muddy ditch they'd passed on the road to the field station. He'd stayed gone far longer than expected, and in his absence, the groans of the cabin and unfamiliar calls coming from the bayou wore at her calm. By the time he'd returned, she'd been close to tears. She'd thrown herself into his arms, just as he'd planned.

Devon's modus operandi hadn't changed.

"Devon told me about you three, how jealous you all are of him, and now I see that every word was true."

Brad hands curled into fists. "You don't know what you're talking about."

Willa turned on him. "You know why Devon got the job you wanted? Because he's brilliant and driven and when he wants something, he goes after it. Whatever it takes. You're lazy. You wait for things to come to you. The job. Her."

At *her*, Willa tossed her head in Kari's direction. Kari winced, and Noah covered her hand with one of his. "We're all worried about Devon, Willa. But we can't do anything until the storm ends."

Devon's new girlfriend regarded Noah through narrowed eyes. "Your so-called friends think you're a fool, you know. They tolerate you because you do the hard work and you make them laugh, but that's all you are to them. A court jester with muscles."

Willa's words hit their mark. Noah withdrew his hand from Kari's and folded in on himself.

"That's enough." Kari snapped. "You don't know us, and you don't know Devon. Not the way we know him."

"And you. You're the worst." Willa wouldn't be stopped, her anxiety overriding her common sense. "You work your ass off to prove you're one of the guys. You're smart and pretty but you use people when they have something you want and discard them when you've wrung every last drop of blood out of them."

"Stop." Both Brad and Noah stood behind Kari now, the three of them against the stranger across the table.

Willa, undaunted, lifted her face to the men. "Do you two think she'll be loyal to you once this is over? Once she doesn't need you, Noah, to help with the physical work or you, Brad, to tell her she looks hot covered in sweat and dirt at the end of the day? Do you?"

The next morning dawned bright and calm. If it weren't for the leaves of trees that glowed soft and green and air that smelled fresh, washed clean of East Texas dirt, Kari could almost believe the storm had been a figment of her imagination. She found Willa waiting on the porch, wearing a determined expression and a borrowed pair of rubber boots several sizes too big.

"The rain stopped an hour ago." Like the bayou, Willa had transformed overnight. She'd grown subdued in the wake of her tirade. "Do you think he's out there?"

Kari followed her gaze to the swamp. Devon had never carried a prank to this extreme before. He might have tried to return to the cabin but given up when tramping through the mud had become too difficult. He might have sought shelter when the storm's second wave hit and decided to wait for them to come back for him. Or, the scenario Kari tried not to think too much about, he might be injured, lying in the elements all night and wondering why his friends hadn't been there to help him. The creak of the cabin's door saved her from answering, and within minutes they were on their way back to the frog pond.

Rain had turned the road into a sucking, slippery mess. Brad wrestled the steering wheel with a death grip to keep them from plunging into the waist-deep water in ditches along both sides. He stopped on the knoll where Kari had last spoken to Devon and the four of them got out.

At night, under the sparkling sky after the worst of the storm passed, the frog pond had felt magical. Now it was just another pool of murky water in a vast expanse of murky water. No sign of their nocturnal adventure remained. No footprints. No tire tracks.

No Devon.

"I thought he'd be here," Willa said. Her earlier determination slipped in the face of the emptiness that surrounded them.

Before them, the path sloped gently downhill for a quarter mile or so to the spot where they'd parked the night before. The far end of the pond was another quarter mile away around a bend in the road. Half a mile altogether. If Devon had stuck to solid ground during the storm, his red shirt should leap out at them amid the palette of greens and browns.

Off the road, cypress trees draped in Spanish moss dotted the bayou, and its dark waters hid untold dangers. Unexpectedly deep holes. Tangled tree limbs. Alligators.

Kari's imagination followed Devon in the dark, furious after their disagreement, only a flashlight to illuminate his path. Swallowed whole by the swamp.

"He probably found a dry place to hole up for the night," Noah said, his forced optimism obvious to anyone who'd known him more than five minutes. "Did he say anything to you when he left, Kari?"

They all stared at her. She shrugged. "He was just Devon being Dev."

"He was as angry as I've ever seen him," Willa said. She still played the sad, bewildered girlfriend but the tight set of her shoulders carried the weight of unvoiced allegations. "He walked away from you so fast I couldn't catch up."

The jealousy that had kindled when Devon arrived at the cabin with Willa and that had smoldered with every minute in the other woman's presence erupted into a full conflagration of bitter resentment tinged with a strong desire to protect the privacy of her last conversation with Devon. Surely, Kari thought, she was entitled to that much? Surely Brad and Noah knew the blame for this mess didn't lie with her?

"Well, we're not going to find him by standing around bickering." She stomped down the middle of the road, mud sucking at her boots until she felt like a cartoon, all exaggerated movement and no forward motion. The others followed, reluctantly she thought, but she heard them behind her.

She stopped at the spot where they'd parked the night before, but here, too, the rain had washed away any signs that might have helped them find Devon. They continued toward the farthest end of the pond, the only direction Devon could have gone and kept to solid ground. Brad grumbled the whole way. "This is pointless. I would have seen him if he'd come this far."

"It was dark—" Noah pointed out, "—and the frogs were really loud. You know how focused you are when you're concentrating on your work. He could have slipped past without you noticing."

They stopped where a tangle of concrete and rebar had been dumped along the water's edge as an erosion barrier to help prevent the road from breaking up and slipping into the swampy water. Given enough time, the swamp would reclaim anything humans built out here.

Kari stared into the clouded water, her gaze caught on a strip of torn denim hooked on a piece of rebar just under the surface. A deep rich blue that indicated the fabric hadn't seen much use, or been there long. From a jacket meant to impress, not work. The others hadn't seen it, not until they'd noticed Kari's stillness. Noah was the first, his body stiffening, becoming unnaturally still. Then Brad, and finally Willa.

"You said you didn't see him." Willa's accusation floated away on the breeze.

No one said anything for what seemed an eternity. Kari barely dared to breathe. Then Brad shoved his hands deep into his pockets and stepped away from the water's edge. Kari turned to him, but he wouldn't meet her eyes.

"When he found me up to my knees in that damn swamp, filling sample bottles, he laughed. Said I could play scientist all I wanted, but it wouldn't make one bit of difference if I didn't learn to play the game. The way he played them."

Devon had been angry at her, Kari thought, and taken his anger out on Brad.

Brad's face hardened. "Then he slipped. When he didn't crawl back out like the slime he is, I figured it was just another game to him, another chance to make me embarrass myself in front of him."

Willa, wide-eyed as if she, too, hadn't been playing games since she arrived, whispered, "You killed him."

"I didn't save him."

Kari's eyes fixed on the swatch of denim under the water. The four of them would report Devon missing. The cops would note the slippery mud, the storm, the lightning. The distraught friends. Willa might tell them about the job, about Brad and Devon's discord, but they wouldn't be able to prove Brad shoved Devon on purpose. In the end, they'd rule Devon's death a tragic accident. What do you expect when you turn a bunch of college kids loose in the wilderness, they'd say. Especially with the weather that came through at this time of the year.

Al drifted by, his eyes mere bumps on the surface, but ripples in his wake caught the sun and sparkled like diamonds, like the stars the night before between the bouts of the wicked storm.

What are we going to do about Devon? Brad had asked.

What can we do? Kari had replied. *Devon will keep on being Devon until the day he dies.*

Mafiosos, crooked FBI agents, missing cash—and a woman. Somebody's scheming someone, or is everybody scheming everyone? There's a pile of cash out there that will walk away at the end of the story...but with who?

CLICK
Dana Haynes

"It ain't rocket surgery."

That's what an old-school grifter named Jack Lisbon told me. Jack was one of those classic long-ball hitters, guys who see around corners. You know what I mean. We'd been acquainted for years. "Rush," he told me, sitting up in his hospital bed. "This thing steals itself."

Jack Lisbon had smoked like a coal-fired power plant and it finally caught up with him. He wasn't around to finish this thing off, but I promised to do it in his honor.

Here are the basics: a Mafioso from Milan, guy name of Lorenzo Romano, got himself into a world of hurt here in the U.S. and was facing indictment. A grand jury had been empaneled in his name. Romano had spent the last couple of years setting up a heroin distribution network, and he'd been squirreling away a little money on the side for himself. The way you do. He was sitting on something a little north of one point three million, cash money, American.

But the noose was tightening. City, state and federal agencies all locking on. The sitting grand jury would meet for he first time this coming Monday.

According to Jack Lisbon, Romano approached a bent FBI agent, Mark Finley. The Feds didn't know about Romano's private stash, and the Milanese Mob didn't know, either. It could become Finley's retirement account provided Romano got out of the U.S. and into a country with no extradition. He just had to do it before the grand jury finished its work.

Follow so far?

Jack Lisbon had been in no shape to follow through with his plan, which—I don't think I ought to have to spell this out for you, but here I go—had been to steal the $1.3 million. Finley wouldn't have been able to make a fuss without revealing himself as being as dirty as Romano. And he would do it after the handoff so Romano would have been long-gone fled. Romano'd be free so what would he care who ended up with the money? The mob in Milan? They hadn't even known about the stuff.

Win-win-win. High-stakes. Dangerous but doable.

Jack Lisbon, rest his soul, could have done it.

I could do it.

But not alone.

"So it's like this." I wait until the third round of drinks arrives. Sitting across from me is Paulo D'Ignazio. From his Roman nose to his slumped shoulders and back to his curved spine, the guy looks like an end parenthesis. He'd been working for Lorenzo Romano. Over-worked, by the look of it. We sit in a faded red vinyl booth in a dark jazz club with absolutely the worst acoustics in the whole of Manhattan. You could pretty much plot anything in these booths and sound would drop like a boat anchor within inches of your elbow. The place was popular, not because of the booze or the hot jazz, but because of the privacy.

I slide something across the table, then sip my Skyy rocks. I sit back, waiting.

D'Ignazio eyes it for a full thirty seconds, left hand gripped tight around his beer as if it were the joystick of a fighter jet. The guy's sweating diamonds. He glances up at me, then again at the tabletop. He gulps about a third of his beer, then uses both hands to open the unsealed envelope and unfurl the twice-folded sheets.

Government documents.

Paulo D'ignazio reads. He slowly sighs out the word, "Shit."

"Yep." I swish ice around my glass, enjoying the musical tone of it.

"Your friend told me about this. Where is he?"

"Emphysema."

"Ah." He nodded. He tapped the document with a dirty fingernail. "This is…this is real?"

"'Fraid so."

"He's leaving me here to rot?"

"Well…" I sit forward, wincing, the truth painful to spit out. I imagine myself as an oncologist, studying X-rays, shaking my head. "Romano's not just leaving you here. He's making sure you take the fall. This is the deal he set up with the FBI. They gotta arrest someone otherwise their own guys look crooked. If someone goes down, the brass won't be asking too many questions. A win's a win, especially if someone's going to prison. Can't be Lorenzo Romano, right? His father's a don. His grandfather was a don. This guy is to the Milanese mob what the Bushes were to American politics. Someone's getting arrested, and it ain't the crown prince. I mean, no one's naïve here. Right? You were born at night but it wasn't last night. That true?"

D'Ignazio drains his beer. He studies the pages. It looks legit. It isn't, but you get what you pay for, and Jack Lisbon's forger is expensive.

D'Ignazio drains his beer in a long gulp. "Shit."

"Precisely."

* * *

"That's the FBI bastard. Finley."

D'Ignazio and I sit in a nondescript Nissan, half a block from a coffee shop in Queens. I have opera glasses that fit into the palm of my hand and use them to study the too-cheerful café, the mint and blush décor, round metal tables and metal chairs that should have been outlawed by the Geneva Convention. Two pale, light-haired men have just entered. One is gym-fit and thin, blond highlights, with narrow jeans and an unstructured jacket hanging elegantly off wide shoulders. The other's more burly, hair cropped short, has an oft-busted nose and cauliflowered ears. They aren't friends.

"Which one?"

"Thin one," D'Ignazio says. "Mark Finley. He is, how you say, the up-and-comer."

"And the bruiser?"

He snorts with derision. "Is a bruiser. Bell. U.S. Marine. Dishonorable discharge. He's Lorenzo's bodyguard."

"Romano doesn't have an Italian watchdog?"

"He is the paranoid, yes? Who can he trust? Who works for his brothers? His father? Other gangs? He hires outsiders for muscle. He pays well. He figures money buys loyalty."

"Well, he's right, I suppose."

I watch the bruiser move to the bar and order something, a coffee probably: Bell. The guy wears a black T-shirt stretched over a barrel chest and massive shoulders. He looks dim.

Finley sits at one of the little round tables. Already seated is a dark-haired, dark-skinned guy in a polo shirt and chinos, lots of product in his coif, skimming foam off the top of a to-go cup with a little spoon. Well, hey there, Lorenzo Romano. Understand you have travel plans, bro. Good luck with those.

"Finley's predictable," I say, mostly to myself. "All crooked people are."

D'Ignazio's laugh isn't kind. "What does that make you?"

I give him my thousand-watt smile. "Put away your lantern. You just found an honest man."

"Really…"

"I'm a thief, Paulo, *mi amico*. I'm totally honest about what I do. Is Bell going to be a problem?" I watched the big man who sat at the bar, an eye on his boss and the FBI agent.

"He's vicious. A rabid dog. As long as he's around, you have a problem."

I lower the glasses and smile at him. "As long as he's around, *we* have a problem."

My old buddy, Jack Lisbon, gave me the most wonderful Easter egg. Mark Finley had an ex-girlfriend who'd been with him most of the year but whom he'd dumped only a few weeks prior.

Hell hath no fucking fury, bubbeleh. It's a cliché for a reason.

Her name's Hailee—hand to God, two e's—and she'd been, in no particular order, a roadie, a barista, a stripper, a college dropout and a web cam girl. The Renaissance slacker. She, also come to find out, is well and truly pissed at FBI Agent Mark Finley. That's my intro. I meet her on the elliptical at a neighborhood gym and tell her I plan to take Finley for a lot of money. Money I'd be willing to share.

That's all it takes.

She's a smoking-hot thing with hair dyed royal blue and plenty of tattoos on her shoulders and across her upper chest. She has a nose ring and she chain-smokes these absolutely nasty Turkish cigarettes that you could use to burn through a bank vault. She's manic, absently clicking a pen, fiddling with her hair and earrings, talking with her acrylic nails, her fingers painting glyphs in mid-air as she speaks.

"Such an asshole! God, I don't know why guys like that do it for me."

I'm having a tough time seeing Mr. Frosted Tips and his narrow-cut jeans as a bad boy but I'd been fooled by looks before. Who among us hasn't?

"Know why he dumped you?"

Hailee sucks down another cigarette and stabs it out in an amber tray. She'd ordered an absinthe. Seriously. I'd never seen one before. I'd ordered an eighteen-year-old Glenmorangie; the booze is maybe two years younger than she was.

She stares at me through artfully smoky eye shadow. I wait. It's important that she ask. That she thinks she's driving the conversation. I clock her accent as South Boston. "He found some other girl?"

"He was about to come into a quarter million dollars." I sip the whiskey. It tastes like a moonlit walk along the Seine. I don't see any reason to tell her it was actually $1.3 million. That would have been like casting a thirty-pound test line to catch a goldfish. A quarter mil would get her attention.

Hailee studies me. Her long nails become still for the first time since we sat.

"Having a girlfriend around means having to share. Mark is not, I take it, a sharer."

"He gave me HPV."

"Aside from that, I mean."

She shakes her head slowly.

"Greed." I tsk. "One of the seven deadly sins."

Her fingers twitch out more arcane symbols in the air. Their varnish was the same color as the absinthe in her glass. She hasn't touched the drink; I think she ordered it to match her nails. She rattles off the others: "Pride, lust, envy, gluttony, wrath and sloth."

"I take it you're a collector."

"But only in mint condition. What do you got in mind, Kurt?"

(Kurt. She'd worn a vintage Nirvana T-shirt in the gym. I pick my *noms de voyage* to appeal to people's pre-existing interests.)

"I got in mind taking his quarter million from him."

"You do know he's in the Fucking Bureau of Investigation."

"And I'll take it from him in a manner that precludes him from chatting about it around the water cooler. The Bureau doesn't know about the dough now and still won't after it's missing. We're not taking legal money."

See what I did there with the *we*?

Her smile comes at me sideways, like a rattler. "And you're the sharing type, are you?"

"Twenty percent of the take. I need to know where Finley will be. Some place nobody in his law enforcement circle knows about. Some place he feels safe."

"How come?"

"Because nobody's ever safe. People who feel safe are the most vulnerable."

"That's deep."

"You're in?"

She says, "Twenty percent of a quarter million is..." Her eye flutter, looking up and to the left. Her lips move a little. I think about suggesting she use her pen and the bar napkin to do her sums, but I sip instead.

She quirks that sidewise smile again.

"I'm in."

Setting up a good heist is like greasing the insides of a complicated but reliable machine. An old, manual typewriter, maybe. You press this key, and click. A letter forms. Press it three dozen times, you get three dozen copies of the same letter. Click Click Click. It's the part of this business I like best. The Click.

Before he took a turn for the worse, Jack Lisbon had installed lipstick cameras in Lorenzo Romano's Upper Eastside condo. He hadn't bothered mic'ing the joint because, like me, he didn't speak Italian. Now I sit cross-legged on the ugly, miasmic carpet of my rented apartment, barefoot and shirtless, bottle of scotch by my kneecap, drinking from a stained coffee cup and watching the black and white images on my laptop.

Romano, all swarthy and wire-thin, tie loosened, wearing

crocodile mocs with a beige suit. He makes it work. He's leaning against an antique desk and speaks directly to Paulo D'Ignazio, the guy old Jack had turned and who's working with me now. Bell, the ex-Marine bouncer, stands off a bit, hands folded in front of his belt buckle, parade rest, T-shirt straining around his deltoids. He doesn't speak, doesn't fidget, doesn't blink near as I can tell. His eyes do not come off his employer.

Guy's a pot roast but I'm getting the sense he's a for-real bodyguard. He takes the job seriously.

He looks like a complication.

I hate complications.

A court clerk tells me the grand jury is hoping to be done by the weekend. They'd be handing down a true bill within days. I have too little time. But I'm nearly ready.

Getting there, at any rate.

Hailee says, "What do you think?"

The apartment's in a redeveloped Brooklyn factory. The old brickwork had been painted a glossy white. The hardwood floors were uneven and warped because, for about eighty years, people had made candy here and sugar had infused itself into the decades of varnish. Tall, narrow baroque windows face out toward Sheepshead Bay. He's got a small desk and it's absolutely pristine; not a piece of paper to be found on it. The art on the walls is cheap-print LeRoy Neiman.

Real estate in this neighborhood has gone nuts the last couple of years. "Finley's been on the take for a while?"

"He didn't earn this on his government payroll, honey." Today she wears a strapless white eyelet dress and vintage red Chuck high-tops, revealing still more ink. She chews gum. She'd put her blue hair in pigtails.

This place was decorated by a guy. For sure. I remember that

Mark Finley's married. "Bachelor pad?"

"If you're asking, does he fuck girls here, yes."

"But his Bureau buddies don't know about this place."

"Nobody does. He called it his Fortress of Soli Dude."

Jesus wept. I'd have been willing to rip Finley off for that alone.

"He keep a gun here?"

Sashaying over to the right side of the bed she puts her hand against the side of an antique wooden nightstand and pushes. The side recedes and she reaches in and withdraws a Glock G19X, coyote-colored. Bought illegally, no doubt, after it fell off a truck destined for Operation Enduring Whatever. An untraceable weapon. A bent agent like Finley would play it no other way.

She hands me the gun, butt first. Her voice drops half an octave. "You're sure he's out of town today?"

"D.C. Back Thursday."

And by Friday, indictments could be in season.

Hailee eyes the low-framed bed with the Egyptian cotton sheets. She drags her eyes from the bed to me. She clicks her tongue. "Doesn't have to be just money you take from him."

I give her the thousand-watt smile again. "When we're done. That'd be nice. I'd really like that."

She shrugs. "Don't know what you're passing up, Kurt."

I think, *Well, there's the HPV.*

Back in the red-vinyl booth again, in the bad acoustics bar. Paulo D'Ignazio's on his third beer, sullen and scared. I tell him, "I'm thinking seventy-thirty."

He gives me the eye. "*Cazzo.* I'm thinking sixty-forty."

"Sixty-forty doesn't sit on the sidelines. Sixty-forty is in the game."

"You think I'm not in the game?"

I lean toward him. "I think I'm the one who knows how to take Lorenzo for his one-point-three. I think I'm the one who will carry the duffel away. I think I'm the one Finley will know stole his money. Way this is working out, you could spend the whole night right here. Start doing this for a living: offering information with no risk, set up a reputation for yourself. Dr. Red Vinyl, Scourge of the Underworld."

He says, "*Cazzo*," again, and again I don't know what it means but assume ill intent.

I sip my drink. I order him a fourth beer.

"What is it needs doing?"

I let the question linger for damn near a full minute. "You like having Bell breathing over your shoulder?"

He shudders a little. "You look into that one's eyes: no soul. One of the heroin distributors, he ran off with the cash, yes? This was last fall. Ran as far as Ohio. The Pacific Coast."

That'd be Oregon, but I let it slide. "Bell?"

"Chased him. Like a dog. You know how much money the distributor took? Six hundred dollars. Six. Hundred. Could have been six cents. Bell, he doesn't care. Lorenzo says go, Bell goes."

"Seems like the kind who takes his job seriously. A guy with pride. He fails to keep Lorenzo Romano safe, that's losing face."

D'Ignazio's eyelids droop as the beer does its work. He looks both scared and fatigued.

He whispers. "I hate that guy."

(Complicated but reliable machine. Click...)

I'd brought a messenger bag, used and untraceable. It was on the table between us. Now I opened the frayed flap, show him a glimpse of blued steel.

"Now that sounds like sixty-forty."

He snorts. "It sounds like fifty-fifty to me."

I lean back, sip. "Fair enough."

So Hailee tells me Finley has a thing for make-up sex. The rougher the better. She just has to convince him that she's jonesing for him. One last time. She does her part perfectly. Finley agrees to meet her at two a.m. at his Bronx bachelor pad.

If my intel's right, Finley and Lorenzo Romano were meeting at midnight to exchange the money. I check my watch. The handoff should have happened twenty minutes ago. Finley would be feeling flush, full of himself. Guy like that, after a big win, he's probably hard as an anvil. Looking to show little Hailee what she's missing.

Self-confident people make mistakes.

I wait in an alley and see Finley arrive at the old Bronx candy factory. He comes on foot. No LoJacked FBI vehicle for him. Not here. He's carrying a satchel.

I meet him on the sidewalk, stumbling a little like I'm drunk. I do a brush pass, a half block from his door. "Sorry, buddy."

He nods but ignores me.

Now I know he's not carrying. He doesn't take a service weapon to the love shack. Doesn't need to. He has the Glock tucked away behind the receding panel of his bed stand.

The Glock with the now missing firing pin.

I get back to my alley. Paulo D'Ignazio's waiting for me. Even in the dark, in the alley, he looked sweat-sheened, twitchy, eyes too dilated, moving his weight from foot to foot. He hands me back the messenger bag. His body is wired with adrenaline. "Fuck him. Fuck Bell. He wasn't so tough."

I take the blued gun out of the bag and smell the cordite and gunpowder. One bullet missing from the carousel. "One and done. Paulo, *mi amico*, I'm impressed."

"This is not my first killing. You think I'm the virgin?"

"I think you're a rich man," I say, and stuff the gun back in the messenger bag.

D'Ignazio puffs up.

I close the bag around my wrist, point the bottom of the messenger bag his direction and shoot him in the chest.

The bag absorbs most of the sound. Paulo D'Ignazio crumples to the asphalt behind a dumpster. I wait in the shadows, listening. Did anyone overhear?

Nope.

The lights blink on in Mark Finley's hideaway. I see Mr. Blond Highlights pass by his window, tumbler in hand, tie loosened. He's had a good night. He's made a killing. Who hasn't? Next, he's going to have some rough make-up sex with Hailee. He looks relaxed, master of the universe.

A Lyft pulls up. Hailee shows a couple acres of thigh stepping out onto platform heels, which click when she steps onto the asphalt. She actually makes the okay symbol in the direction of the alley and winks, fake lashes fluttering. Jesus H. Christ on a moped. If Finley had been at the window still, I'd have been actuating Plan B, which included a night train to Montreal.

But he isn't, and I don't.

I wait for her to enter first. I don't wait long, though. No romance for Mark Finley. He likes to get right to it. He should be ripping her clothes off just about now.

I check the street. No traffic. No pedestrians. No silhouettes in windows.

I cross.

I'd already mastered the ten-key lock for the building. How do you think Hailee and I got in the first time? I'm take the stairs slowly, walking near the edge—not the middle—of each step. I get to his door. I take the blued handgun out of the messenger bag, set the bag at my feet.

I very slowly pick his lock.

I've got the door open and I'm three steps in before Mark Finley walks out of the bathroom, heading toward his bed and toward an old sweatshirt and pair of jeans he's laid out. He's wearing a towel wrapped around his well-crafted torso. I take it he screwed Hailee in the shower. A porn classic.

I spot the satchel on his desk chair; the satchel he picked up from Lorenzo Romano.

Finley stops, water dripping from his blond highlights, eyes on me.

He doesn't look scared. Or surprised. I'm more than a little impressed.

I close the door quietly behind me. The barrel of my revolver doesn't waver. "Hi, Mark. I need what's in that bag, please. No need for this to get any messier than it already is."

He eyes the gun, then turns his gaze to me.

"*Che cazzo è questo?*"

I'm...wait. What?

"*Tu chi sei?*"

Does he think I'm from Lorenzo Romano? I let that play out in my head. You know, that scans. That could be good. I nod.

He makes a beeline toward the nightstand with its retracting side panel. I don't mind. Like a chess master, I let him move to my right while I shift to my left, three steps, and retrieve the satchel.

The weight feels perfect. One-point-three million perfect.

He's retrieved the Glock, turns on me.

"*Nessuna pistola!*"

I edge toward the door.

He pulls the trigger.

The bullet is more heat than impact, more shock than pain. Blood begins to seep into my shirt, just above my belt. I stumble, blink, shock coming on.

This...this isn't right. That gun doesn't have a firing pin.

I pull my own trigger.

The sound is more painful than the bullet I took. My ears ring. He collapses back against the nightstand, lamp and digital clock radio crashing to the floor. He fires again and his second bullet gouges a chunk out of the warped wooden floor, sugary finish mushrooming into the air.

He flops half onto the bed, legs akimbo, blood everywhere.

I put a hand to my stomach and it comes away beet red. That means the blood's oxygenated, right? Is that good or bad?

How the fuck'd he shoot me without the firing pin for the Glock?

The shots were loud. I need to get out of here. I set the satchel down on his small desk, scattering the already messy mounds of papers and documents, ledgers, envelopes, opened mail. I move to the bed, whisk away his towel, leaving him naked. I feel behind me; find an exit wound. Still not much pain. But it's coming. Boy, is it coming. I wrap the towel around my torso, same way he had. Then I tuck it into my belt, cinch my belt tight.

I return to the desk and the satchel. I unzip it. It's filled with money. American money.

I glance at the desk. The desk that, two days earlier, had been pristine. I remember now. No paper on it at all. Nothing.

Now it's scattered with documents.

Covered with Italian writing.

I throw my gun in the bag, grab it and head out.

I am not bleeding out in this man's love shack. I'm not. End of fucking discussion.

I can barely drive. The pain ratchets up. I lean over and puke onto the passenger-side floor mat. Leaning over increases the pain. I'm drenched in sweat, the towel now a puttanesca red. I stagger into my apartment.

I know a doc upstate who can patch me up. I can pay; that's no problem.

The TV's on in my place and that's just plain weird. I'm nauseous, shaking, and I'm almost inside before I realize it. I draw the revolver, hold it in my sticky, blood-caked left hand, push open the door.

A woman lies on my bed, leaning back on her elbows, eyes on my TV. She's watching the news. She doesn't look in my direction. She's wearing jeans tucked into suede ankle boots with stiletto heels, plus a navy sweater. Her hair's long, straight and black, held back in a complicated French braid. Her hair isn't blue and I can't spot a nose ring or acrylic nails. I can see a bit of her shoulder and a band of her abs with no tattoos. But it's definitely Hailee.

I point the gun at her, a palsied shake rattling my aim.

She clicks the remote to turn off the sound. She says, "Wait. Here it is."

Her accent is mid-European something.

I blink sweat out of my eyes, look at the screen. A lectern. A Justice Department insignia. Two American flags. Three officials are speaking. One of them is Lorenzo Romano. The chyron beneath his image reads *Mark Finley, FBI.* But that's Romano. Not Finley. I left Finley dead in his... Finley. The blond-highlights in the love shack had spoken to me in Italian. His desk had been cluttered with Italian documents.

My bathroom door opens on my left and the ex-Marine, Bell, steps out. He gently takes the satchel from me. I'm too stunned even to fight. "Take care of that, why don't I, mate."

He sounds British. Working class, Midlands.

Paulo D'Ignazio steps out of the bathroom, too. The same Paulo D'Ignazio I killed behind the dumpster in the alley. The same Paulo D'Ignazio I'd talked into killing Bell. He looks taller now, his spine straight. He moves like a dancer.

He studies the sopping red towel bulging from my trousers, belted tight around my torso. He looks at the bruiser.

The big man says, "Romano got a shot off. Told ye."

The guy I knew as D'Ignazio sighs, pulls a twenty out of his pocket, hands it over.

I back into the corner, so I can cover all three of them with the revolver. But all three of whom? Hailee, Bell and D'Ignazio? Fuck that. Or fuck me, as it were.

Hailee stands and uses the remote to kill the video. She looks a little older. A lot more sophisticated. When she speaks, she cants her head sideways, as if studying an animal in a zoo.

"Lorenzo Romano was showering to get ready for his meeting with Agent Finley," she says. The eyes that stare at me don't blink. They don't register any emotion. "They were meeting at three a.m. to exchange that."

Her eyes pivot to the satchel in the big Englishman's hand, then back to me.

"I don't…who…"

"Romano was killed in his flat. Shot by a thief. A thief Romano also shot. The thief fled the scene. Fortunately, Romano was paranoid. He had CC cameras inside and outside his flat. The thief will be easy enough to identify."

"Fuck…you're…" I point the gun at her chest. "What is this! Who the fuck are you?"

The thin dark man whose name obviously isn't Paulo D'Ignazio smiles a red velvet smile. "First shot was a blank, love. That one was for me. Second wasn't, as poor Lorenzo found out. Third one…?"

I turned the gun to the big man with the satchel and pulled the trigger.

Click.

The woman—the woman not Hailee without two e's—nods. "Finley was about to accept a bribe, so he can't report what's missing. So either you bleed out, Mr. Rush, or you survive and have a very, very angry Special Agent Mark Finley waiting to take back what he thinks is his. If you evade both those fates? Well, you killed the heir presumptive of the Milanese mob, Mr. Rush. They have an awfully long memory."

The three of them head for the door. Her heels click as she walks. I pull the trigger two more times. Click Click.

My left leg gives out and I slump down on my ass, my back against the wall, legs sprawled out on the ugly, miasmic carpet. The edges of my vision blur.

The dark-haired guy wasn't Romano, he was Finley. He'll be after me now. The blond highlights was Romano. I survive this and I'll have the mob on my ass.

I'd been confident, safe. Remember what I told you? People who feel safe are the most vulnerable.

The thin man's phone vibrates and he pulls it from his pocket, checks a text. He smiles. "Finnigan and Fiero. Needing a hand."

The woman smiles at him. "Where?"

I pull the trigger. Click.

"Would you believe, Belgrade?"

"Be a nice change, that," the big man says. "What d'you want to do?"

The guys look at her to make the decision. She's in charge here.

"We owe them," the woman says. "We should help."

Click.

They hit the door.

Click.

Before she leaves, she turns back to me.

"The emphysema would have killed Jack Lisbon in due course, Mr. Rush. You didn't have to smother him. That was just bad form."

Click.

"Best of luck."

Click.

Two women, one husband, one diamond—and one big lie. Somebody's going to get hurt...

PRINCESS CUT
Tim P. Walker

Yes, everything does sparkle, doesn't it? In this neighborhood, under these blue white streetlamps, when it's raining. Sure a drop of moisture on the windshield can make any light shine like a gemstone, it's that the cut of it in this neighborhood is so much more brilliant. Maybe it's the way the glow from the streetlamps tears through the leaves of the elms and the palms that line the boulevards. Maybe it's those floodlights over every garage and the way they light up the cars parked in their driveways. Maybe it's the raindrops in those heavy beams of light, glowing like a shower of sparks as they bounce off the cars' curvy frames, their glossy bodies shimmering all cherry red and grapefruit pink and vanilla white. Or maybe it's just his house, with those tall windows and the hot white glow behind them. Prince Charming and his palace. The man and his Princess.

The shape of the windows that line the palace walls all around give the building its impression of an ovoid shape. Unlike most of the houses on this street, those old beige monoliths of stone and clay crafted in the Spanish mold, this one is modern, its style stainless. It wasn't built so much as landed here, on this flat stretch of ground overlooking the black water bay. Every curve and every angle—from its pointed roof to the slate black car park—is so measured, so precise, that it could give the second

71

hand of Prince Charming's Rolex watch the nervous sweats. The way the place is made up of so much glass seems to dare or even beg someone to throw stones, from both the inside and out. It sparkles, this place. It sparkles so much.

Becky pulls the Chevette over beneath a palmetto tree just at the edge of the property. Then she throws the gear into first and cuts the engine, which shakes and sputters itself to death. Most of the properties on this street have yards full of trees, but not this place. No, Prince Charming and his Princess have their grounds completely cleared of them, as though they'd meant to open up the view, not for them but of any other thing. Because what's the point of living in such a sparkly monument to modern living if nobody can see it?

It's all about spectacle with these people, isn't it? Wasn't it Prince Charming's big-wheeled white Bronco she'd glimpsed through her rapidly swelling eye from the floor of the Courtsquare Tavern that day, honking spastically as it peeled out from its parking spot and tore away down Church Street? And weren't those some big windows they had at the Courtsquare, too? Not only at the right time of day can a person see everything going on inside as clear as a bell, but anybody inside can see just as clearly everything going on outside, even with their rear end planted firmly on the ground next to their barstool.

But his Bronco's not here tonight. No doubt he's on the prowl, looking for another silly fool. But she's home tonight. Yes, indeed she is. The Princess herself. Somewhere in those amber shadows dancing in that glass palace. Becky feels around for the lump in her pocket, just to make sure it's still there, and she slowly begins the walk down the slate driveway toward the house. The driveway's so flat, so slick, that the rain drops bounce from the surface, soaking her canvas Keds and the ankle hem of her jeans. Still she moves slowly, pulling the hood of her crimson sweatshirt over her head and shoving her hands as deep in her pockets as they can go.

As open as the house is, for as many windows there are, the

door is as imposing as any palace gate should be. It's tall, bulky, and colored the blackest shade of walnut. With the probing overhead light trained down at the doorstep like a spotlight, it only added to the impression. Becky presses the glowing button to the left of the door and shoves her hands back in her pockets. The doorbell chimes loudly, its lonely tune sending echoes throughout the house. Its echoes still resonate as the door opens and a bronzed and narrow face peers through the crack; a pair of dark brown, deep-set eyes fixing themselves on Becky. It's the same narrow face, same set of eyes that were fixed dead on her that afternoon at the Courtsquare. It's the same shock of black wavy hair rushing at her like a fast rising tide. All those people in that place, and it was Becky she was coming for. This woman at the door—the Princess herself.

"Can I help you?" the Princess asks.

Standing as she is with her hood over her head, without her makeup on, with a bandage under her eye and the rain dripping down her nose, she was sure the Princess wouldn't recognize her. What could she be to her but one of who knew how many faces? She sputters something about car trouble, something about a phone that she can maybe use or any kind of help or some such thing. There are words dribbling from her mouth.

The Princess's eyes dart over Becky's shoulder and off into the distance. "Do you mean that piece of shit right there?" she hisses, nodding toward the beige hatchback outlined in bright blue streetlight. "Is that the car you speak of? Exactly what business would a piece of shit like that have breaking down in this particular neighborhood?"

Well, this certainly wasn't something Becky had planned for, let alone rehearsed. Becky starts to sputter again, spinning sounds off her tongue that don't even begin to cohere into complete sentences. Of course the Princess has to go and throw her for another loop when a look of recognition crosses her bony face. She flings the door open completely, wrapping her fingers around her hips as her eyes suck in Becky like she's made of tobacco and lit on fire. She has on a black pullover speckled with gold spots all over like the pelt of a leopard, the neckline cut to the point where her breasts meet. It's tucked into a dark pair of tight jeans with a coiled golden wire slipped around her waist through the belt loops. Same outfit she wore that day at the Courtsquare.

"I know you, don't I?" the Princess says, her red-painted fingernail tapping the silver-threaded bull's head embroidered on the hip pocket of her jeans, as though attempting to agitate it. She lifts her other hand to her chin, strokes it, and there it is, glittering in the searing overhead light, that platinum engagement band fixed with a square-cut rock the size of one of her own knuckles. The sight of it makes the scab under the Becky's bandage twitch. It sparkles, that thing. Oh yes, it sparkles.

"Wait a minute." The Princess snaps her fingers and a hungry smile creeps across her lips. It's that same smile Becky saw just before the sudden burst of stars, when the whole world shimmered for a brief moment, before suddenly nothing did. She knew Becky's name then. She knew who she'd been in town to meet. So now it's—"You're that little bitch from the bar, aren't you?"

"I..." But there's nothing in the script for this. The way that Randy who poured the drinks talked about this woman, about her and her husband's exploits, maybe Becky should've figured that the Princess keeps a mental rolodex of every woman's face that had ever been ensnared in their little game. Simple memories to flip through every once in a lonely afternoon. That's how these things are supposed to work, aren't they? This woman, the Princess, probably has better memory for faces than her own husband. It would be just like Prince Charming to have forgotten Becky's face already, wouldn't it?

"I'm sorry to have bothered you. I think I have the wrong..."

"Bullshit, darling," the Princess purrs wickedly through her toothy Cheshire grin. "You know why you came." Her eyes take another drag off Becky. "You'd better come in. You're getting all wet."

That honey-tinged drawl she's put on, like a black velvet glove for her tongue, wasn't there a minute ago when she answered the door. It sure as hell hadn't been there for the run-in at the Courtsquare, but it's here now and seeing as how Becky's following this woman into her home, into the very chambers of her palace, then it must be doing what it's meant to do. Her arms close by her side, gripping tight that cylindrical lump in her pocket, Becky tiptoes across the floor in the woman's wake, aware of the tracks her wet Keds were making. The Princess doesn't seem to pay any mind as she slowly strides through the foyer and down the hall, the wineglass stem heels of her shoes clacking on the chessboard marble floor. It's a strange sight, this woman, the Princess, dressed like she's bound for the ball, or at least the disco. It's a Tuesday night, and she's wearing heels in her own home.

The palace is both smaller and larger than it appears from the outside. The blinding whiteness of the walls and the sparse furnishings lend the space an open feeling but the curved aspect of the rooms seem to close them in, as though the whole place were a massive arm curling around prey it only means to toy with for a while. At the center of it is a large circular room covered with coal black carpet, two steps lower than the main level of the house, like a miniature gladiator arena. This is the living room.

"It's very white, isn't it?" the Princess asks. When Becky turns, the Princess has a stemmed glass held out to her, filled nearly to the brim with wine, its hue as golden as one of the spots on her shirt. "White wine? That is what you prefer, isn't it?"

"It is." Becky struggles to answer. It was what she'd been drinking as she'd stood at the bar at the Courtsquare, waiting for Prince Charming before the Princess strolled in. Truth is that most of the time she couldn't care less what kind of wine she was drinking. White—of whichever variant—had seemed like the right choice at the time. The right choice now—well, that would be a cold hard shot of tequila. Something to steady her nerves, keep her hands from shaking so much as she reached for the glass.

The Princess suddenly yanks it out of reach and takes first one sip, then another, slowly. "Apologies, darling. I'd thought I'd relieve you of a few drops before you drip something else all over my carpet. Cheers." She hands the glass back to Becky then raises her own and offers a wink and a toast before downing half its contents in a single gulp. Judging by the two empty bottles sitting on the silver-wheeled cart by the window, Becky's personal preferences would never have been a factor.

"Come," the Princess says, taking a few steps down to one of the ivory leather sofas around the large plate glass coffee table. "Sit," she adds, patting the cushion next to hers. Becky does so, gingerly planting herself as the Princess leans back and lights a very long, very skinny cigarette. "Drink," she says then, and Becky tips the glass slowly to her mouth, taking a tiny sip, the dryness of it seeming to suck all moisture from her lips.

The Princess asks her what she thinks and gulping hard between heavy breaths Becky tells her it's good. "Chardonnay, is it?" she asks, to which the Princess merely cackles.

"Pinot Grigio, darling." She flicks an ash somewhere in the direction of the glass ashtray on the coffee table. "Chardonnay is for those dried-up ol' house fraus who sit around all day playing stupid card games and bitching about their husbands. How boring is that? Or is that what brings you here? You've come to play cards and bitch about my husband, haven't you? Come on, fess up. I know you're not here to see him. Surely you would've noticed that his truck is gone." Her eyes go wide with intensity as that peculiar grin stretches across her face a second time. She leans forward and grabs Becky's knee, rough and playful at first, then shifts it to a soft caress. Becky must be giving off some serious nervous vibes, because the Princess tells her to relax.

"I'm only teasing. You're going to have to lighten up, darling."

Maybe it's the needling, or maybe it's the fact that the Princess is sliding her hand up her thigh, but Becky takes a bigger swig of her wine.

"That's the spirit. You know, I can't believe my manners," the Princess says, drawing her hand back to Becky's knee. "I didn't even get your name."

Except she did. Once. Becky heard her say it. *Are you Becky?* she'd said. *The same Becky here to meet with Henry?* Those were the words, the exact words the Princess uttered just before she laid every carat of that rock into her face. And all those people sitting around, standing around, all those eyes pretending not to notice her flat on her ass next to the bar, blood pouring from her nose as well as the gash below her eye. And this bitch, the Princess, has the luxury of forgetting her *name?*

"It's Becky."

"Oh, that's right." The Princess points and waves the lit end of her cigarette at her. "You're one of the Beckys. How could I forget? So tell me, Becky, where did you and my husband meet?"

Had there been a hesitation? "Work," Becky answers, not knowing, as she stares out into the rainy darkness beyond the windows. With windows as tall as these, it makes for a lot of darkness and rain to take in.

"Well I could've told you that. Where exactly do you work, darling?"

"King Motors." Becky sighs again.

"Oh, for that ol' Trent King? Henry told me he'd been pitching him on that high rise over off the Seventeen. You'll have to pardon me, but you don't strike me as quite the salesman type."

"Well, I'm not. I…"

"Let me guess—a secretary then? My apologies, I meant a personal assistant. For an automobile dealership, too." The Princess shakes her head piteously as her eyes scan Becky from the greasy strands of her mousy hair down to her Keds sneakers. With a frown, she runs a lone finger up the copper-threaded seam of Becky's Kmart-bought jeans, stopping at the hem of her crimson sweatshirt. "Must not pay you very well either."

"He didn't," Becky mutters, thinking about the disgusted

look on King's face that only grown more and more hardened each day the bandage had graced her face. He finally told her that if he found her that repellent then other folks—meaning the customers—would surely feel the same way. He cut her one last check and told her to go be hideous somewhere else.

"So sorry to hear that, darling." The Princess pats Becky's leg patronizingly, then she grabs her knee again, squeezing lightly. "Now if you don't mind me asking—if it's not to see my husband, just what the fuck is it that brought you here?"

No. Him and that white Ford Bronco of his weren't there. She'd been following that thing around town all week enough to know where it was and when. From his office to some building site somewhere to another building site somewhere else to some other office and to a bar and to yet another office and then yet another bar—she followed him all over the city. All the while she wondered if the next joint he parked in front of would be the next one where he'd sit in his Bronco and just wait. Would he sit and wait for his wife to walk into this one? Would his windows fog up then the way bartender Randy had described them before? Would he hoot and holler and hammer on his horn as he peeled out of this parking space?

Eventually she'd follow him home to his sparkly castle night after night. To his Princess. Becky knew he wouldn't be here tonight.

So why is she here?

The room and everything in it—it all goes sparkly as her eyes fill. "I don't know," Becky admits with a sniffle. "I guess I just wanted to know why."

"Why what, darling?" To which Becky only tilts her head to show off her bandage.

"Well, darling, in all fairness that is my husband you were trying to fuck," the Princess coolly tells her, inspecting her nails as the cigarette burns away between her fingers.

"But you knew," Becky mutters, and all the shiny things start to melt and blur. "You knew the whole time and you did

everything to me on purpose because you wanted...because..."
She stops, because even sitting here the whole thing is too absurd
for her to believe, much less describe. Prince Charming set her
up. There's no other way to see it. All the winks, all the ways
he'd sneak a tickle of her wrist, her elbow, her hip; all the cup-
cakes he'd buy special from the crosstown bakery that he'd leave
on her desk when he'd visit—all of it just a setup. And when he
finally asked her out on a lunch date at the Courtsquare—none
of it was real. He set her up like tenpins so the Princess could
step in and knock them down.

"You had to have known he was married, darling."

"You planned it that way."

"You had to have seen his ring. He doesn't take it off."

"But I..." Or did she? Granted, a man's wedding band doesn't
sparkle like this rock on the woman's fingers, but it's surely something she would've noticed. Right? And oh, for that twinkle in
his cobalt blue eyes, and that big million-dollar set of pearly
whites in his mouth, that chiseled chin, that blonde flip of pres-
idential hair—who'd be looking at some junk-hunk of metal on
his finger?

"There, there," the Princess says in a soothing voice, patting
Becky's back as Becky tosses back the rest of her Pinot. Then
the Princess pours the rest of the wine from her own glass into
Becky's. "It's all right. All is forgiven, darling. Drink up."

Becky tilts the refilled glass to her lips as the Princess starts
to stroke her hair. But then she stops suddenly, pulling herself
out of the woman's royal grasp. "I still need to know why."

The Princess sighs cuttingly, smashing her cigarette out in the
ashtray. The honey in her voice seemed to have been rinsed away
in a mouthful of vinegar. "You wanted to fuck my husband and
I put you in your place." She sounds just like she had when
Becky was on the floor of the Courtsquare, hearing that same
voice dressing her down loud enough for the entire tavern to get
the message.

Stay away from my husband, bitch. Those were the words.

"No," Becky snaps. She pushes away, further from the Princess, her eyes moist, her heart thrumming rapidly. "You tricked me. Both of you. You wanted to hurt me like that. And he... he..."

"Got off on it?" the Princess says with a shrug. "Of course he did, and I did, too. So what?"

"But why?"

"I don't know, darling," she answers with a huff. "You know what it is that really annoys me about people like you? It's that you require a reason for every damn little thing in the world. You can't ever let things just *be*. You know—be as they are, as they're better off being." She inches closer to Becky, reaching out to stroke her hair once more. "And just what is it that makes you think that you're the innocent in this scenario? You wanted to fuck my husband, so in return—I'll admit it—it certainly seems like we went and done fucked you." The Princess plucks a single strand of hair from Becky's scalp without a warning. "So just how did it feel, might I ask?"

Becky swallows her answer with another gulp of wine.

"It does help, doesn't it? The wine? Dulls the pain a little?" Becky nods, but a tiny pinprick in the side of her head disagrees, to say nothing of the scab beneath her bandage. "You know, darling," the Princess goes on, giving Becky's cheek a pinch, "for whatever fate that's brought us together, I must say that I do enjoy the company." A wry grin creases across her face as a sparkly glint flashes in her eye. That's when the flat of her palm flies across the space between them and hits Becky square in the cheek, the crackling sound echoing around and around the funneling walls and on to the ceiling high above.

The impact isn't so hard though the shock of it knocks Becky to the floor as her vision fills with sparks. She crawls briskly away as the Princess stands up, cackling again.

"Don't go anywhere yet, my darling," the Princess says, nudging her in the butt with the pointed end of a black pump. "Not when we're just starting to get all worked up."

Becky turns herself over, writhing on her back as she squeezes the lump out of her jeans pocket. The Princess stands over her, smiling, mocking, her hands on her hips, her fingernail scratching the bull's head emblazoned on her hip pocket, its threads charging electric in the hot white glow of the room. Becky grabs the arm of the couch and pulls herself to her knees, then all the way to her feet. The Princess breaks into a prizefighter's stance, that rock on her finger twinkling wildly, hungrily.

"C'mon, darling, show me what you're made of," she taunts. "You're not just gonna let me fuck you again, now are you?"

But Becky slips the lump from her pocket and palms it. The urge to pull the ripcord, to turn and run pokes at her rear like it's wearing the Princess's shoes, but she stands her ground, raising the brown paper-wrapped cylindrical object over her head.

The Princess lowers her fists slightly. Taking in the sight, penciled brows knit together, she tilts her head the way an animal would.

There's not a lot of heavy objects laying around Becky's apartment, at least none that could be pocketed easily. She thought about buying a baseball bat, one of those Louisville Sluggers; or even a hammer, a simple claw hammer. But for the same reason she didn't just empty her knife drawer and pick out something to use on the Princess, she nixed buying either. She needed something to hurt the woman the same as the woman had hurt her. She'd been sizing up her keys and how they would feel tucked between her knuckles when she saw the roll of quarters. They felt just right when she slapped the leaden roll against her palm. At least they did at the time. Now though...

"You better be careful with that, darling. You lose 'em you won't have anything to do the wash with."

A sudden smoldering heat surges within Becky and steam feels as though it's hissing out of every pore. That little remark—she doesn't know just what it is that pisses her off except for the fact that it's absolutely true.

Becky lets out a scream, a loud throat-searing bellow, as she cocks her arm back and lets the roll fly, straight at the Princess's face. The more experienced woman raises her hands at the last and the roll flies away, a crack sounding as it ricochets off the glass tabletop.

The Princess curses and shakes her wrist, clearly stung. "Ooh, you bitch, you've done it now," she growls, sounding almost gleeful in her pain. Her eyes go wide, as do her lips as they peel back to reveal large gleaming teeth. Then she steps into Becky, jabbing her fists once, twice.

The first one Becky catches. The second one catches her too, right where the first blow at the Courtsquare had, east of her nose and south of her eye. Lights again fill her eyes, blood runs to her nose, but she keeps her feet. She stays on them when the Princess delivers another right-handed blow, this one to her other cheek, and yet another to her chin. Becky thinks of the floor under the bar, next to the barstool, and all those faces looking away from her, as far away from her as they could, and how cool and comfortable it was there, in that place.

"Having fun yet?" the Princess taunts, feinting a few more jabs. "I am. Shame Henry isn't here to see this. He would've blown his load by now for sure. It's so good of you to come over tonight, darling. I can't tell you how pleased I am. You know, we really should get together more often. I could get used to this." She lifts her left fist and that same square cut stone sparkles and teases, like it's wagging its tongue and taunting Becky with silly names. If it's sticking its tongue out it's because it's tasted her blood once and the thing's hungry for more. The Princess, panting, fakes a few jabs with her left. "Are you ready for this, you little bitch?"

But Becky reaches out and grabs the fist, sinking her fingernails into the flesh around the wedding band. The Princess growls and snorts and jerks her wrist as she hammers Becky's gut with her right. Becky yelps but keeps tearing at her majesty's hand. She opens her jaw and launches her teeth at the ring but before she can bite the Princess throws herself backward.

She hadn't time to consider those high-heeled shoes. Becky feels it, too—the weight of the woman coming down on those shaky wine-glass stem heels, and those heels giving out beneath her. She flaps her arm and twists her legs to find her balance but it's too late. Her legs wrap around each other at the knees and she goes down, the bull's head emblazoned on her hip pocket leading the charge as she plummets face first into the plate glass top of the coffee table.

Yes, it does sparkle. All of it. All those shards of glass flying everywhere glittering in the hot white glow. But it doesn't last. It couldn't. Not with all that blood spraying everywhere. Blood—yes, there's something unique about it and its thickness and the way it smothers everything it touches. It's spreading across everything that sparkles, every jagged piece of broken glass. Even that rock on the Princess's finger is dimmed as the hand it's attached to wraps around the metallic frame of the table. It seeks a grip, something it can use, only to catch another shard, a splinter that pierces the Princess's skin where the lines intersect in her palm. There are shards everywhere, protruding from that perfect ivory skin—her hands, her wrists, her ankles, her cheeks, that soft spot under her chin, the softest part of her neck…all around her forehead.

And everywhere they sparkled there's blood. So much of it.

Her eyes are wide though that look of hunger, the violent lust, doesn't flash in them anymore. There's another look, a look filled with awe, marvel, even. She's caught sight of the thing that sparkles most in this world, floating above her and locking her in, drifting with her toward the void. Or maybe it's reeling her in, pulling. Everything shimmers when you've lost that much blood.

Angela continues her father's stories of Blacklin County with a new sheriff, Ruth Grady, stepping up after Dan Rhodes' retirement. Here she faces a mystery at a funeral parlor, or just another day at the Blacklin County Sheriff's Office...

BAD JEANS
Angela Crider Neary

"My husband is dead!" Althea Hardison announced as she stalked into the Blacklin County Sheriff's Office. The seventy-five-year-old matriarch made a formidable, if slightly farcical, image in a form-fitting dark denim jumpsuit, the collar and pockets of which were studded with rhinestones, and high-heeled denim boots, similarly adorned. Her white hair was blown back and up into a bouffanty beehive, projecting the effect that a tiny twister had landed on top of her head for a brief moment, swept her hair into a cylindrical shape, then skedaddled off to parts unknown. Sparkles glistened and popped from the rhinestone pins placed strategically in the expanse of her up-do. Or, knowing Althea Hardison, the pins could have been made of real diamonds. Her lips were an unnatural slash of crimson that bled into the lines around her mouth.

Sheriff Ruth Grady, who had been tapping out a report on her laptop when the storm that was Althea Hardison blew in, put her head between her hands, then quickly recovered, running her fingers through her short, practical hair as if she were adjusting it. She had come to find out all too quickly why Sheriff Dan Rhodes had chosen to retire. Since she had taken the reins, the people and cases in the county had gotten exponentially more bizarre. Or maybe this was the norm, and she hadn't realized it until now since Sheriff Rhodes had done such a good job of managing law enforcement in Blacklin County. She only hoped she could do half as good a job as he had. At this rate, however, she would lose all of her hair before being in office a year.

"Percy's dead, and this is what they've done to him." Althea blustered up to Ruth's desk.

"My condolences for your loss, Mrs. Hardison," Ruth said. "But why is this a matter for the sheriff's department? It's my understanding that your husband's death was an accident."

Ruth had read in the paper and, of course, heard through the local grapevine that Percy Hardison, the self-proclaimed "Denim Magnate of East Texas," had passed away in a tragedy out at his farm. A tractor he had been working underneath had crushed him when the hydraulic jack had failed.

Percy Hardison had come from a family of wealth, but had never let that affect his work ethic. The denim empire he had inherited had been established several generations before him. His ancestors had crafted hard-wearing work pants that had outfitted many a cowboy herding cattle out on the ranges of Texas for decades. Hardison had continued the tradition of developing and selling work trousers, as well as ushering the company into the current generation with every-day denim fashions, including premium "artisanal" jeans that went for over two-hundred dollars a pop, all the while working almost full-time as a rancher. He had expired doing what he loved—and while wearing his beloved dungarees.

"Pfft," Althea snorted. "I'm not talking about his death, of course."

"Of course," Ruth said, agreeing with her. She had learned through her years of working in law enforcement that it paid to go along and listen rather than trying to jump in with her own interpretations or questions. Ruth waited patiently until the older woman finally spoke.

"Don't you see, they've desecrated his body!" Althea swooned and took a seat in a nearby chair, flapping her hand in front of her face like a Southern belle with the vapors.

"Try to calm down, Mrs. Hardison." Ruth walked over to the water cooler, filled a paper cup, and handed it to Althea. "Now, tell me what happened." Ruth felt for a moment like she was talking to Hack and Lawton. The dispatcher and jailer were famous for failing to come to the point, instead choosing to provide information little by little in a long, drawn out and often rambling manner. She looked around the room and found them conspicuously absent, although Hack had been sitting behind his desk only moments before, shooting the breeze with Lawton, who had been perched on the desk's corner. The intimidating denim maven must have given even those two a run for their money and spooked them out of the immediate vicinity. They were likely eavesdropping nearby, however, not being ones to miss out on a good story. They always insisted on being kept in the loop.

"They took his gold and diamond bedazzled boots," Althea said. "Right off his feet. While he was lying in his coffin during the visitation at the funeral home, no less! Left him with nothing but his Dallas Cowboys socks a'showin'. You know, I just took the top pair out of his drawer, of course not thinking they would be the last things folks would see of him. But there he was, in his favorite denim tuxedo and cowboy hat, his feet sporting nothing but the blue and silver stars of America's Team."

Ruth wondered why someone would lay a loved one to rest in gold and diamond boots but not bother to think about what socks to put on him, although Percy, a publicly avid Cowboys fan, would likely not have minded—at least about the socks. The boot snatching was another matter entirely. And how valuable could these boots really be? She hated to ask, but she did.

"I'm sorry to hear that, Mrs. Hardison. How much were these boots worth?"

"I think they were valued at fifty-thousand dollars, although

I'm sure Percy paid more for them. They were commemorative boots to celebrate the hundredth anniversary of his favorite boot company. They weren't for general sale, but he was able to buy them at a charity auction."

Ruth drew in a sharp breath at the figure. She started to lower her head between her hands again, but stopped herself before completing the gesture. As a public servant, spending that much money on footwear—or a car for that matter—was beyond her comprehension, although the fact that it was technically a charitable donation made it a little easier to swallow. But only a little.

"That makes it a felony offense, right?" Althea said.

"The amount itself, would make it a felony, yes," Ruth said. "In fact, any theft from a corpse would be a felony, even if the items were only worth, say, twenty dollars." Althea flinched when Ruth said "corpse," and Ruth instantly regretted her word choice.

"Did you plan to bury your husband in those boots," Ruth continued, "or was he only wearing them for the viewing?"

"He was to be buried in them," Althea said.

"I have to ask, Mrs. Hardison, why would you bury your husband in something so valuable?"

"Are you saying this is my fault?" Althea asked in a huff.

"Of course not, Mrs. Hardison. It just helps me to have all the background I can get." Ruth wasn't sure about the relevance of why Percy would be interred in such attire, but you never knew what could be significant in such cases. And besides, she was plain curious now.

"If you must know, Percy requested that he be buried in his favorite denim tuxedo, his cowboy hat, and those boots. They were his prized possessions and he kept them in the safe in our home. He never got to wear them in life, and now some scuzzbucket has deprived him of wearing them in the afterlife." Althea sniffled and took a tissue out of her denim clutch.

"When did you first notice the boots were gone?" Ruth asked.

"Not until after most of the guests had left," Althea said. "I was up front greeting people, and not in the viewing area where they had the casket displayed. I never dreamed someone would get away with stealing clothing from my dear Percy's body. I guess I should have been more careful."

"Did you or anyone you know see anything suspicious, or was there anyone there who seemed out of place?"

"I didn't see a thing," Althea said. "But I'll admit I wasn't in my right mind with all the grief I was feeling. And I'd had a few drinks to take the edge off."

At least she was honest about it, Ruth thought. She nodded her head to encourage Althea to continue.

"No one I've talked to in the family saw anything, either," Althea said, "but there were hundreds of folks packed into a small area—they don't have sufficient facilities in this town for an event of this magnitude—which might have made it easier for someone to make off with the boots without being noticed. I'm sure it was one of those funeral home employees. You can't trust anyone these days."

"All right, Mrs. Hardison," Ruth said when it became apparent that Althea had provided all the information she had. "Thank you for coming in. I'll need a photo of the missing property if you have one."

"I thought you might say that." Althea took a photo out of her purse and slapped it down in front of Ruth. It depicted a pair of black cowboy boots decked out with glimmering diamonds and bright gold plates and buckles. "I hope you'll find out who did this to my poor Percy."

"I'll do my best, ma'am."

Ruth squinted up at the immaculate brick façade between the towering white columns on the front porch as she entered the dignified mansion that housed Ballinger's Funeral Home. Clyde Ballinger, the funeral director and owner, met her at the door as she walked in. Ruth had called ahead, so Clyde had been expecting her. He was wearing his usual dark suit and tie with a crisp white shirt.

"Hi, Deputy," Clyde said. Ruth stared at him without saying anything for a few moments, then the realization hit him. "I mean, Sheriff," he said, shaking his head. "Sorry about that. It's hard to get used to a new sheriff after being around Dan for so long."

Ruth had found herself in this situation quite a few times since she had assumed her new title. She tried not to take offense since she had previously worked as a deputy with Rhodes, and he had been the sheriff with whom most of the county had become familiar after his many years of service. She knew she had some big shoes to fill, as Rhodes had been respected and very well-liked. She also knew, or at least hoped, people would get used to it after a period of time.

"Don't worry about it," Ruth said.

"I guess you're here to ask me about the Hardison visitation." Clyde led Ruth into a small room that held a big glass-topped desk with nothing on its smooth surface. Two chairs covered in red leather faced the desk. Clyde sat behind it and motioned for Ruth to have a seat in one of the red leather chairs.

"That's right," Ruth said. "Where were you during the event?"

Clyde sighed. "I've talked to the sheriff's department about dozens and dozens of cases, but never as a suspect before."

Ruth nodded, but made no verbal response. She would be surprised if Clyde had been involved in any malfeasance, but you never knew what someone might do in the right circumstances. It was her job to investigate thoroughly and talk to everyone involved. Besides, it had happened at Clyde's funeral home under his very nose.

"I was here that evening," Clyde said. "I don't attend every viewing, but for something involving a prominent resident like Percy Hardison, I felt like it would be best for me to put in an appearance.

Ruth said nothing and Clyde continued, filling the silence, like many were prone to do during an awkward pause. Another law enforcement trick.

"There must have been over five-hundred people here," Clyde said. "And they were all imbibing heavily. It was quite chaotic. Mrs. Hardison insisted on catering the event with hor d'oeurves and alcohol."

"Is that common for something like this?" Ruth asked.

"Not around here. And it was against my better judgment, but Mrs. Hardison sort of bullied me into it. Have you met that woman? She could spook the Devil himself." Clyde rubbed a hand across his forehead.

Ruth's lip twitched, but she managed to keep from smiling. "Yes, I've met her. Did you see anyone or anything that seemed abnormal or unusual?"

"No, but I didn't know most of the people who attended. They must have come from far and wide. I didn't know anything was wrong until close to the end of the night when I heard Mrs. Hardison shrieking. She was bent over Mr. Hardison's body, and I thought she'd become overcome with emotion. Turns out, she was overcome with the looting of her husband's casket."

"Is it normal to bury someone in something so valuable?" Ruth asked.

"No. But believe me, this is no regular family. I advised strongly against using such costly apparel while the public was about, but you've met the woman. I told her she could bury Mr. Hardison in anything she wanted but that it was extremely inadvisable to put those temptations on him during the viewing. But she wasn't having any of it. Personally, I think it was sheer vanity—she wanted all her fancy friends to see those things."

"Who else was working with you that night?" Ruth asked.

"Normally we only have one staff member at an event like this, but since I thought this one might be larger than usual, I scheduled Alice Oates and Isaac Grayson to be here with me. Alice got a bout of the stomach flu that afternoon, so it was only me and Isaac. And to be up front with you, Isaac does have a criminal record. I like to do my part to help the down and out. And before you say it, yes, I do take advantage of the tax credit."

Ruth was glad Clyde had given her this information. She would have found out anyway, and Clyde's revelation saved her time. "What did Isaac do?"

Clyde peered down at the shiny desktop, then looked up at Ruth and said, "He did a stretch for robbery. But I swear to you, he's been rehabilitated. He wouldn't have done this. He's one of the best employees I've ever had."

And tax credits, Ruth thought. "I'll need to talk to him. Is he in today?"

"Yes, I'll go see if I can find—"

"There you are!" came a voice from the doorway.

Ruth and Clyde looked up to see a tall, dark-haired man entering the room. Although he wasn't flashy, everything about him exuded affluence, right down to his fingernails, which had an unnaturally healthy gleam. He probably got manicures, Ruth thought, feeling a spark of envy. She had tried to talk her boyfriend, Seepy Benton, into trying a manicure, along with a pedicure, to no avail. The man looked dapper in dark jeans, a sport coat over an indigo chambray shirt and bolo tie, a tan cowboy hat, and exotic ostrich leather cowboy boots. Ruth thought he was quite attractive, until he talked some more.

"I've been looking all over for you, Ballinger. Have you found those boots? We're gonna sue you to kingdom come for emotional distress and have you prosecuted for abuse of a corpse and theft from a corpse, and anything else of a corpse we can think of. You'll be done in this town if you don't make things right."

As he spoke, the man marched over to the desk where Ruth and Clyde were sitting and slammed his fist down on its transparent surface to emphasize his last point. Clyde jumped and sweat sprung out around his temples, his appearance much different from the quiet, assured professional Ruth was used to seeing.

Clyde pulled himself together, stood, and said, "Why don't you have a seat, Mr. Steadman. This is Sheriff Ruth Grady, and she's here to investigate what happened. I have all confidence that she'll get to the bottom of it soon. Sheriff Grady, this is Kenneth Steadman, Althea Hardison's nephew."

Ruth stood, expecting Kenneth to offer his hand for a shake. He didn't do that, nor did he sit down. Instead he looked at her and said, "What are you doing to solve this crime, Sheriff?"

"My office is doing everything it can to investigate and ascertain who the perpetrator was, Mr. Steadman," Ruth said. "But you need to manage your expectations. Although we'll make every effort to find out what occurred and recover the missing property if we can, these cases don't always get solved immediately."

"How long are we talking?" Kenneth asked. "My Aunt Althy has been to hell and back. And we're not burying my uncle until those boots are retrieved."

Clyde's face turned as white as a sheet. "Mr. Steadman, we can't keep a bod—uh, your uncle, preserved for much longer. The funeral and interment are planned for tomorrow. I highly recommend going forward with the services and choosing some alternative footwear for your uncle."

"My Aunt Althy won't hear of it, and neither will I. You'd better figure this out."

"I assume you were at the ceremony, Mr. Steadman?" Ruth said.

"Of course I was. Along with about five-hundred friends and relations. You have a lot of people to investigate, Sheriff."

"But where were you, exactly?" Ruth said.

"What do you mean where was I? I never left the building. As a representative of the family, it was my duty to mingle and speak to everyone. I also had to be there to support my Aunt Althy."

"Did you see anything out of the ordinary, anyone lingering around your uncle's coffin for an unnatural period of time?"

Ruth asked, although she thought that any amount of time spent hanging around a person's embalmed body probably wasn't in any way natural.

"How would I know? It was *his* job to make sure no one interfered with my uncle." Kenneth pointed at Clyde. "Why are you interrogating me?"

"I'm only asking a few questions," Ruth said.

"Well if you want to ask any more, you can make an appointment with my secretary." Kenneth flipped a white business card onto the glass. "I don't have all day to stand around here and chit chat. You just find those boots." He turned on his own boot heel, the leather strings of his bolo tie whipping through the air and strode out of the room.

Clyde let out a long sigh. "We generally can't keep an embalmed body much more than a week. I don't know what we're going to do if they refuse to bury him until everything is recovered."

"I hate to give you more bad news, Clyde, but whoever the thief is has probably already taken them apart for the diamonds and gold. And even if we retrieve them intact, they would have to be held as evidence."

Clyde nodded, resolved.

"I'll need to see the visitation room and talk to Mr. Grayson," Ruth said.

"If you want to go on over to Room 3, I'll find Isaac and have him meet you there."

Ruth walked into the expansive space. She assumed it was the funeral home's largest visitation parlor, and even then, the bereaved had probably spilled out into the foyer. In keeping with the atmosphere of the entire structure, the area was nicely appointed and clean, if not a little dated, with puffy floral sofas and chairs set around the walls. In the back was an alcove for the casket surrounded by easels that could hold enlarged photos or sprays of flowers, and several pillar stands that could support potted plants and bouquets. There were folding chairs where mourners could sit and have moments of peace and reflection with the dearly departed. Ruth noticed a door in the corner, behind where the coffin would be placed.

"Ahem." Ruth heard a meek sound.

She turned and saw what at first appeared to be a large man looming in the entryway. As the man shuffled toward her, however, he seemed to be shrunken into himself, with a bit of a slump and thinning grayish-blond hair. No one you would suspect of criminal activity. Ruth was always surprised at how innocent and non-threatening some people who had committed even the most heinous transgressions could look.

"Hi, Mr. Grayson. I'm Sheriff Ruth Grady."

"Hi, Sheriff," Isaac said, his head down in an ingratiating stance. Prison did that to some folks, Ruth knew.

"What can you tell me about the night of Percy Hardison's service?"

"Well, Sheriff, there were sure a lot of people here, and they were drinkin' and cuttin' up quite a bit. They were a handful for me and Clyde. We did our best to keep things under control."

"Did you see anything suspicious or anyone paying too much attention to Mr. Hardison's casket?"

"I didn't see anything uncommon, ma'am." Still with the dereference. Ruth wasn't sure if it was an act or the effects of time served. "But there was such a big crowd and so much drinkin' goin' on, it wouldn't have been too hard for someone to sneak out with the boots, I'm afraid."

"Mr. Grayson," Ruth said. "Did you have anything to do with the theft of Mr. Hardison's boots?"

Isaac's light blue eyes met Ruth's for the first time. "No, ma'am. I wouldn't do anything to risk my parole. And besides, I've left that life behind me."

"What did you do your time for, Mr. Grayson?" Ruth asked.

Isaac's glance darted back and forth, then he looked down

again, falling back to reverential. Or was it cagey? Ruth couldn't quite tell. "I robbed a house of some valuables. It was mostly jewelry—a lot of Western-style stuff, like turquoise, and you know, those leather string ties. Prob'ly not even worth that much, when I think back on it. Got wind that the owners would be out of town so it seemed like easy pickin's from some rich folks who could afford the loss and had a lot of insurance, besides."

"Kind of like the Hardisons?" Ruth said. Something Isaac had said made the synapses in her mind perk up and tingle, but she wasn't quite sure why.

"No, ma'am. I swear I didn't have anything to do with this. I wouldn't want to let Mr. Ballinger down, after him takin' a chance on me and all."

"I notice there's a door here behind where the coffin would be," Ruth said, turning. "Where does it lead?"

Isaac walked over to the door and opened it. "It goes down this hall with a couple of offices on the left here. Then out that way into the back parking lot." Isaac pointed toward the end of the hall at a red "Exit" sign.

"I guess that could be an easy escape route," Ruth said.

"Yes, ma'am," Isaac said.

"All right, Mr. Grayson. Thank you for your time."

Isaac nodded and Ruth walked out through the front entry. She ran into Clyde in the vestibule.

"Can I do anything else for you, Sheriff?" Clyde asked.

"Not right now," Ruth said. "But I'll keep you in the loop."

"Sheriff Ruth Grady to see Kenneth Steadman," Ruth said to the young, hip-looking receptionist behind the polished marble counter at Hardison Denim and Apparel. Kenneth hadn't done too bad for himself, joining the family company, Ruth thought as she gazed around the opulent reception area. "I called earlier to say I was coming in."

"Please have a seat and I'll let him know you're here."

Ruth stepped over to a modern gray chaise longue that didn't look comfortable in the least, but when she sat down, it enveloped her in cozy luxury. At least she would be comfy if Kenneth made her wait, which he did. A classic power play, Ruth thought, but she wouldn't let it get to her. She tried to channel former Sheriff Rhodes's temperate attitude. She didn't know how he had always maintained his unflappable demeanor, but she had found that meditation, which she had been trying recently at Seepy's suggestion, worked quite well for her.

After about twenty minutes, Kenneth entered the lobby. "What can I do for you, Sheriff?" He made a point of looking at his Cartier watch. Ruth got the message—your time is more important than mine.

"Hi, Mr. Steadman. You said if I had any further inquiries to make an appointment with your secretary. So I did."

"Yes," Kenneth said. "But I didn't think I would be seeing you so soon."

"Or you hoped not." Ruth smiled. "Can we talk somewhere in private?"

Kenneth looked behind him as if he wanted to say, "No," but shrugged his shoulders and motioned for Ruth to follow him down a plush hallway into an expansive corner office. The third-floor room was surrounded on two sides by floor-to-ceiling windows. The view of some fields and a few small hills wasn't much, but it was likely the best there was in Clearview. Ruth had learned from an online search that this was a satellite corporation from the headquarters in Dallas that the family had set up when they decided to move to a ranch on the outskirts of the city. They had left the bigwigs in Dallas to run the main operation and depended on their trusted nephew to head up the smaller facility.

Kenneth walked around a spacious table and sat behind it, leaving Ruth to sit on an elegant silver leather chair, not unlike the chaise longue she had enjoyed in the reception area. "What can I do for you, Sheriff?" Kenneth said. "I've got a busy day, so I don't have much time."

"Just a few standard questions, if you don't mind," Ruth said.

"Go ahead."

"You're the sole heir to the Hardison fortune, is that right?" Ruth asked.

"Well, yes," Kenneth said, "but my Aunt Althy is still alive, and everything my uncle had went to her. I'm not sure what you're getting at, Sheriff."

"Bear with me if you would, Mr. Steadman. I want to make sure to clear up any loose ends. That's a beautiful tie, by the way, if you don't mind my saying."

A broad smile crossed Kenneth's face and he fingered a large white stone from which two black leather braided strings dangled. "This here's a White Buffalo rock. Found in only one place in the world—at a mine in Nevada."

"So you got it in Nevada?" Ruth asked.

"No, my Aunt Althy gave it to me just the other day."

"Seems strange that your aunt would give you a gift so soon after your uncle passed. What was the occasion?"

Kenneth's smile fell away. "She doesn't need an occasion to express her love and appreciation for everything I do for the family. She and my uncle have given me everything I have." Kenneth spread his arms wide to indicate the spacious office and, Ruth assumed, the entire denim business. "Now, can we get back to your questions so I can get on with my day?"

"Such a nice tie, though, Mr. Steadman. Is the bezel that the stone's set in made of real gold?"

Kenneth looked down at it and said, "I assume so, but how would I know what it's made of?"

"That's an interesting shape, too," Ruth said, leaning in to examine the polygonal shield-shape more closely. "And it looks like it has some sort of filigree design underneath the White Buffalo. That's odd, don't you think, since the gem covers up all of that detail?"

"Again, how would I know?" Kenneth placed his palm over

the tie. "I'm no jeweler."

"I think you would know, Mr. Steadman, since you had the tie made yourself from a bezel from one of your uncle's boots. Pretty quick work on your part. And also quite brazen to be wearing it around so soon after the heist." Ruth had noticed something about the tie when Kenneth had confronted Clyde at the funeral home that had stuck in her subconscious until Isaac had shaken it loose when he mentioned what it was he had stolen.

"That's ridiculous," Kenneth said. "Have you lost your mind, Sheriff, coming into my place of business and accusing me of stealing from my own uncle's casket? Preposterous!"

"You said your aunt and uncle gave you everything," Ruth continued, "but not quite all you wanted. They didn't give you those boots, did they? Must have been disappointing to know that those beauties would be buried in the ground forever when they really ought to have gone to someone so dedicated to the family as yourself."

"Kenny, is this true?" Althea Hardison said from the doorway. "But we took you in, raised you as our own. Why would you do something like this to us? You don't need the money."

Kenneth looked down for a few seconds then back up, a quiet rage seething behind his eyes. "Uncle Percy promised me those boots. And then you have the complete audacity and temerity to have him buried in them—after all I do for this company? I couldn't let it happen."

Althea looked faint, but Deputy Andy Shelby caught her arm to steady her and stationed her on another posh settee to recover. He had been standing by in a squad car as backup, and Ruth had hit "send" on a text to signal him to man the waiting room when she had gone to speak to Kenneth.

"Mr. Steadman, you're under arrest for theft." Ruth cuffed Kenneth's hands behind his back while she Mirandized him.

"What's going to happen?" Althea said as Ruth led Kenneth into the hallway.

"Your nephew will likely be serving some time," Ruth said.

"He's disassembled the boots, and we'll have to hold anything we find as evidence in his criminal case."

"Too bad Mr. Hardison won't get his wish to be buried in his most prized possessions," Andy said.

Althea, still dazed, said, "That's okay. I think I'll just leave him in his Cowboys socks. In fact, if the hereafter's anything like his living room, he'll be happier in those old things anyway."

"And to quote Neil Diamond," Ruth said, "at least he'll be 'Forever in Blue Jeans.'"

Evidence? What evidence? Let Michael show you. He'll start with a corpse and move on to what's missing…

THE MAN WHO WASN'T THERE
Michael Allan Mallory

They should not have gone down to the beach, but they did, never suspecting for a moment so much heartache would come from an innocent walk under the sun. And it really was too nice a day to stay indoors.

"C'mon—" Claudette tugged Peter's arm, "—we've been cooped up for hours. I need some air."

He didn't resist. There was no point. She was an unstoppable force when she put her mind to it. Though small in stature, she had big expressive eyes and an even bigger personality that came at you like a tsunami. You were either swept along with her or got the hell out of the way.

They left the posh confines of the big house through the French patio doors and strolled through Marco's tropical garden, turning at the huge philodendrons and towering purple bougainvillea to follow the flagstone path that curved down to the beach.

"This is more like it." Claudette luxuriated in the feeling of warm sand between her toes and the soothing sound of the surf washing ashore.

"It's a private beach," Peter said, surprised, then corrected himself. "Of course Marco has a private beach. What was I thinking?"

"Comes with the fancy house and exclusive address. For sure out of our price range."

"True that!"

Before them lay fifty yards of flat, unblemished sugar-white sand that ran into calm gulf waters. Empty sand save for a pair of green Adirondack chairs eighty feet ahead and a lone occupant whose head they could see just above the scalloped chair back. As they got within earshot, Peter called out, "Hey, Marco, getting enough sun? You've been baking out here all morning!"

Claudette laughed. One of the things their host prided himself on was his deep South Texas tan. Marco Navarro spent hours on it. Peter was right, though, Marco had been sunning himself for hours. When no reply came, Claudette nudged Peter with the back of her hand. "I bet he's dozed off."

Peter snorted. "We didn't stay up that late last night. Your boss has no stamina. Hang on." With a playful grin, Peter trotted across the sand. The chair on the left was unoccupied. Marco was slumped in the chair beside it. "Dude, wake up, you have guests." Peter's lanky frame veered toward the right-hand chair and rounded to the front.

"Holy crap!" He jumped back in horror.

"What? What is it?"

In a shaken voice he said, "Marco's dead. His throat's been cut."

She moved to join him but halted at his upraised hand.

"No! Don't come any closer. You don't want to see this."

"But—"

"It's bad. Lots of blood."

"What if he's still alive?"

Peter gave a rueful shake of his head. "I really doubt that. I'll spare you the gory details. Let's just say the wound isn't pretty."

"We have to make sure. Check his pulse."

From the look on his face Peter wasn't keen to do that. But

he did. Setting his jaw, he stepped in. Marco's right arm dangled over the wooden arm rest, his fingers inches above the sand. Kneeling, Peter reached out and gingerly felt for a pulse. After a while he shook his head and released the lifeless hand. "He's gone," came the grim verdict. Then Peter lurched to his feet and trudged back to Claudette with a shell-shocked expression.

She was beside herself. "This is terrible! Who'd do this?"

"You'd know better than me. You worked for the guy."

Yes, she worked for Marco but she knew next to nothing about his personal life. Had no idea who might want to hurt him, let alone kill him. What she did have was a keen eye for detail, an eye that had scanned the beach and noticed a terrible truth. Praying she was mistaken, Claudette studied the white sand again. What she saw unnerved her. She swallowed hard and spun round to Peter. "Could this have been suicide?"

His gray eyes narrowed on the chair backs a short distance away. "I doubt it. I'm no expert but that rip in his throat is deep. People can't do that to themselves. Besides—" he motioned toward the chairs, "—where's the knife? Marco's hands are empty. Nothing's in the sand except a pocket Sudoku book and a baseball cap."

A cold shiver ran through her.

Peter inhaled sharply. "We have to call the cops."

"No! Not yet." She grabbed his arm.

"Claudette?"

Her gaze fixed on the beach as a rising panic caught in her chest. "The sand, look at the sand."

"What about it?"

"You see Marco's footprints?"

A set of fresh, clear impressions led from behind them across the sand in a direct path to the left chair and disappeared out of view in front of it.

"Yeah. So?"

"Those are Marco's prints. Yours are over there on the right. *Peter, where are the murderer's footprints?*"

"What d'you mean? They're—" he faltered.

"D'you see?" she went on. "There's a set of footprints missing, the killer's."

Peter studied the sand. "Damn, you're right."

"But your prints are there as plain as day, going out to Marco and back."

The color drained from Peter's face as the realization hit him. Still clutching his arm, her slender fingers dug in deeper. "The police aren't going to believe us. Your prints complete the picture, one that says you did it."

"Maybe not. Those prints could belong to anybody."

She shook her head. "Like me you came down here barefoot. Take another look, Mr. Fallen Arches. Your prints stand out."

It was true. Peter suffered from flat feet and his sand impressions were notable for having no arches. He groaned, demoralized. "What do we do?"

"We'll call the police. Just not yet. We need to think this through, find an alternate explanation."

Peter was all for that. "We should talk to the others. Get fresh eyes."

"Good idea."

A short time later Claudette and Peter returned to the beach, joined by a thickset man in a tangerine Hawaiian shirt and a dark-haired woman in a floral sun dress. The quartet came to a halt thirty feet from the Adirondack chairs. The newcomers stood uncomfortably as they viewed the frightful scene before them.

"This is bad," Ruben grumbled, visibly shaken.

Olivia stood beside him. Her dark hair was cut in a shoulder length bob. Blunt bangs nearly concealed eyebrows that drew down. She turned away. "Don't make me do this."

Claudette felt guilty. This would be tough on someone like Olivia who could barely stand the sight of blood. "I'm sorry. If you can bear with it for a minute, we need your help."

"I don't know," the other replied, still averting her gaze.

"We're hoping you or Ruben might see something we missed."

Ruben shot her a disapproving look. "Something you missed? Shouldn't we be calling the police? It is their job."

The rancor in his voice stung, yet Claudette chose to ignore it. The stakes were too high. "We *will* call the police. I explained that at the house. First, we're looking for a way out for Peter."

Ruben looked back skeptically.

It was clear she wasn't going to get much empathy from him. That left her with only one other avenue. "Olivia?" Claudette implored.

Olivia glanced at Peter and, after moment's hesitation, gave a slow nod of assent. She forced herself to view the body and the nearby sand. "You say the killer's footprints are missing," she said as one puzzling out an incomplete thought.

"Right."

"Could the killer have erased them?"

"Erased them?" Ruben mocked. "Let me get this straight. You've just murdered a man in a wide open space. Rather than waste time erasing footprints, you should get the hell outta there before someone sees you!"

A sullen Peter grunted. "He makes a good point."

It pained Claudette to hear the defeat in Peter's voice. For the past few minutes he'd been standing in silence, gaunt and dispirited, barely keeping it together. She couldn't stand seeing him like this. He was her rock, the person who kept her grounded. Now she had to be strong for him.

A passing seagull screamed overhead. Near the water's edge a sandpiper skittered across the damp sand. A moment of tranquility. It didn't last.

Count on Ruben to make things worse. "And if you're thinking the tide washed away any footprints, wrong. High tide wouldn't get within thirty feet of Marco." His mouth stretched into the most irritatingly self-satisfied smirk.

Claudette wanted to smack him. Never mind that Ruben was more than a head taller than her and a hundred pounds heavier, right now she felt feisty enough to take on anybody. But she didn't. Jamming shut her eyes, she counted silently to five. Confronting Ruben would be counterproductive. What she needed was his support. She took a different tack, one she'd learned from Peter. "Maybe we're going about this the wrong way," she said, mustering up her calmest, most rational voice. "Forget the beach. Perhaps you guys saw or heard something unusual earlier." She looked expectantly between them.

Ruben's burly shoulders hitched beneath his colorful shirt. "I got nothing. I was out all morning. Left after breakfast. Rode my Kawasaki into Corpus Christi. Didn't get back until twenty minutes ago."

No surprise there. She'd heard the roar of his motorcycle as it had sped off that morning. She nodded back solemnly and with diminished expectations turned to Olivia.

"Any thoughts?" she asked.

Olivia's forehead creased as she cast her mind back. "I don't remember anything unusual. I was on the front terrace all morning working on a watercolor, saw Ruben ride off, a woman walking her dog, and a FedEx delivery a few doors down."

A disappointed Claudette could only turn away. She was out of ideas and avoided looking at Peter. Things looked bleak.

Then Oliva made a sound, a tiny, introspective grunt that offered a glimmer of hope. "There is one thing..."

Claudette seized on this. "What?"

"It could be nothing."

"Just say it. Please."

Olivia gestured at the green beach chairs. "See how Marco's arm is hanging?"

"What about it?"

"The magazine and ball cap are—what?—four feet away. They seem out of reach."

"So?"

"They aren't handy, are they? I mean, if Marco wanted them he would've had to climb out of his chair and walk a couple of steps. Not at all convenient."

Claudette saw it now. "They *are* out of reach." Her brow furrowed. "Is that important? Perhaps Marco fell asleep and the magazine dropped to the ground."

"Or the wind blew them," Peter offered.

"Not likely." Olivia shook her head. "There was no wind. Not even a light breeze. I was outside all morning."

Ruben brought up a pudgy hand to shield his eyes from the sun. "I think Claudette had it right. Marco dropped those things and they bounced a few feet over."

"No, it's *sand*," Olivia objected. "Loose sand. Objects with any weight to them like that magazine sink a little after they hit sand."

The ghost of a smile played on Claudette's lips. Ruben had been condescending and it pleased her to see Olivia stand her ground.

Ruben took the rebuke in stride. "Fine. Who the hell cares? It's not gonna change what people think."

That was the last straw. Claudette glared at him. "Why are you so hostile?"

With a glance to Peter, Ruben squared his shoulders. His dark eyes locked on hers. "Look, I've tried to play along but the truth is I don't buy the whole killer's missing footprints thing. What I see in the sand makes total sense. What I see says Peter killed Marco."

Peter nearly screamed, *"I didn't kill Marco!"*

"So you say. The evidence doesn't lie, man."

"I had no reason to kill Marco. I barely knew the guy."

In a cold hard voice Ruben countered, "Last night you seemed ready to take off his head."

There was an uneasy silence.

Claudette glanced between the two men. "What are you talking about?"

A snort from Ruben. "Yeah, I bet Peter didn't share that with you. It was after midnight. You and Oliva had turned in. Marco, Peter, and I were playing Grand Theft Auto on Marco's hundred-inch TV. We'd all had a few beers and talk was easy, like how it was when you used to date Marco."

"That was a long time ago. I broke it off after a month. It was amicable."

"Must've been! You went to work for him."

"Two years later. He respected my skills. I made it clear if I worked for him it'd be strictly business. *Nothing more.*"

"He said you were a fine piece of ass."

Peter cleared his throat. His face hardened. "I told Marco not to talk about you that way. He came back and said you still had feelings for him."

Claudette shook her head violently. "No! He's yanking your chain, Peter. I bet I know where this came from. Last week Marco 'accidentally' brushed up against me. Made a lame apology. I didn't let him get away with it. I told him if he ever did that again I'd quit and would sue him for sexual harassment." The memory of it still pissed her off. "Marco's like a misbehaving puppy—he annoys you one moment and does something endearing the next."

Peter shrugged philosophically. "It was late and there was alcohol. Marco's a competitive gamer. He was trying to unsettle me. He apologized. We parted as friends. It was a moment, that's all." This last to Ruben, who remained unconvinced.

"Sorry," he said," but that still gives you a motive. And your footprints are the only ones I see. If it wasn't you then explain where this magical killer came from and how he killed Marco without leaving a trace. Where'd he go? People don't just drop out of sight. Show me proof!"

Proof was something Claudette didn't have and it was a stake through her heart, because without it she'd never convince a hardcore skeptic of their story. She had hoped for a little under-standing from Ruben. Guess not. Annoying as that was she couldn't blame him. Anyone who objectively examined the sand impressions would likely reach the same conclusion.

And that frightened her.

With the arrival of the Corpus Christi police an hour later, her worst fears came to pass. They didn't accept her "fact-defying" version of events as the first detective on the scene put it. Detective Judy Stoffel was marginally more receptive, although not enough to deter her, a day later, from charging Peter for the murder of Marco Navarro.

"More iced tea?"

"I'm good." Claudette smiled and took another long drink before setting the glass on the little mission table beside her. She snuggled into the embrace of the padded arm chair, closed her eyes and drew in a deep calming breath, releasing it in a slow purge. Opening her eyes, she saw Olivia's concerned oval face regarding her from the sofa.

"It's been a long week," Claudette explained. "This is the first time I've had to sit and relax with a friend. Thanks for inviting me over."

Olivia, clad in a tank top and denim roll shorts, sat back herself and nodded. "I can't imagine what you're going through."

"It's been brutal."

"People at work asked about you. They send their thoughts and prayers."

"Thank them for me." Claudette managed a wan smile. She was more frazzled than she cared to let on. Since Peter's arrest she'd faced long aggravating days and sleepless nights trying to find people who'd help him. There'd been too much to deal with and too little time; she'd been forced to take a leave of absence from work. "Tell them I'm hanging in there," she added with a labored breath.

"Have you found a lawyer?"

"Yeah."

"You don't sound optimistic."

"I'm not. Neither is he."

"Oh?"

"At least he was honest. It looks bad for Peter. There's no way to dispute the evidence. That's a big hurdle to get over. Peter's footprints go to Marco's chair and back. No one else's. He argued with Marco the night before. A jury will react the same way Ruben did." She sighed. "And there's the problem twenty minutes."

Twenty minutes that spelled real trouble for Peter. On the morning of the murder, after breakfast, Claudette and Olivia had enjoyed coffee in the front parlor as they poured through a home design catalog. Ruben had been adjusting the throttle to his motorcycle in the driveway and Claudette and Oliva had both watched—and heard—him. Marco had already gone out to the beach. And at the same time Peter was meditating in the back garden, alone and unseen.

He could have slipped away...

Drawing up her legs, Claudette hugged her knees. Cascades of long black hair draped over her shins, a curtain behind which to hide. "Without proof no one will listen. People would rather believe a simple lie than a complex truth." It felt good to say that to someone after the week she'd been living.

Olivia exhaled in frustration. "I wish there was something I could do."

"There is. You are. You're being a good friend."

With a slow nod Olivia added, "Detective Stoffel spoke to me. She asked if I thought you were a credible person. I said you were one of the most honest, ethical people I know. You don't lie."

"Stoffel's been more receptive the last couple of days. I think she feels sorry for me. I learned she interviewed the neighbors on either side of Marco."

"Anything there?"

"The woman on one side was on her patio Saturday morning

doing yoga. Didn't see or hear anything. She was too much in the zone, apparently."

"And the other neighbor?"

"Those are the Ginellies. Mrs. Ginelli was away last weekend, visiting her sister in New Jersey. The Ginellies are from Jersey. When Mrs. G got home on Monday her husband wasn't there."

"What d'you mean not there?"

"As in gone. Missing. Left no note. Didn't answer his cell. Hasn't turned up yet."

"He's done a runner?"

"Or something. He didn't even pack a bag. His car's still in the garage. He just...disappeared."

Olivia sat up. "That's too much of a coincidence!"

"It gets better. According to Detective Stoffel, Gino, the husband, is a hothead. He and Marco have a history of complaints against each other. Most recently, Marco was trying to get a building variance for changes he wanted to make to his property. Ginelli was pissed off."

"Oh. My. God." Olivia's eyebrows went nearly vertical. "Bad blood between the neighbors. That's huge! And Ginelli vanishes the same weekend Marco's killed. There's gotta be a connection there."

"Yeah," Claudette agreed in a subdued manner, barely changing her expression.

"What's wrong?" Olivia shot her a sidelong glance. "Isn't that exactly the kind of thing you need for reasonable doubt for Peter? I'd think you'd be excited."

"I was at first. Then the lawyer reminded me we're still stuck at square one. If Ginelli killed Marco, where are his footprints?" Claudette's arms still encircled her legs. In dismay she rested her forehead against her knees and uttered a muffled groan. "Nothing's changed. Physical evidence still points to Peter."

"Oh."

"But you're right. Ginelli may not be much but he's all we've got," she admitted with raw honesty. She was near the end of her rope and not in a mood to sugar coat reality, and too wound up to sit still for long. Claudette lowered her legs and pushed herself out of the chair. "I gotta stop thinking about this for a while. I'm losing my mind."

"We could go for a walk."

"Let's do." Claudette ambled to the kitchen counter and set down her empty glass, where she paused to take in a watercolor hanging on the nearby wall. The lush pine landscape spoke to her, gave her a sense of well-being she hadn't felt in days. "Olivia, this is good. You have so much talent. You've captured a mood."

"That's so nice of you to say."

"I'm serious. This is first rate. It makes me want to step into it and live there. I adore pine forests."

"Me too. This was from a trip to Oregon."

"And this one." Claudette moved to the adjacent landscape, one of an empty beach that looked oddly familiar. "Should I know where this is?"

"It's Marco's beach," Olivia answered, by now at her side.

"*Really?* I'd never've guessed. I've not seen it from this angle. And no green chairs."

"I did it a year ago. Marco added the chairs later."

Claudette leaned in closer, scrunching her nose at the watercolor. Now she recognized the coastline, the white sand, behind which lay a ridge of grass thinning out to the beach through ripples of small dunes. She took a step back. "Something looks different. Did Marco do some landscaping?"

"To the beach? Not that I know of."

"I'm too fried to think straight. I don't remember Marco's beach having those little dunes."

"You've had a tough week."

Claudette grunted in agreement. "Let's go for that walk. First, I gotta visit the bathroom. That iced tea ran through me."

A few minutes later Claudette stood in front of the vanity and washed her hands. She eyed her reflection and was disturbed

112

at the worn out, ragged woman who looked back at her: a woman with little left to give, a woman who longed to hear the laugh of her husband once more, to hold him close at night. She had nothing good to say to the woman in the glass and so averted her gaze to the vanity sink. The tap water spiraled down the drain, pulling elongated lines of soap suds with it. Away and gone. Claudette released a heartfelt sigh. If only the water could carry her and Peter away from the mess they were in.

She straightened abruptly, a fragment of conversation echoing from her memory. "Ruben," she murmured at a sudden realization. "*What was it you said?*"

The hot afternoon sun baked the white sand and everything standing on top of it. A pair of diggers stood ready, dressed in coveralls and sun hats. They looked for the go ahead signal from the woman in charge. Fortyish, round-faced with canny hazel-green eyes, Detective Judy Stoffel turned to the petite woman who stood next to her on Marco's beach.

"That look good to you?" Stoffel said in an agreeably husky voice.

Claudette was surprised even to be asked. "Yeah. Fine."

The detective motioned for the diggers to begin.

For a while the only sound Claudette could hear was the chuff of metal spades biting into dry sand. She watched the excavation intently, anxious and grateful, her veneer of outward calm as fragile as an eggshell. "Thank you for doing this," she said. "You could've said no."

"I almost did."

"You didn't, though."

"This ain't my first rodeo and you're a credible person, Mrs. Miranda. I'm not heartless. Only an idiot would tell the story you and Peter did and expect it to be believed—unless it were true. That was the thing that kept gnawing at me. You deserved a chance."

Claudette smiled back with gratitude.

Stoffel cautioned. "I still think it's a longshot, you understand."

"I know. Fingers crossed."

The excavators started a few yards to the right of the Adirondack chairs. The sand was loose and dry. They worked with the care of an archeological dig. After ten minutes one of the operators—bespectacled with a light brown goatee—paused and looked over. "We're at four feet. How much deeper you want to go?"

The detective shrugged. "A little more. Try another spot if you don't find anything."

"We'll keep going but it's not easy. The sand's so loose it keeps falling back in the hole."

"Do what you can."

Claudette shifted uncomfortably. She felt sorry for the workmen as they labored under the hot sun. She was standing still and even she felt a bead of perspiration trickle down the back of her neck. After several minutes the diggers stopped again, still having found nothing. They took a short break and set their spades in new locations, neither of which looked any more promising, until—

"Detective." The workman with the goatee spoke in a way that got their attention.

Stoffel craned her neck. "Something?" Excitement edged her smoky voice.

"Looks like some hair. With a head connected to it."

The two women edged closer for a better look. Three feet into this new excavation thick tufts of black hair protruded from the sand. The second workman joined the first. Both set aside their spades in favor of garden trowels and dropped to their knees to scoop away the sticky white grains. For Claudette, whose nerves teetered on a razor's edge, the process was painfully slow. It was a crime scene, she understood, and care had to be taken not to compromise whatever was down there. Eventually the workers uncovered the head and shoulders of a middle-aged man with

Mediterranean features.

"He was buried standing?" A surprised Detective Stoffel studied the sand-caked face. "That sure looks like the photo I saw of Gino Ginelli." She paged through images on her cell phone. "Keep going. See what else you can find."

What they discovered five minutes later was a razor knife with dried blood stains on the blade and handle.

"And there's the murder weapon." Stoffel gave a fist pump and looked at Claudette. "That seals the deal for me. Ginelli's our killer. You were right, Mrs. Miranda. There was something buried here."

Hearing those words after the week she'd had made Claudette's eyes well up. She couldn't stop herself.

Stoffel shook her head in disbelief. "This is the damnedest thing! What made you think someone was buried here?"

Still startled she'd been right, Claudette gave a muted laugh. "This will sound weird but I got the idea from a bathroom sink drain and a watercolor landscape." At the detective's puzzled expression Claudette went on. "Last evening I was at Olivia's apartment, trying to wind down from a terrible few days. I was tired and feeling pretty low. So I'm in her bathroom washing up, watching the water run down the sink, when something had Ruben said popped into my head."

"What was that?"

"He wouldn't believe our story about the missing footprints. Thought Peter and I were lying because we couldn't explain how Marco's killer could've come and gone without leaving a trace. 'People don't just drop out of sight,' Ruben told us." Claudette's dark brown eyes widened. "*But what if someone did?*"

Stoffel nodded.

Claudette continued. "The drain reminded me of a tiny sink-hole. West Texas is notorious for them."

"Big ones. The kind that leave craters."

"Right, house eaters. Even though we're on the Gulf, I wondered if there were other kinds. I had a vague memory of a story

I'd read in the paper years ago about a boy in Oregon who'd walked out on a beach and disappeared. The sand beneath him collapsed from his weight and swallowed him whole. He was totally buried by the sand, which filled in after him. Could that have happened here?" Her eyes lit up with inspiration. "It'd explain everything. Someone—Mr. Ginelli, we know now—decided to kill Marco. Ginelli saw him sunbathing alone and walked over from his house, snuck up behind Marco and cut his throat. You'll figure that part out, I'm sure. As he started back to his property the sand underneath him gave way and sucked him down. It was a preposterous idea at first but one that made sense the more I thought about it. And I knew it *could* happen. I Googled it and found other examples of sinkholes like this."

Detective Stoffel marveled at the idea. "I'd never've thought of it. Yet there's Ginelli buried upright in the sand right in front of us."

"And then, what came next was even stranger. The hole was deep and the sand dry and loose, so when Ginelli fell in the surrounding sand got sucked in after him, taking away his footprints. It's why Marco's Sudoku book and cap ended up where they were. They were light enough to be carried a few feet by the moving sand, like the soap suds I saw pulled down by the water in Olivia's drain."

Stoffel passed a hand through her unruly, wheat-colored hair, eyes incredulous. "A one in a million freak accident that simultaneously removed the killer from the crime scene and the evidence of his being here! Wow."

"I know!"

Stoffel's eyes narrowed as she remembered. "Wait. You mentioned a watercolor."

"The watercolor was of this beach. Olivia painted it a year ago. At first I didn't recognize the landscape; it had been done from a different angle. But there was more than that. Eventually I figured out what it was. Olivia's landscape shows several small dunes running along the grassy side of the property leading to the Ginellies." Claudette gestured to the stretch of beach to the right of the green chairs. "It doesn't look like that now. It's all flat. Where did the sand go?"

Stoffel laughed. "Sucked into sinkholes."

"Yup."

As the workmen continued to dig behind her, Judy Stoffel turned to her cell phone. "I'm calling the station to have them start the paperwork. The charges against Peter will be dropped."

Claudette stood a little straighter even as her knees buckled.

The detective's hand shot out to steady her. "You okay?"

It had been the worst week of Claudette's life, purged now in one wonderful instant. She and Peter could resume their lives together. She could finally relax. Her body, which had kept her worst fears at bay for so long, was unprepared for the sudden release of emotion. Claudette regained her balance with Stoffel's support. Relief and gratitude washed over her like a cleansing spring rain.

"Oh, yes," she grinned back. "I'm okay."

A vinegaroon sounds like a nickname for a type of soldier in the Napoleonic wars, or maybe a sort of herb found in gardens in households in the northeast, something like that. Good thing it doesn't sound like a giant scorpion or anything really scary...

VINEGAROON
John Shepphird

The old lady didn't trust banks. She buried her money. I was there to take it.

I stood outside the farmhouse in the dark trying my best to be quiet. My shovel struck something hard. It felt like a coffee can. I thought *bingo* and shined the light of my iPhone into the hardened Amarillo soil. I could see something there. I jumped down into the hole, picked it up and brushed off the dirt.

That's when I saw it was a skull.

At first I thought it was a Halloween decoration. It wasn't. I dropped it just as a creepy-looking bug scurried at my feet—a huge scorpion. Only later would I learn it wasn't a scorpion but rather a vinegaroon.

I'd been set up.

Randall County sheriffs were waiting by my car. I ran but their German shepherd got me. Fighting off a police dog is considered resisting arrest so they hit me with Tasers. You don't want to get arrested in the Texas Panhandle.

"I've been set up," I told the cops.

A paramedic tended to the bites on my leg and they sat me in their interrogation room. A middle-aged guy wearing a short-

119

sleeve button-down introduced himself as Detective Parsons. To me he looked like a Mormon. Or maybe he was a Methodist, I don't know, reminded me of a by the book, Bible-thumping type of guy. I told him that I'd been set up.

"By who?"

"A Texas Ranger."

That piqued his interest.

I added, "It's a long story."

"We've got nothing but time, son," he said. "Can I get you something to drink? Coffee? Water? Pop?" I wondered why he was being so nice. They brought me a Dr Pepper and I asked him, "Who is that buried out there?"

"I was going to ask you," Detective Parsons said.

"I wasn't expecting a grave."

"Why don't we start at the beginning?"

I sipped the lukewarm Dr Pepper. "There's a bar outside where I live in Austin. I met this old guy, Jimmy, there."

"Jimmy who?"

"Jimmy Lane."

He wrote that down. "What bar?"

"The Orchid Room, a dive near where I live with my girl-friend Cindy."

"And Cindy's full name?"

"Cindy Farris."

He wrote her name down too. "Your girlfriend."

"After she graduated from UT we moved in with each other." I didn't tell him I had been meaning to pop the question when I found a decent job, but diamond rings weren't cheap. Cindy worked a corporate gig downtown, got up early, dressed for success and was off while I slept in...or more often slept it off.

I was in between jobs and hadn't had much luck. Cindy said it was because I'm artistic by nature and that makes me "overly selective." I'm a singer-songwriter and to get out of bed it's got to be for something that inspires me. Nothing inspired me then, not even Cindy. Not until Jimmy told me about the buried treasure.

I explained, "There was this old guy sitting at the bar all the time. He was a Texas Ranger back when GW owned the team."

"As in GW Bush?"

"That's right. Who else?"

He leaned back and asked, "So this man doesn't work in law enforcement?"

"Like *Walker, Texas Ranger*? Hell no. He played baseball."

Detective Parsons let out a sigh of relief. I realized he must have thought I was talking about an actual Texas Ranger. I added, "He played in the early nineties, had a baseball card in his wallet and showed it off from time to time."

"Go on."

"Most days after Cindy is off I get up and finish the pot of coffee while searching the internet for jobs. I go to the gym, pick up groceries and her dry cleaning, whatever needs to be done."

"How is that pertinent here?"

"Getting to that. Most days I drop in the Orchid Room for lunch and a couple of beers."

"And Jimmy Lane told you about the grave?"

"Not a grave, buried money," I said. "I had a map but you guys took it."

After a brief discussion with the other cops they produced the map, the one I'd had in my pocket. Detective Parsons spread it on the table and gave it a look. I asked, "Your sheriffs were waiting for me. How did you guys know I was out there?"

"The homeowner reported you," he said.

"Gladis? She saw me?"

"You know Gladis?"

"Jimmy told me about her."

"Tell me more about this Jimmy."

"He didn't talk much, drank Seagram's Seven and blended into the place like a chameleon so you wouldn't give him a second glance. From the lines on his cheeks I suspected while at home he breathed with the assistance of bottled oxygen. That didn't stop him from ducking outside for a smoke now and again."

"So he was a smoker. Is that important?" he asked.

"Well…no. I'm setting the scene."

"I see. Why?"

"It's because I'm a songwriter."

"Okay, but let's just stick to the facts," he said. "So former baseball player Jimmy Lane gave you this map. How'd you end up in Amarillo?"

"Drink enough beers next to a guy and you'll hear all sorts of stories." The Irish charm I got from my mother's side of the family. I've always been one to talk to strangers. "One day he proposed the caper."

"The caper?"

"He told me about his ex-girlfriend from years ago, Gladis. He said she'd been a stunning beauty in her day, drop-dead gorgeous, but also entirely crazy. One day she got a big settlement check while he was on the road playing the Angels."

"Settlement for what?"

"She was a widow, married real young. Her husband died from an accident out at the Randall County Feedyard and they paid her some sort of settlement. Jimmy said she treated herself to a few things, a new car, TV and refrigerator. When Jimmy returned he was surprised to learn she pulled the cash out of the bank and buried it. He said she had always been incredibly cheap, wouldn't spend a dime on anything unless she had to and Gladis didn't tell him where it was. They had talked about marriage. She'd sell the house and move to Fort Worth, close to Arlington Stadium, but Gladis grew stubborn and didn't want to give up the family property."

"And why did Jimmy send you?"

"I guess because he couldn't do it himself. Jimmy's sort of a half-cripple, uses crutches and has a handicap sticker. The deal was we were going to split it by thirds with his niece, Fiona."

"Fiona who?"

"I never got her last name."

I could tell he was getting frustrated. He wrote her name on his pad. "And please explain how this Fiona fits into the picture."

"She's Jimmy's only surviving relative."

"Go on."

"Back then Jimmy decided to leave Gladis for good, but not before scanning all around the property. He found a spot of soil that looked like it had been dug up, the scrub brush cleared away, and such. He realized he couldn't take the money and leave her because she'd know it was him. He had to wait it out. So instead he drew himself a treasure map—" I motioned to the tattered paper on the table, "—figured he'd go back to get it after enough time had passed. Then he got into a nasty car accident. A drunk driver on the wrong side of the road put Jimmy in a coma and then a wheelchair for a while. That ended his career. While in the hospital he gave the map to his sister for safe keeping. She lost it so Jimmy figured it wasn't meant to be. But his sister died of cancer a few months back and cleaning out the garage her daughter Fiona found it. I got the map from her."

"When was that?"

"Yesterday. She lives in Lubbock. Jimmy warned me that Gladis keeps a Remington in the house and said, 'She's skilled at trap and skeet and knows how to shoot, but don't worry none, Gladis is as old as me and likely can't see for shit.' Something like that. The shotgun made me nervous. I'd repossessed cars and have been shot at before, but this was different because digging for treasure takes a lot more time than driving off in a car."

Detective Parsons leaned back and sized me up. "You repossess cars?"

"A part-time job I had, yeah. Bar talk, I'd bragged about how I was on a job liberating a Dodge Ram down in San Marcos when the deadbeat came out of his trailer with an AK-47. He unloaded the magazine as I sped off."

He seemed mildly impressed. "How long were you in the repo business?"

"Couple of years, but I'm out of that racket now. I served

subpoenas too. That's why Jimmy thought I'd be right for the job."

"This sounds like you willfully agreed to burglarize this woman's property."

"I saw it more like a maritime salvage operation."

He raised an eyebrow, dubious. "How's that?"

"Like when a ship sinks it becomes the property of whoever recovers it."

"It's nothing like that."

"Well, that's how I justified it. At least to myself. It was a crapshoot. It had been buried so long Jimmy wasn't sure the money was there anymore, but he set up the meeting so I could get the map from Fiona."

One of the cops came in and summoned Detective Parsons. I sat there alone for a while and thought about Cindy. I hadn't told her about any of this because I knew she'd judge me and wouldn't approve.

Cindy and I met one night while I was playing a gig at Antone's in Austin. She was there with her college girlfriends. I was that guy on stage. We hit it off and were really close until she got corporate day jobs which meant she had to get to bed early. I'd always been a night owl. Because of that we fell out of sync.

The Friday I set out for Lubbock Cindy looked great in her dark grey suit, the one with the skirt cut high. I noticed her heels were different that morning and realized I'd never seen them before. She said, "I'm still on that crazy deadline so you're going to have to eat without me."

"I'm not here tonight, or this weekend," I reminded her. "Driving up to help my brother out with the house, hitting Home Depot and leaving around ten." This was a lie I'd planted earlier in the week. My brother Brian watches way too many home improvement shows. He'd bought a fixer-upper in Fort Worth and spends weekends working on the damn thing. I'd helped him with other houses before. When he sells them I get a reward for my effort.

"Don't drink and drive," Cindy said.

"I won't," I told her.

None of that was true except for my planned trip to Home Depot. There I picked up a shovel and a pick axe. At the PetSmart next door I got a bell-encrusted dog collar. Then I bought a twelve pack of Coors and drank most of it on the drive up, pulling alongside the road to pee: it's about a six-hour drive to Lubbock.

I found the Starbucks where Fiona worked as a barista. I had no idea what to expect but she was a beauty. She had red hair and vivid green eyes. I was taken aback.

"I get off in a half hour," she said. "Meet me at Nicky's." She gave me directions to a sports bar across the highway.

When she arrived she was out of her apron and into a clingy, burgundy knit thing that hugged in all the right places. I've got to admit it's because of women like Fiona that kept me from going to Zales and buying Cindy that engagement ring. Well, that and the fact I couldn't afford one.

Fiona sat on the barstool next to me, ordered a double Jack and Diet Coke and said, "Since Jimmy referred you, I guess you must be good."

"I used to repossess cars."

"Used to?"

"Technology killed the repo man," I lamented.

"How's that?"

"It all depends on the risk assessment determined by the dealer running your credit score."

She sipped and waited for me to elaborate.

"If your credit is questionable, dealers install GPS vehicle tracker kill switches in cars now."

"What are those?"

"Electronic devices tied into the ignitions. Stop making payments and returning their phone calls and all of a sudden your car won't start. They can track where it is and send a tow truck."

She seemed surprised and asked, "So now every new car has

one of these?"

"No, they're only installed if the dealer suspects you may be a credit risk. Most people aren't, but they're in the business of selling cars so they're usually willing to roll the dice. Some rental cars have them, too."

"Okay, but what I'm wondering," she asked, brushing the auburn hair out of her eyes, "after all these years why does my uncle choose you?"

"Because I'm the best," I said.

"All I see is piss and vinegar," she said accusingly.

"What's that mean?" I didn't know what had made Fiona's attitude change so quickly.

"Arrogance and bravado," she said. "Digging up the money barely merits a third. What makes you so special?"

I caught the scent of some kind of perfume, or maybe it was her shampoo, sexy, nothing like Cindy's flowery little girl essence. I said, "You can always get it yourself."

"My uncle won't let me. He said it's a man's, job which is total bullshit."

"Keeping you clear of the buck shot from that twelve-gauge Remington," I said. "Probably not a bad idea."

"You don't have to do this, you know."

"I'm up for a challenge," I said. What I really meant was, *I need the money.*

"When will you go?" she asked.

"Tonight after dark. I understand there's a dog."

She nodded. "There is, some sort of Rottweiler or something. I've driven by there a few times."

"Can't have the thing barking at me," I said. "It's surprising how fast raw hamburger mixed with Benadryl puts dogs to sleep." I'd brought along a vial of crushed Benadryl that I had in my pocket and showed it to her. "Back in my repo man days this was the go-to trick to eliminate the threat of junkyard dogs."

She eyed the vial before admitting, "Sounds like you *are* the right man for the job."

"Just a matter of experience." I could tell she'd warmed up to me, her confidence seemingly restored.

We laid out a plan. I'd dig up the money and we would meet back at the bar the next morning when they opened. I'd shave off expenses for gas, tools, and miscellaneous before she'd get her third. Then I'd take the remainder back to the Orchid Room and split it with Jimmy.

"Good luck."

The curve of Fiona's waist caught my eye as she walked out. I couldn't wait to see her again.

I drove up to Amarillo and found the house just as dusk had set in. There was junk everywhere. Overgrown weeds. The once white house was the color of its surrounding dirt and in desperate need of repair. This was a Boo Radley house, for sure. It made sense since Jimmy had said Gladis was nuts.

I couldn't just hang out because there's no cover in the flatlands. To kill time I found a Denny's and ate there. It was past eleven when I drove back to the house and parked up the road. The lights were on. I waited.

Then Cindy sent me a text message: *I called your brother. WHERE ARE YOU?*

I dialed her from my car. She said my brother had phoned and she'd learned I wasn't with him in Fort Worth. "What's going on?" she asked.

"In Amarillo on a business trip."

"Why didn't you tell me?"

"It's complicated."

"You lied to me."

I could tell she was hurt. "I didn't want you to worry."

"Worry about what?"

"It's work…sort of like what I used to do."

"A repossession?"

"Exactly."

"You promised not to do those anymore."

I explained how the job paid really well. I sensed she could tell I wasn't telling the entire truth so finally I spilled the beans and told her everything.

Cindy said, "It sounds like you're stealing money."

"This old lady's got Alzheimer's," I fabricated. "She's forgotten where it's buried."

Cindy began to cry. I begged her to stop. I thought this came from nowhere but she told me it was over between us.

"It's no big deal. I'll be back tomorrow."

"It *is* a big deal. You lied to me." Then she hung up.

I called back. Cindy wouldn't pick up. I texted. Nothing. It wasn't like her to break up on the phone. We'd been together too long. I got to wondering maybe all those late nights at work hadn't entirely been spent in the office. Was there another guy in her life? Had she been looking for a way out? Why couldn't I be honest with her?

After what seemed like forever, Detective Parsons returned with another Dr Pepper. He said, "Okay, now tell me what happened out at the Unger place."

"I heard the barking so I made a sleeping pill laced with the raw hamburger I'd brought in the cooler in my trunk."

"A sleeping pill?"

I explained the Benadryl routine and how I went to the driveway and set the treat by the mailbox. Sure enough, the dog appeared and gobbled it down.

"The lights finally went out and I waited another hour. Then I got out of the car and went to the house. The first thing I did was duct tape the dog collar bell I'd bought at PetSmart to the door. If the lady came out I'd hear it for sure. Next I followed the instructions on the map and found the spot. I began to dig.

"Since I'd been drinking beers I had to pee again. When I took a break I heard a noise coming from the darkened house. I was ready to make a break for it at any moment. I thought I saw a shadow move on the porch but didn't know if my mind was playing tricks on me. I stood there, not moving an inch, for at least half an hour. There wasn't any more movement or noise, so I resumed the dig. That's when I came up with the skull. And there, in the bones, was this really weird bug that totally freaked me out. A huge scorpion. That's when I got out of there."

"Probably a vinegaroon."

"It looked to me like a scorpion."

"How big was it?"

I demonstrated with my hand.

"*Mastigophora giganteus*, also known as a whip scorpion. They don't have a stinger but rather claws and tentacles at the head and tail. There are millions of them in West Texas."

"Whatever it was freaked me out. I don't like bugs."

"Did you catch a scent of vinegar?"

"No."

"Vinegaroons keep predators away by spaying acetic acid in the eyes of the assailant, temporarily blinding them. That's how it found its nickname."

It was ironic that I'd been blinded too, only by the greed of a fast buck.

"Vinegaroon," I said.

"That's right."

"How do you know so much about them?"

"Studied entomology at A&M."

I wondered how learning about bugs had led to a career in law enforcement, but didn't ask. I said, "That's when your boys got me."

"Thank you for your candor," he said, putting his pen inside his legal pad and getting up once again to leave me by myself.

The bite marks on my leg began to ache. Maybe it was a kind of canine karma—payback for all the dogs I'd drugged over the years. I thought about Cindy and how I'd messed things up.

They arrested me for attempted burglary, criminal trespassing and animal cruelty. I got to make a phone call. I called Cindy but she didn't answer. I wasn't really surprised. I tried my brother and he told me he'd be on his way.

The next morning Brian hired an attorney, Rhonda Gomez, a middle-aged woman that reminded me of Gloria Estefan. She put on the professional-face but I got the impression she didn't care for me. She admitted that the majority of her cases were handing DUIs and I got really nervous. I wondered where Brian had found her. He said, "The internet, where else?"

On Rhonda's advice, we pleaded not guilty at the arraignment.

After Brian posted bail I was free to go. While we were going through the process of reclaiming my impounded car, I told him everything, including how Cindy was dealing with it. He said I should have clued him in and he would have covered for me.

On the way back home I stopped in Lubbock, went to the Starbucks and asked for Fiona. They told me she'd quit and didn't work there anymore.

By the time I returned to Austin, Cindy had moved out. She'd taken her couch. She didn't really have any guy friends and I wondered who had helped her carry it out. Was it a new boyfriend? I went to the Orchid Room. Jimmy was not there. The afternoon bartender said he'd not seen him in a while.

As my trial approached I became a complete wreck. I couldn't sleep. Everything in my life was falling apart. I replayed all my bad decisions over and over in my mind. I started writing a song about it, sort of a Tom T. Hall thing.

The day before my trial I drove up to Amarillo and checked into a fleabag motel because it was all I could afford. Early the next morning I met Rhonda Gomez in the courtroom hallway. Detective Parsons was there, too. I wondered if he was going to testify. Parsons and Gomez were laughing and seemed chummy, like old friends. Had they ganged up against me? I was certain I was doomed.

Gomez took me aside and said, "The district attorney offered a deal. I think we should take it."

"What sort of deal?"

"They're willing to drop the trespassing and attempted burglary charge but not the animal cruelty. That's a misdemeanor. You'll have to pay a hefty fine."

I couldn't believe it. "Why'd they drop the charges?"

"Through dental records they've identified the corpse as Wallace Unger, Gladis's deceased husband."

"Did she kill him?"

"No. Back in the nineties a work-related accident took his life." I vaguely remembered Jimmy telling me something about that, the money being her settlement. "Gladis Unger admitted she hadn't wanted to pay the funeral expenses back then. It appears the woman suffers from chrometophobia."

"What's that?" I asked.

"The fear of money, a condition that makes her extremely frugal. Also a hoarder." I recalled all the clutter on the property and the condition of that house. Gomez explained, "It's an obsessive-compulsive personality disorder. She didn't even purchase a coffin and buried her husband on the property, next to the remains of his favorite dog. The county has assigned a social worker to help her sort things out."

That's when it all made sense. The freshly dug soil Jimmy saw and put on his treasure map wasn't the buried money at all. It was her former husband's shallow, unmarked grave that Gladis was compelled to keep hidden.

I signed the plea bargain. I had to beg my credit card company to raise my limit so I could pay Gomez's legal fee and the animal cruelty fine. Unless I hit it big as a songwriter it would take years to pay off. Even now, every month as I cut those checks, I wonder where that fabled settlement money is buried. And I think about Fiona and Jimmy. They're out there too, somewhere, but only one of them is worth looking for. Unlike the money.

There's one thing I'm certain—down in the dirt that buried cash is guarded by a sentry of vinegaroons.

There have always been myths and legends of people who kill. Thomas gives us a version of a modern-day tale of someone who kills, a ghost, an unseen assassin...

INVISIBLE SHADOW
Thomas Luka

THEN—

The meeting was held at one of the oldest hotels in the oldest cities in France on the night of the last full moon of summer. Marseilles was a city so ancient it was already heavily in use when the Romans landed in Gaul more than a thousand years ago. The hotel sat on top of a seawall near the port but fashionably far enough away not to attract drunken sailors and the vice that followed them.

The woman was dressed in culotte pants tucked into knee-high leather boots and a thin white blouse that did not cause her discomfort in the warm climate. She wore a scarf to cover her blonde hair, and large tortoise-shell sunglasses that hid stunning green eyes and blocked the dying sun. She smoked a cigarette in a holder, one leg crossed over the other, a glass of chardonnay on the table, looking like a woman who had never seen a hard day in her life. Although in her forties, her early forties, she looked a decade younger at least.

The man met her just after sundown, portly and red-faced, his jacket off and tucked under one arm, tie blowing in the breeze, sweat stains under his arms and around the band of his hat. He sat down at the table without being asked, the woman's only acknowledgement of his presence the removal of her sunglasses.

"Is it always this hot?" he asked in English.

"I would not know. I live in Cannes, further up the coast. It does not get so warm."

"Why didn't we meet there?"

"There would be the possibility of recognition. I did not think you would want to be noticed with me."

The man shrugged, slipping a thin square of paper from his coat pocket, placing it on the table and sliding it towards her, his hand never leaving the sheet. Without picking it up, the woman read the few sentences it contained before the man gave it to the flickering candle, turning it to ash. "We are going, sometime in the fall. It is a one off: cold bore. Can it be done?"

The woman hesitated with a drag on the cigarette, and spoke casually through the exhale. "It can, but it will be expensive."

"How much?"

"Five million, in uncut diamonds. Half in advance, half when the job is completed."

"How will that work?"

"I will give you the address of a bank. You will have the stones delivered to said bank within five days from. The second half will be delivered to the same institution five days after. If full payment is not received, I will reluctantly be forced to... take measures."

"Where is the bank?"

Another puff of the cigarette. "Switzerland. Where else would it be?"

The man pretended to hesitate, but the hook was set. "The strike point must be at a location we designate."

The woman said nothing, accepting with another ring of smoke. "What else?"

"And after, will you need an exfiltration plan?"

Of course, the woman thought, *so your men can ambush me just out the door or have a driver kill me to obscure your own conspiracy.* "I will handle my own departure."

"That is not an option, I'm afraid. We have to ensure you cannot be captured. There can be no chance of it."

"Then we have wasted each other's time." The woman made to leave, until a hand touched her arm lightly.

"Wait."

She hesitated before re-taking her seat with a small sigh. "It must have taken tremendous effort to find me. I am one of the few people in the world who can succeed in this operation, or in failing, can sufficiently muddy the waters enough to insulate you from any blowback or consequences. I may even be unique."

The man's silence confirmed her story. "When can you begin?" he said, finally.

"When the diamonds have been deposited. The same box will act as our dead drop for instructions. All communication will go through the box as well."

"Do we need to discuss the alternatives to success? Not to mention any sign of betrayal."

"If you are who I think you are, that would be very bad for me, indeed."

LATER—

The six-story concrete edifice was indistinguishable from the buildings around it, commercial offices filled with attorneys and oil lobbyists hoping to one day make their way to the massive structures being constructed in downtown Houston.

Each floor consisted of four suites: two private offices with a reception area and adjoining conference room. Two suites were on one side of the elevator bank, and two on the other. Thick walls separated the suites.

For security reasons, the men sitting in the conference room of the north side suite had rented the entire fifth floor. Six men sat at the table dressed similarly in dark suits and dark ties, some wearing glasses, some not. Their ages ranged from up and coming to octogenarian, and all were somber and serious about their purpose.

"Are you kidding?" one of the older men asked one of the younger.

"You asked me to come up with a plan, one that must succeed and without the chance of exposure. This cannot be done without considerable cost."

"Like before?"

"If you recall, you wouldn't let me take the steps I recommended. Now we are here."

"I think you are being dramatic."

"Am I? You asked me to come up with a more workable scenario."

"But a woman? Really?"

"If this fails, if we are discovered, everyone in this room as well as everyone we represent will be doomed," another of the older men said.

"Which is why I have brought you this. Your original plan would have never worked. All your eggs had been placed in one basket and too many variables could have shifted their values by the time of the mission itself. This plan is different. Redundancy often means success over failure."

"Why diamonds?"

"Makes sense. Can't deposit that much money in a bank account, any bank account, without somebody getting wise. Gold is too heavy; look what the Nazis tried to do. It took entire train cars even to move a million dollars' worth. That amount in diamonds can be carried in a pocket. Uncut stones add an extra level of anonymity."

"How so?"

"Whether you sell them in Antwerp, or Johannesburg, or Brooklyn, there are maybe a hundred quality gemcutters and setters in the world. You take a finished stone to any jeweler in any one of those cities and they would be able to tell you where the work was done."

"Strings that need to be severed. You are saying she knows what she is doing."

"No, I am saying she is *professional*. For years she operated in enemy territory, often alone, and they never got close to her, and that was while they were looking *specifically* for her. I am saying that she has thought this work through and wants as little connection with us as we want with her. If discovered, she can give nothing because she knows nothing, but I don't think she is going to get caught. It is my opinion that this is how the job gets done, and no one finds her or even suspects her existence."

"And if you're wrong? If she is captured?"

"Then they will have caught a woman officially dead for nearly twenty years."

NOW—

The woman stepped off the bus at the stop with a slight hitch in her walk, still not comfortable in the pencil skirt and pumps after wearing them every day for the last month. The Texas autumn morning was sunny and cool, with little humidity. *A fine day for work*, she thought, strolling to the seven-story building on the corner. Despite the early hour, crowds were beginning to line up along both sides of the street for the impending parade, some blocking the doors to her building. It took a policeman to force the people to make way.

After taking the elevator to the third floor the woman moved demurely to her desk. Laid out in a bullpen style, the large room contained fifty or so desks for clerks, typists, and receptionists. They were surrounded on four sides by offices for owners, advertising men, and the best of the salesmen working for a variety of companies and enterprises.

All of those working in the bullpen were women of varying ages, colors and creeds ranging from the very young to the very old. The third floor was reserved specifically for clothing manufacturers, brokers, and their support staff. Marie, a heavyset black woman, sat at the desk directly to the woman's right. Over the past few weeks the two of them had become friendly, if not actual friends. Marie spent all day typing out invoices, demands for payment, and affixing labels to envelopes for a fashion wholesaler. The woman, called Rose, copied Marie's style of endless repetition as she went about her own tasks, the better to maintain her identity.

"How are you, today?" Rose asked.

"Just fine, sugar," the black woman responded with a sigh. "Another day, another fifty cents." Things had been hard on Marie since her husband had been laid off at the rail yards. There had been promise of more work to come, but nothing yet.

Rose had rented space in the building a month before for an absentee textile company owner in New Hampshire wishing to try his hand at the ever-growing blue jeans market. It was an easy story to sell, as hardly anyone in Texas could point to New Hampshire on a map. The leasing agent was happy to take six months' rent in advance, all cash of course. She took her desk at her assigned place in the pen and began typing up a meaningless invoice for the purchase of raw denim for processing. The Hollywood movies of the past decade had made the material the most popular clothing with young people in the world. Children and adults alike were buying denim pants, shirts and jackets as fast as they could be made but Rose found the material to be too thick and inflexible for comfort.

The rent included a desk in the bullpen and an office for design and manufacturing staff. For the last month she had mostly sat in the pen from 8:30 a.m. to 4:30 p.m. Monday through Friday typing meaningless reports, letters, and invoices that would ultimately go nowhere.

On this Friday morning at 11:45, Rose got up from her desk to take her regular lunch break. Others working in the pen asked if she was going outside to watch the parade, but she told them she did not wish to fight the crowds. Instead she took her brown paper bag and slipped into the office she had rented for her imaginary boss on the East coast, a not uncommon thing for her to do during this time, and locked the door behind her.

The office was on the western edge of the third floor, large enough for design tables and machinery. Denim material was thick and coarse, the rolls of it so heavy-duty sewing machines with their thickened needles were needed to stitch it into clothing.

The woman kicked off her shoes, unzipped her skirt and let it fall to the floor. She unfastened her garters and removed her stockings as well. Stepping out of her slip and pulling off her blouse, she pulled on a pair of worn woolen pants she retrieved from her purse.

Two burlap sacks, filled with railyard sand smuggled into the building one purseful at a time, rested in the middle of the office space, benign on their own. The sacks were measured to be precisely four inches above the windowsill, where the shade had been drawn to keep the sun away, despite the noon hour.

From a compartment beneath the sewing machine the woman removed first a rifle and then a scope, which she deftly screwed onto the top of the weapon. Although the woman preferred a different grade of rifle altogether, she had been clearly instructed to use this exact model, as well as quite specific ammunition. After securing the telescopic sight she placed the gun sideways on the sandbags. Wearing only a brassiere and the wool pants, still with no shoes, she lay face down behind the sandbags, controlled her breathing and picked up the rifle, sighting through the scope.

Settling into position, Rose contemplated her life, as well as her three deaths.

THEN—

She had died the first time after returning home from teaching kindergarten when she was nineteen. She found her mother crumpled on the floor, sobbing uncontrollably, clutching a single piece of brown paper in her hand. That telegram informed the family their youngest son had died heroically on the front. The girl had felt a cold fist grip her heart, and she sank to the kitchen floor next to her mother, unable to breathe.

The girl enlisted in the Army the following day, the young teacher remade into a remorseless killer from a distance.

Other brothers would die in the war but they would not kill her as the first telegram had. Instead, the pain of those losses stoked the furnace in her breast, the heat and pressure of such sacrifice fueling the hate for the enemy within her. It made her heart a lump of charred coal, and then cold and hard as a diamond, unbreakable, and she vented that rage against her opponents. And then, amidst the rage and the hate, she met Gregor.

Poor, sweet Gregor; another soldier, with his doe eyes and chiseled features, but he was not like her, not a shooter. He could not hit a target outside of thirty meters but he shared her gift of total stillness and lack of panic under fire. He had impeccable eyesight he used to find targets even the girl missed with a spotter scope.

It started as many battlefield romances do; in cold nights in dark trenches bodies naturally seek each other for warmth and companionship. The need for something more eventually turned to lust, quick couplings mostly clothed, one eye looking for the enemy, the other for superior officers. The lust of desperation can sometimes seed deep roots, turning slowly without either knowing, into a great and powerful love affair.

Their love was the love that can only be found in war: fierce, passionate, consuming. For love is the enemy of war, it replaces that which war takes away—hope. Hope for survival, hope for victory, hope even for the war to end. Most importantly, hope for a future.

She died a second time one year later on a frozen battlefield far from home when Gregor was shot in the head as they moved cross an open stretch of land deep in enemy territory.

He was killed by a counter-sniper, shot as the pair of them were relocating from one hide to a new one. He lifted his head the width of his hand too high and the bullet struck him at that moment. He lived for a day and a night before finally dying in her arms.

Her last death occurred two years later on another freezing January day. It had leaked to the enemy that the "Invisible Terror," a name she had acquired following the death of Gregor, was facing them across the field. The enemy commanders pulled back their infantry, well beyond rifle range, and pounded her fellows' position with mortar fire. On the third day, after the shelling had been its most intense and seventy-seven of seventy-eight men of the unit had been killed, she watched an incoming round arcing toward herself and the commanding officer. Without thinking, she threw herself on top of the man just as the shell hit.

When she regained consciousness, she was in a field hospital. Her entire midsection wrapped in gauze, the screams of the wounded and dying were the same in any language. A nurse, noticing she was awake, came over and injected her with something, sending her out again.

When she awoke the next time, she found herself in a real hospital, not a tent hastily erected in in the rear of some battle-field. The air smelled clean and septic and it was quiet. The walls were made of thick concrete, and the floors and walls and bed sheets all shimmered in white. A bag of plasma hung on a pole near her left ear. Her abdomen was still swathed in bandages, but she lacked the strength to sit up even had she been free. She tried to call out, but her voice came out as a muffled croak.

Someone must have heard her because a heavyset woman entered the room, dressed in a white nurse's uniform, crying out in the language of the enemy.

That quickly decided where she was, and her fate.

The nurse then ran from the room, leaving the girl to stare at the ceiling for a time.

Minutes or hours later, an officer in a grey uniform with major's stripes entered room with his cap tucked under his arm.

"You can understand me?" he asked in his own language.

"A little," she replied.

He responded in her native tongue. "Then this will give me an opportunity for practice. I spent two years in your country as a young man, for study."

"If you are going to torture me, I will not make it easy for you."

The major took a step back and smiled, pointing at a chair in one corner. "May I sit?"

She nodded, as though there was an actual choice. The major sat as if for parade, his back ramrod straight, holding his cap in his hands. "Thank you. Do you know why you were saved?"

"To wring me of information, I assume," she replied, with more bravery than she possessed.

His smile was genuine. "No. It was your eyes, my dear. After the battle, our soldiers were scouring the field for our own wounded when they came across what they thought was another dead fighter. Fortunately, one of them recognized you from the flyers we had circulated. Their orders had been to capture you, not kill. Sadly, artillery shells do not follow orders as well as a man."

The girl only nodded in response. The enemy loved propaganda as much as her own country. She knew every enemy soldier with a rifle had a paper with her picture on it. It was known she'd been receiving fan mail and marriage proposals from enemy troops at her headquarters for over a year.

"You were severely injured. Our surgeons had to remove part of your intestine, but I am told you will make a full recovery. Happily, the war is over for you, though others fight on. Your country holds several thousand of our men as prisoners of war. This fight cannot last forever. We want as many of those men as we can returned safely. You can help with that."

The girl was stunned. "How?"

"My dear, you are famous. You have killed more than fifty of our men with a rifle and hardly anyone caught more than part of your shadow. Others surrendered out of spinechilling fear of nothing more than reports that you were in the area. It is said you can kill two men with one bullet, waiting until they are lined up in your scope, and even four with two. You fire your rifle so fast it sounds like a single shot: four soldiers dead with one crack of the rifle, a literal bolt from the blue. Do you know how disheartening that is to a man in the field?"

"That is why I do it," she said. The girl reasoned keeping silent would serve no purpose. Officially she had killed fifty-eight men, but the real number was at least four times that. That did not count the ones she'd killed in close quarter with a bayonet, which would have been six, or possibly seven, more. Her fear had always been that the higher the body count the enemy could confirm, the more energy and resources they would expend to make her their trophy. She would be captured or killed, and her vengeance stilled.

The major tamped down his fear of the small girl with a slight cough. "In any case, this war *will* end, in defeat or victory. When it does, we intend to show how well we have treated our enemies in the hope that our prisoners of war have been given equal treatment. Believe it or not, you have the hard-won respect of your enemy, which is rare, and others idolize you, which is rarer still."

This man does not know our leaders, the girl thought, as the major nodded and left the room, never to be seen again.

In the end it was not the enemy who traded her, or even her own countrymen who liberated her. After the hospital, she was moved to a women's camp in the northwest corner of the city, then freed only a month later by a group of resistance fighters led by a double agent named Jean Chenault.

With the resistance, she was smuggled west, not east, to allied lines. Along the way she confessed to her liberators who she was, and it was decided by all parties that the west might be a safer landing place. Her own country was not one for captured heroes—the capture itself seen as a failure of mission—and a prison camp was just as likely as a victory parade to mark her achievements. En route, the girl learned that her superiors had declared her dead that past January. It was far from uncommon for high command to make mistakes, but it was more likely that she have more value to the motherland as a martyr rather than a prisoner of war.

Predictably, Chenault had fallen in love with her. He was only a man. And she did love him back, after a time and in her own way, at least as much as she could after the loss of Gregor. He was a man of means with homes and property in the south of France. Papers were arranged showing she had been a refugee of the war born in a small town she'd never seen. She became Rose Chenault, sophisticated bohemian socialite and for a time she and her husband became the toast of the Riviera during the post-war years.

Her wounds were such that they had left her unable to bear children. It was a disappointment to her Chenault, but the woman called Rose convinced him otherwise. Her heart was so irrevocably broken she did not think she had the love necessary to raise a healthy and happy child. In the end, he made his own peace with it and satisfied himself with the affections of his wife.

NOW—

Rose did not want a radio or spotter with her. Additional points of contact could only increase her chances of exposure. She set her slim watch on the top sandbag, watching the minutes pass by, and waiting. Every thirty seconds she put her eye to the scope to view the scene. More and more people were gathering, the crowd sounds increasing in volume, but she tuned them out, as she'd been trained on the battlefield so long ago. The light from the sun would not be a problem and the distance so short the slight breeze not a factor. She was required to take two shots and only two shots—not one, and not more than two. Both shots must count. Her specialty was needed: she would shoot twice, so fast the shots would sound like one.

It was why they had chosen her, after all.

Waiting, she thought of her husband, a good man who had found a broken young woman all those years ago and used his not inconsiderable wealth to nurse her back to health and normalcy. Those resources had nearly been expended however, after ventures in parts of the world had not worked out according to plan. Castles were expensive to maintain, and her work today would go far to solve their money concerns. She had told Chenault she was visiting a sister she had once thought perished in the war, who was now ill, and that she would be gone for a month, possibly a few weeks more. She called him every day to make sure he was getting along, assuring him she would be returning home soon.

Rose settled in, absorbing the rifle into her body, the perfect melding of human and machine. Her cheek was pressed softly to the small of the wooden stock. Her elbow set, she swiveled right, picked up the line of cars approaching. The crowd noises quieted in her mind with the acquisition of the target, capturing and tracking the parade in the scope as it approached from the north; the trajectory was low and flat.

The lead vehicle was a Cadillac convertible, so large in the scope she could read the registration sticker on the corner of the front windshield. The target vehicle, also a convertible, followed just behind, the four people inside minus the driver waving to both sides of the street. Four policemen on motorcycles, two on each side, stayed just behind its rear bumper and ahead of the third car, another black convertible. The procession moved along slowly, giving everyone a look at the passengers. The shooter tracked the target car from one window to the other with the rifle as it made the turn southeast and slowed further. The subject was moving away from her while working its way into the center of the sight's reticule.

She kept the target low in the scope, knowing the rifle would kick up slightly, the bullet not dropping significantly at this range. She found that cold hard place deep inside her heart where now rested an indestructible jewel of the hardest substance. Her grip relaxed on the rifle rather than tightened, allowing muscle memory to take over.

At a particular moment, the woman willed the trigger to break, and it simply did, easily and smoothly for a smooth, clean shot. The target's head dipped forward. Rose threw the bolt and the trigger broke again before the echo of the first shot had dissipated, this time kicking up a bloom of flesh and red mist from the head.

The world returned to normal speed. There were screams, sirens, people pointing in all directions as expected. Rose the assassin stood and pulled heavy plastic gloves over her hands. Taking off the wool pants, she used them to wrap the rifle, soaking the packing with the contents of a bottle marked "solvent." The acid was useful for destroying trace evidence. She placed the rifle back into the compartment inside the immense sewing machine, arrangements for which had already been made. Regardless, there was nothing there that could be traced back directly to her.

Rose ripped each burlap sandbag open and spread its contents over the floor, resembling little more than construction debris, before stepping back into her skirt, slip, hose, and shoes. She finished the buttons on her blouse, smoothing the wrinkles, and opened the door to the hallway. The corridor was empty on the way back to the bullpen, so she slipped into the bathroom to check her appearance. Her hair was a bit mussed, and her makeup could use some touching up, but after what had just happened, no one would question how she looked.

She covered her mouth with one hand as she stepped into the hallway, smearing her lipstick she crashed into Marie rushing out of the pen. The large and overweight woman grabbed her in a great bear hug and squeezed Rose tight against her ample bosom.

"Oh, honey," she said. "It is just terrible, terrible, I know."

Rose sank into the embrace, intentionally losing her footing for a moment. "Oh, God. Oh God," she repeated, forcing the tears to her eyes.

People were rushing past them to get out of the building while police officers were trying to work their way in.

One officer stopped before the pair of women, gun in hand but low at his side. "Is she alright?" he asked with concern. "Has she been hit?"

"I-I'm alright," Rose responded with a sob. "I'm not injured."

"Best clear out of the building, now," the officer said, his own anxiety plain.

Rose broke the embrace. "I will be fine, Marie. You see if any of the others need help. I will take the bus home now, I think. I am just in shock." On the way out, Rose saw her "co-workers" weeping, sobbing, or shrieking. Rose knew of dying, and she knew that she had killed not just a man, but an ideal. She had ended a movement.

"We all are, honey. We all are," the black woman replied.

The woman born Roza Sherapova, in Yedma, Russia, 1924, nicknamed the "Invisible Shadow of East Prussia" in the Second World War by a Canadian newspaper, decorated Soviet sniper, reported killed in action January of 1945, dispatcher of hundreds of men yet none so impactful as this last one, kept a tissue to her mouth as she exited the building. The dozen policemen outside her "place of work," nicknamed the "Dal-Tex" building, did not give her a second look, for it was a very shocking and sad day for everyone that would only get worse with time.

After all, who would be looking for just one more woman among many, crying over the death of Camelot, in Dealey Plaza, Dallas, Texas, on November 22, 1963?

Crime fiction writers and readers like to get together for readings at bookshops, bars and libraries across the country. Usually nothing really bad goes on there (depending on the readings themselves). In this case, there's much more going on than anyone would know...

THE TALENT KILLER
Mark Wisniewski

The tape and the wire are making my chest itch, the basement of the Cornelius far less crowded than it was for the readings I attended before the twenty-nine minutes in which I lost my mind and committed homicide myself. So far tonight, only eight people have shown, including the six writers scheduled to read. In the air is a sense that, really, most people here would prefer to be home playing on Facebook.

Jonas, my partner in this undercover operation, takes a seat, on a folding chair in the very back row. As a supposed literary upstart, he's already sneaking peeks at everyone, but as a long-employed full-timer for the Bureau, he's here to support me as I seek one more damning piece of evidence on the man the Bureau believes is The Talent Killer, Ethan Hendee.

Two rubs, though.

Hendee's been a client of mine since back when I was only a literary agent and not a convicted killer. In fact, this is why I've been released from prison to sting him; the Bureau's theory is that if anyone can help them establish probable cause, it's me.

But there's also the second rub, the one neither Jonas nor anyone in the Bureau knows—I believe Hendee is innocent.

And, yes, I believe this because Hendee's been one of my favorite clients, personally speaking, for more than twenty years. Though I also believe it because I can't imagine the man ever hurting anybody. Let alone killing and dismembering three women and dropping the pieces one at a time in the East River.

It's with all of this in mind, and with Jonas doubtless sneaking peeks at me, too, that I claim a chair halfway up the aisle. Tonight's readers have created two huddles on opposite sides of the stage. On the left and chatting politely enough are the four women, dressed in blacks and grays. On the right two men with apparently nothing to say to each other stand with hands in pockets. Hendee, a second look around assures me, is nowhere.

A third glance of mine back toward Jonas tells me that, between us sits the sexiest human being I've ever seen. Then again, I warn myself, *you just got out*. But none of the four women onstage, young and dolled up as they are, attract me. So it's all this older one's doing, I think. This forty-something with a shiny black bob.

Ignore her, I think. Focus. I wonder if she herself could be The Talent Killer, and with this mistrust of her in mind, I check her out again, and immediately we make eye contact. Deep, optical communion in which she lets only me know she's both seen and done a few things, good and bad. She's traveled a lot, these slightly grave yet bright ebony eyes suggest to me; she might have tamed lions; she might have done some dancing, and I don't mean in ballrooms.

Certainly she's broken some hearts, I think as I force myself to face ahead. But no way is she The Talent Killer. Too sexy. No one that hot has the frustration to kill.

And no diamond. In fact, no rings whatsoever. And in faded jeans, with holes apparently made by time and wear and tear, not by some fashionista factory.

I shake off our eye contact—it's overwhelming—to study the two men onstage. They're young. They exude tamped-down nervousness. Though they are, I remind myself, minutes away from reading their work in public.

Behind me some calls my name. "Matt?"

I look over my shoulder. At the bottom of the stairs stands a robot of a man whose name I can't remember, much as his voice strikes me as familiar. Suspect material, I think, because his arms remain flat against his sides, his entire being stiffening more the longer he stands there.

"It's Mitch!" he says.

"Mitch!" I say.

"Of *The Pelican Crypt*," he says, enthusiasm lost.

I still can't remember his last name, but now his face is growing familiar, even though his mane of thick black hair has been shaved off and he's grown a fluffy gray beard—and it all comes pounding back. The "novel" that, after I took it on, proved to be so autobiographical it could only be called non-fiction. The compromise he and I made to dub the book "creative memoir." His theory that if the title included words from both *The Pelican Brief* and *Tales from the Crypt*, I'd be able to auction the manuscript overnight—without him deleting dozens of pages that were not only irrelevant but also boring as hell. My failure to sell it to any house whatsoever, the hit my reputation took as a result, the subsequent years of estrangement with this Mitch guy.

I put my personal estimate that he's The Talent Killer at eighty-eight. In any case, in my mind he has infinitely more leanings toward being a psycho than Hendee will ever have. I stand and walk over, and we shake. In his eyes is sharp disappointment or dashed expectation or anger or maybe all three. He tries to smile but can't.

"They let you out early," he says.

"Yes, they did."

"For good behavior?"

"For excellent behavior. Anyhow it's truly great to see you, Mitch. What're you working on?"

"A few things, actually."

"I imagine you have representation elsewhere by now?"

"I don't. Will you be…are you still…how does that go when a literary agent gets out of prison?"

I want to glance back at Jonas. I crave moral support from him; already I prefer the company of FBI agents to the writers of books, and I wish Jonas would rush up here and slap cuffs on Mitch, who the more I think about it, always did sort of creep me out.

But I keep on with Mitch and Mitch alone: "Kind of up to me, I guess."

I meant this as a joke to soften him up, but his face is not in the least that of a humored, reasonable man. He grabs my wrist, squeezes it hard, very hard, then lets go as he says, "Maybe I'll shoot you an email," and heads over to the two guys standing beside the stage.

They shrink from him slightly as they notice his approach. It's as if, in their rumor mill, he's done something objectionable socially or sexually or worse. He picks up on this, his demeanor now fidgety. Why doesn't the Bureau want him rather than Hendee? Clearly he, this Mitch, is losing the writing game. And shaving off all that great hair and growing the full beard? Isn't that what sociopaths do, change their looks?

I glance back at Jonas, who grimaces slightly, shakes his head. The "no" clearly means he disagrees with me that Mitch should replace Hendee as our prime suspect, but what did the grimace mean? Is he ticked off? At me? If so, for what?

Then I notice it. Ethan Hendee is here. Behind all of us, standing on the stairs, one step above everyone else, taking stock. His own appearance haggard, unshaven, the fret on his face suggesting he has a chip on his shoulder the size of an OED.

But maybe that's only because he's sixty-some years old without a published book, I tell myself. He's diminutive as ever (I've always put him at about five-four, but tonight he seems shorter), faded jeans sagging more on one side of his waist, the left. From clicking a mouse eighteen hours a day with his right hand? In any case, my assessment of him now is that more than anything, he's still writing stellar plainspoken poems. No way does he have blood from a dead woman anywhere in his apartment.

But when his eyes meet mine, he looks away immediately.

Much as Jonas is still playing it cool, he appears to be struggling to. He still believes Hendee's appearance has put us in the presence of evil.

I brace myself. Swallow. As per Jonas's earlier instructions, place my hand on my chest and scratch it briefly. Jonas scratches his left ear, our code to assure me the wire's transmission is fine. I mosey toward Hendee hoping he'll say hello first.

He does not. He's one with his thoughts, which, yes, given his penchant for inner focus, may well be focused on how to conduct himself so he can snuff out the most talented woman onstage. I remember what Jonas mentioned in the Falcon during our ride here: it's notable that Hendee, whose name is known by most every poet alive, would bother to show at a reading held for six neophytes and not him. I do not want the Bureau to be correct; I want this conversation I'm about to have to prove that he—my most talented client without a book, Ethan Hendee—is innocent.

"Hend!" I say when I'm six feet away.

He sees me. Recognition does not register on his face.

"It's Matt!" I say.

"Hey, Matt."

We do not shake. We hug, gingerly. But I find myself still liking him, if tentatively.

"Criminal justice—finally," he says.

To test him about what he meant by this, I say, "Either that or another violent homicide is in the works?"

He does not flinch. He laughs, and not with the chuckle of a murderer trying to live a double life. It's a hearty laugh, genuine. Like the more effusive half of a pair of old pals who cherish each other at least as much as friends in publishing can.

Sounding earnest, he says, "What are you doing here, man? Scouting out that young female talent?"

"Just…putting a toe back in the water."

"You hear what's been going on?"

"Regarding what?"

"Big houses've been handing out book deals left and right."

"To poets?"

"To novelists. Young ones. Female ones. In the past few months, three very young women hit the jackpot."

And there it is, smack in front me, something in Ethan Hendee's eyes I've never seen. Hopelessness. Though it does remind me of what I saw in those same eyes eighteen years ago, when Chronic Fatigue Syndrome was a misunderstood thing and he told me he'd been diagnosed with it—and that a doctor had said he could die from it one day.

But the only true elephant in the room here, in the Cornelius Café's basement, is the fact that he brought up the subject of the three big book contracts without mentioning that the women who signed them have each been killed and butchered and disposed of piece by piece.

"So you're telling me you haven't copped one," I say.

"A woman?" he asks.

"I meant a book deal, but—"

He looks off. He's studying the four young women who are about to read. Jesus, I think, because if I'm honest with myself, he's indeed giving off the vibe that if he could get away with running any of them through a meat grinder, he'd do so in a heartbeat. Is he that starved for more recognition from the publishing world?

Then his expression returns to the melancholic one I've always identified as Hendee's.

"I got nothin'," he says.

"Meaning no book deal, or…?"

"Meaning no women. As far as book deals, I've been sending around manuscripts of my better poems on my own. I mean, I hope you don't mind me doing so without your permission."

"Of course I don't mind, Hend. I was in jail for Christ's

sake. I mean, what were you supposed to do?"

"Anyhow, no takers. Not even from the tiniest press out there. It's like it's become required among the young hipster editors to ding me. And this business of me never having had a book—it hasn't helped with my...love life."

"Yeah, well, I haven't been having much success with women either," I say, intending this as a recently released convict's quip.

"Yeah, I heard about your ex getting married to Blaine Davis and all."

I shrug as if I've never cared about my ex. Despite the twinge of malice inside me, and somehow forced through a rush of thoughts that is drying out my mouth, I say, "True love, I guess."

It's just after I say this that Hendee regards me more closely. Maybe to see if I'm as cool about my obliterated marriage as I pretended to be. Maybe to see deeper into my sincerity—it's hard to tell.

"You know, I'm thinking of trying fiction all over again," he says.

I glance over at Jonas, who nods almost imperceptibly. Meaning he figures this is it. Maybe not the heart of it but at least an edge of it. Hendee's explicit statement of his desire to succeed as a novelist and thus kill the three women—this, as the magistrate might see it, is Hendee's admission of motive, slim as it is.

"Short stories?" I ask nonchalantly.

"A novel," Hendee says. "Now if I could just do something about my gender," he adds, and he sets his jaw and clenches it, causing me to suffer not only a mental blur but also all manner of feelings. Because I not only sense he is murderous, I also feel he needs to confess his murders to me, his agent and maybe the only person on earth who might understand him, the person with a history of understanding his work.

Not to mention I'm foreseeing him trying to survive unharmed behind bars: for him, a poet who weighs in at a hundred thirty tops, the chances of remaining untouched by the grabbier inmates would be zilch.

"Hey, great to see you, Hend," is all I can think to say, since the flurry in me is growing worse. There's shock because of his guilt, and there's shock because of my guilt for agreeing to be in a position to betray him.

"I need to make sure I end up with a decent seat, Hend," I say. "Let's talk later."

And with that inanity hanging in the air, I start toward the folding chairs, Jonas pinning me with a quick, razor-sharp glare—clearly he thinks I've backed off too soon. Have I really blown things, though? I wonder. Isn't it best to investigate cautiously? Or have I operated so ham-handedly I'll be back in Sing Sing before midnight?

I brace myself best I can as I turn to Hendee and call, "Coffee soon?"

"Still drink the stuff," he says, smiling wanly.

I flash him a thumbs-up. Again I glance past Jonas, whose jaw hangs in disappointment and disbelief. I claim the chair two away from the woman with the shiny bob out of animal instinct: a blur of thoughts in me has me wanting to leave with her to some place safe and far away and quiet.

No, I think. *Focus.*

The two men onstage continue to refuse to speak to each other. As it was before my arrest and conviction and incarceration and early release to join this investigation, it's still a cutthroat world—writing—and clearly they've been through it. The befriending merely for the sake of making inroads toward agents; the back-stabbing to thin the playing field; the online sabotaging of others' published books with early scathing one-star customer reviews under pseudonyms.

Is Jonas checking these guys out? I ask myself. *If not, why not?*

In any case, I now smell, and adore the smell, of the woman with the bob. There's a warmth to her scent, but it's also fresh and floral, like lilacs, the best French lilacs, I decide, and I crave it and want to breathe in more of her.

But The Talent Killer might be here. Maybe. And onstage, the four young women are being approached by a young man with a goatee. A newbie literary agent, I think, and Mitch Parker confirms my guess by taking a seat in the front row, a foot and a half to the right of the guy. Mitch is gazing up at him as he and the women chat. Mitch Parker Wannabe Author is angling for representation by someone other than yours truly.

Or figuring out which of these women he'll try to take home.

"Excuse me," I hear.

It's the woman with the bob. Facing me. Allowing those obsidian eyes of hers to study my features as intently as I am savoring her scent. I like feeling her eyes on my jaw.

"Yes?" I manage to say.

She smiles, kindly but teasingly. God, does she know what she's doing. There are words coming out of her mouth I care little about compared with how much I want her mouth smothering mine: "Am I correct in assuming, given what I just overheard, that you represent writers of books?"

I am taken. I cannot return her smile. "You are," I say.

"Do you ever consider PhD dissertations?"

"Never been opposed to them," I say, a lie of sorts, but not an out-and-out lie since, in my mind, there are always exceptions.

"Written by women my age?"

"Never had the pleasure, but I imagine we could make it work."

She is now, in this moment of my low, low life, flat-out riveting. "Are you hitting on a stranger?" she asks.

"Are you?"

"Well, I do adore those wingtips," she says, and she beams, and Jonas clears his throat loudly, letting me know that some FBI regulation or other forbids this kind of fraternization with potential suspects of whichever gender.

But this woman, I think, is no suspect. And any guilt in her, I'm sure, is the kind I'd understand, even enjoy. *I'm not really in the FBI*, I think. *Not forever.*

"I'm Elise by the way," she says.

"Matt," I say. "I'd give you my card, but I just got out of prison."

"Seriously?"

I nod, blushing from my cheekbones on out.

"That fellow up there wasn't just joking with you?"

"He was not."

"What did you...do?"

"Choked the man who slept with my now-ex-wife."

"To death?"

We share a moment right then of searching each other's faces in that unflinching way spouses do now and then. She seems open to me having ended a life, which to me during this moment means it's possible she's killed someone herself. Notions both terrifying and pleasant bottleneck in me; I need to share one of them with someone or make some kind of move physically, so I nod.

"Interesting," she says.

"That's what the jury thought."

"So then you got a divorce in prison?"

"Yes."

"I never knew a man who got a divorce in prison."

"Well, here you are."

"Are you telling me you're no longer on good terms with your ex?"

"Actually I'm not telling you that. I loved her, and I'm still fond of her. It's just that a year or so after my incarceration began, certain, you know, exigencies made it clear she no longer loved me. So...boom."

"Boom what?"

"Boom divorce."

"But no hatred."

"Not on my part, no."

Nails painted teal flip some of that bob over an ear. It's a new bob, perhaps cut within the past few hours. She's showing herself off, this Elise.

"When did you get out?" she asks.

"Of the marriage?"

"Of prison."

"About four and a half hours ago."

"Which prison was this?"

"The one up in Ossining."

"You mean *Sing* Sing?"

I nod.

"Wow," she says. "That's so...exciting!"

"You really think so, or are you just being polite?"

Her eyes hold mine long enough to let me know she's been in some hells, too. *Hopefully not because she's created any*, the FBI guy in me thinks. But, damn, do I want this woman.

"I do think so," she says. "More than I can express publicly, if you catch my drift."

I'm tongue-tied. It's hitting me inside, on a level deeper than thought, that she might be trying to lure me to some dungeon of chains and poisons and knives and table saws.

Plus she seems fine with the wordlessness growing between us, in which I now remind myself that I, too, am high-risk, so really, we are peas in a pod. In any case I'd forgotten what this feels like. This kind of desire for a stranger: lust.

The reading begins. The emcee prattles about his own bio, his coming of age. *Must everyone?* I think. To me now, in the presence of this Elise, youth is silliness.

Focus, I think.

The Talent Killer.

I search the authors onstage for tells. They appear more or less innocent; Jonas is typing something into his phone. Then the first "author" is up, a woman, redheaded, twenty-something, beauteous. The sentences she imparts are impressively lyrical, suggesting she's well-read but her prose will never earn a publisher a profit. Several phrases she reads are so poetic and bland I neither understand them nor want to. Pass. As both a suspect and potential client.

Second comes the next female reader, this one in high heels. Her teeth are shockingly crooked, implying a lack of family wealth some publishers de facto require. Does this mean she could feel enough frustration to murder a fellow writer? In any case I give her a chance. As a literary agent I've always given underdogs a chance. She's reading what she's called "snippets," which are, to her, neither poems nor stories. Her best (in her opinion) snippet boasts the refrain "sunshine on my face," which eds my age will know was used in the film *Mask*. Pass with regret in both regards.

Then the host works in one of the men. His pages detail his experiences as a waiter in Brooklyn. So difficult! And being single in Brooklyn—so lonely! But no tension, no reveals, no dialogue, no reversals, and no killer instinct of any sort whatsoever, I decide. Good luck, young man.

The third woman walks to the stage as if on a cloud of pride. She announces she wants to keep the contents of her "nearly done" novel secret until it's published, a sure sign she's written none of it. As she reads "a series of short-shorts" about her mother's hands, I write her off as too sweet to conjure enough envy to be a suspect, and nearly doze off.

Then comes the fourth woman, who's slightly cross-eyed and speaks with a wise amount of fear. Better still, she reads from a thick, dogeared manuscript she's called her "stupid-assed novel." Within fewer than ten pages, a toddler falls out of a window but survives, octogenarians conduct a threesome in a sauna, a business executive silently abandons his religion in a city council meeting and thus leaves it early and escapes an explosion. Somehow she makes all of these plot twists jibe.

Surprising prose that clicks and flows and keeps me listening—if she hasn't plagiarized, she's a natural. Jill Klugman is her name, and her author photo won't move thousands of copies on its own, but if I had my little CVS notepad with me (as I always had before my arrest) I would jot her name immediately and underline it three times. Instead I create a mnemonic device: Klugman as in Jack Klugman of *The Odd Couple*, she and I precisely that—an odd couple—if we go on to become client and agent, since here I am, an aging ex-con while she's a young genius whose prose in the hands of the right publisher would sell like coffee in October. Whether or not she's committed crimes, I want to represent Jill Klugman.

The second guy finishes it. A poet named Cal-something with stunningly large and white teeth. Cal is twenty-five, yet his third book has just been brought out by an Ivy League press, so publishing-wise he's set—no motive to kill, even dentally speaking. I personally believe his work has nothing on Hendee's; to be sure, as this Cal's incisors underscore yet more alliterative similes, I don't see why Hendee doesn't charge the stage to pummel the guy.

But Hendee remains seated.

Other than his failure to leave the premises, he seems disinterested completely in this young man's musings.

All of his focus is instead on Jill Klugman. *Because she has talent and he's The Talent Killer?* the undercover agent in me wonders.

No, the literary agent in me thinks.

He's just impressed with her.

But then, just like that, without anything irritating being read by the young man onstage, I notice Hendee's face overtaken by something I've never seen on it before. Something serious and wolflike, perhaps vitriol. His eyes remain set on Jill Klugman.

He is truly glaring at her.

While he remains steadfastly focused on her, I have to admit to myself that, dammit, Jonas and the Bureau are right: he, Ethan Hendee, is probably the killer.

As I stare, he removes a jackknife from his jeans pocket. He uses that knife to clean the undersides of a fingernail, then another, but from what I can see from where I sit, his nails are not only spotless, he's bitten them down to the quick. He again glares at Jill Klugman, clutching the knife, which is still open. He holds it as if it means as much to him as the lucky pen he used to tell me about, the one he drafted his best poems with.

Worse still, his focus on Jill Klugman reminds me of how I felt for the hour or so before my fateful twenty-nine minutes. Homed in. With mechanical intensity. A heartless, cold steadiness in my mind.

Hend! the literary agent in me wants to shout. *Stop thinking whatever it is you're thinking!*

But I don't shout this.

Of course I don't.

If I did, I'd be back in that cell before the eleven o'clock news.

Hendee keeps on, glaring at Klugman with that same intensity, incriminating himself in my heart all the more.

On top of which I also consider the possibility that if the Bureau doesn't cuff Hendee tonight, there's no guarantee he won't turn his wrath on Elise.

He heard me talking with her here, could see the looks on our faces. Because he's known me, he knows there'd be more than physical attraction at play. He knows that, like Jill Klugman, she has potential if not already realized talent galore.

I want to see Elise, merely glance at her again, but I can't. Not if I'm going to be a pro for the Bureau and help stop the monster. Thoughts in me whirl. *Am I falling in love? Am I finally seeing for real who this frustrated client of mine is and maybe has been all along? Am I going crazy?*

In need of calm, I glance over my shoulder at Jonas. He's not facing me, but his Bureau-issued smart phone is on a palm on his lap—with one tap of an icon, he can have this place teeming with our backups.

I cough loudly, and he glances away from the stage and over at me.

He nods at Hendee, then raises his eyebrows as he mouths, *Now?*

I glance back at Hendee, who's closing the jackknife, returning it to his pocket; this I will never be able to deny honestly.

Nor can I deny that I feel even crazier about Elise than I did when I was flirting with her.

I lower my chin until it all but touches my chest.

Goodbye, pal, I want to shout to Hendee.

I say nothing to anyone. I reach to my left and feel for Elise's hand. She neither hesitates nor hedges as she grips mine back.

I listen to the poem being read.

I realize that, thanks to Hendee, I will probably never again enjoy poetry, and through the wire that will take my voice to Jonas, I say two quiet words:

The first is, "Yes," though it strikes me as flat. The second, more resounding, is, *"Now."*

We've known since the radio days of The Shadow *that the weeds of crime bear bitter fruit and that crime does not pay. But maybe it can, for a little while…?*

THE MIDNIGHT CHILD
John M. Floyd

East Texas
5:30 p.m.

It was quiet at the edge of the lake. Somewhere in the forest, an owl hooted. A whippoorwill called. The sun, fat and orange and low in the sky, glinted off the window of an empty car, one of two parked in the gravel at the end of the dirt road. High overhead, a lone crow perched on a pine branch.

Then the silence was interrupted: a blue Toyota Camry rumbled up the road through the surrounding woods and parked beside the two other vehicles. Four people climbed out of the car—three men and a woman, all dressed in jeans and jackets. One of the men was taller and older than the others, with a thick beard and dark hair. He and the woman—a thin blonde carrying a shotgun—were tense and watchful, their eyes checking everything around them. The driver was short and solemn, and wore an orange Tennessee baseball cap; the fourth member of the group was pudgy, redheaded, and rosy-cheeked. The two younger men carried heavy brown duffel bags. Without a word they all made their way toward an old wooden picnic table sitting in a grassy patch near the water. As soon as they reached it, they paired off, the tall man and the woman standing on one side and the two young guys—the redhead and the driver—on the other. At a nod from the tall man, both bags were unzipped and emptied. Still no one spoke. For the moment, all eyes were fixed on the neatly-bound packets of cash that covered the tabletop. Best guess, according to the woman, was around six hundred thousand. A hundred and fifty grand apiece.

"Before I forget," the redhaired man said finally, looking at the tall man, "I have something for you—" and pulled a revolver from his coat pocket.

The tall man's reaction was swift: he snatched at his own gun—a black automatic—and fired twice into the redhead's chest. Before the body hit the grass the driver ducked, pulled out a pistol of his own, and shot the tall man in the forehead. His head snapped back as if he were looking for heaven, then he toppled forward and bounced off the tabletop on the way to the ground.

Silence fell, broken only by the driver's heavy breathing and the echoes of the gunshots off the forest wall across the far side of the lake. But the noise wasn't finished. When the young driver turned to look down at the redhaired man's body, the woman raised her shotgun and fired it into the side of the driver's head. His orange ball cap spun away into the gathering twilight.

This time it stayed quiet. The woman, her chest heaving and her eyes wide and her disheveled hair shining in the last rays of the sun, lowered her smoking gun and stared at the three bodies lying on the bloodstained grass around the table.

The crow floated down from the pine tree, lit on a fencepost nearby, and cawed to her.

She paid him no attention.

One Hour Earlier
4:30 p.m.

They found only a sparse crowd in the lobby of the bank. As Twelve had predicted, there was no security guard, and when the customers and staff saw the firepower in the hands of Twelve Becker and Eddie Farris—and the no-nonsense looks in their eyes—they lay face down on the floor as ordered, and stayed there. With a stocking-masked Red McLain covering the back entrance and Mark Wiley parked and waiting behind the wheel of the Toyota out front, a similarly masked Farris and Twelve cleaned out the registers and much of the vault within the ten minutes they had allotted themselves. No shots were fired and few words were spoken. Then they took off, with Wiley roaring down Main and Cypress and then up the ramp to the interstate and off again onto surface roads five miles later. And finally, half an hour after that, they made a screeching left turn onto the four-mile dirt road that led to the end of the line, the little clearing they'd found in the woods along the lake shore. It was a long-abandoned picnic area surrounded on three sides by miles and miles of thick pine forest, not to mention a reportedly impressive population of bobcats and wild hogs and snakes and gators.

From the front passenger seat, Eddie Farris turned to study the faces of his team as they bounced along the rutted track. Wiley, in his silly orange baseball cap, had his eyes on the road and his hands on the wheel, where they were supposed to be; Red was grinning from ear to ear in the back seat, his plump cheeks glowing even brighter than usual; and Twelve was gazing calmly out the window, a shotgun across her lap and a pleased little smile on her lips. Hell, all of them were pleased, Farris most of all.

He faced front again and saw, through the windshield of the blue Camry, the road's end, and the shimmering blue water beyond. It was time for dividing the loot, changing clothes, switching to the other vehicles, and splitting up. On the one hand, he hated to leave the getaway car behind, but it was stolen anyway, and after ten minutes of idling in front of the bank it was extremely possible that the cops were looking everywhere for it by now. Farris and Twelve would take the Ford and the other two would take the Jeep, and by the time the Toyota was located out here in the middle of nowhere, all four of them would be long gone.

It had been a good day.

3:40 p.m.

"You think we're ready?" Twelve asked.

Farris put down his bottle of Budweiser and looked across the dimly-lit room at Red and Wiley, the men he'd recruited weeks ago for this job. They were standing beside one of the pool tables at the other end of the barroom, talking. Doing more talking than playing, actually, even though each of them held a cue stick in his hand. But they looked upbeat to Farris. Not excited exactly, but upbeat. And that was good.

Farris had suggested they come here from the motel where they'd stayed the past two days, even though it was mid-afternoon and nobody really needed a drink. What they needed was a break from all the preparations. The bank was only three blocks away—all they had to do now was wait until 4:30. That, they had decided together, was zero hour.

"Yeah, we're ready," Farris answered. "I've been a little worried about Wiley—we don't know much about him, even after all this time. But he's a crack shot, and the best driver I ever saw." He turned to Twelve. "What do you think?"

"I agree. He ain't a Texan, but he's from Shreveport, so he almost is. Besides, Dave Pennington vouched for him—he'll be fine. He seems a little slow sometimes, but he's capable, and that's what we need. We don't necessarily want a deep thinker."

"Good point." So far Farris and Twelve had worked together on three robberies in two states, and although they weren't on anybody's Most Wanted list—probably because they'd not yet shot or killed anyone—they were notorious enough to attract attention. But everything had to be done well and done fast.

"The one I'm worried about," Twelve said, "is Red."

Farris frowned. "Why? He's a Tyler boy, and he has Pennington's blessing too."

"I know." She took a sip of her drink and studied their two partners a moment more. "I'm just not sure I trust him. Keep a close eye on him, when we get to where we split up."

"You think he might try something?"

"I just think you should watch him."

"How about at the bank?"

"I think he'll do fine at the bank," she said, putting her glass down. "If he tries anything at all, it'd probably be after we're done and we have the money and we're off by ourselves."

"You're not making a lot of sense here. You sure that's your first drink?"

"Will you watch him, or not?" Twelve said. "Especially at the lake."

"I'll watch him." Farris smiled and scratched absently at his beard. "Seriously, though. The way we've got all this mapped out, you think we're ready? You think it'll work?"

She nodded. "It'll work. It's a good plan." She clicked her glass against his beer bottle. "Well done."

He shrugged. "I'm a Saturday's child—I work hard for a living."

She grinned.

"What are you smiling about? What day are *you*?"

"I'm indeterminate," she said. "I was born exactly between Wednesday and Thursday. Right on the stroke of midnight, Mama said. That's why she named me Twelve."

"You never told me that before."

"Well, it's true."

"Educate me," he said. "I know Wednesday's child is full of woe. But Thursday's—"

"Has far to go. So I'm straddling the fence. I have a little of both in me. Woeful sometimes, but ambitious, too."

"Yeah, well. If I really believed in that kinda thing, I'd read my horoscope every morning instead of the funnies."

"You probably should," she said.

"Should what?" Red asked. He and Wiley had finally hung up their cues and drifted back to that half of the room.

"Should get something to eat," Twelve said to them. "We got a long drive after this is done, and I sure as hell didn't pack a supper for you."

Wiley grinned. "I thought you would, Twelve. You look like the motherly type to me."

"Obviously that's not your first beer," she said.

Farris waved to two empty seats. "Sit down, we'll all order some burgers." He studied the two men as they dropped into the chairs. "You guys okay? Wiley, you look tired already."

"You would too, if you'd been listening to Red run his mouth for half an hour."

"Well, now you can watch him eat." Farris raised a hand to signal a waitress.

"I'll just be glad when we're done with this, and gone, and safe," Red said. His voice sounded shaky.

"Me, too," Wiley said.

Farris and Twelve exchanged a glance.

2:55 p.m.

"The cars are in place?" Twelve asked.

"They're there. Gassed up and ready." Mark Wiley was leaning against the Camry, which he and Red and Farris had used to bring them back from delivering what Farris called their "fresh horses"—Twelve's Ford Focus and Wiley's Jeep Wrangler—to the meeting place, a remote picnic area on the east side of Hardy Lake. As he spoke, Wiley noticed Farris beckoning to him from the other end of the motel parking lot. He headed in that direction, leaving Twelve and Red McLain standing together.

"You got a minute?" Twelve said to Red. "I need to ask you something important."

"Okay."

"Why does Wiley always wear that stupid cap?"

He grinned. "That's your important question?"

"No," she said, smiling too. "My question is, is everything all right between you and Farris?"

Red looked surprised. "Sure it is. Why?"

"You two don't seem to talk much."

"I guess I hang out mostly with Wiley." He frowned. "Has Farris said anything to you, about me?"

"Nothing serious. The thing is…he's a little insecure. He's the leader and we all know it, but he doesn't think he gets much respect. He likes to feel appreciated."

"So what am I supposed to do?"

"I don't know. If I were you, I think I'd give him something, when all this is done. Something to thank him, I guess, something to remember you by."

Red gaped at her. "This ain't the Garden Club, Twelve."

She sighed. "It's just a suggestion, okay? Farris isn't somebody you want to cross."

Red ran a hand through his hair and turned to look at Farris and Wiley, sitting now at a round plastic table beside the swimming pool. Both of them looked back at him. To Twelve he said, "What did you have in mind?"

She pointed to his coat pocket. "That gun of yours? The revolver?"

"What about it?"

"It's a Colt Peacemaker, right?"

"Well, it's a lookalike. Shorter and newer, but yeah, it's a single action forty-five. Why?"

"Farris has been talking about it. Said he wished he could find one like it."

Red shrugged. "It's nothing to me. I found it in a pawn shop in Dallas."

"So why don't you give it to him?"

"Give it to him?"

171

"Why not? You have a thirty-eight too—I've seen you cleaning it. And you'd make a friend for life."

Red thought that over. At last he nodded. "I can do that. Yeah, I *will* do it. Thanks."

"One thing, though." She leaned closer, lowered her voice. "Wait till we get to the meeting place, at the lake. Till just before we split the money and go our separate ways. At that point you won't need an extra gun anymore anyway. Give it to him then. A nice surprise."

"Okay, good idea. Thanks again, Twelve."

They both turned as Wiley walked up to them. Beyond him, in the distance, Twelve saw Farris rise from his plastic chair, prop his forearms on the top of the chain-link fence that encircled the pool area, and light a cigarette. She wondered what he was thinking.

"Everything's all set," Wiley said. "Farris says we load up in ten minutes. We're going to a bar first, near the bank, and wait there. It's got pool tables."

"Okay," Twelve said.

She hung back a moment while Red and Wiley ambled back across the parking lot to chat with Farris. For a long moment she stood there, watching the three of them and thinking hard. That had gone well, she thought. The only thing that worried her about this whole enterprise was that a fourth of the take, today, might not be enough for her. It was a lot, yes, a lot more than she could earn elsewhere. But if she had even more...

She felt herself smile.

It just might work.

5:40 p.m.

Twelve Becker couldn't believe it herself. It had worked. Some of it had been planning and some had been luck, but it had worked. And it was over. She stood there a moment in the gathering darkness beside the lake, studying the dead bodies of her three unsuspecting partners in crime. Their three handguns, one fully loaded and two with spent rounds, lay in the grass beside them. The money, scattered there across the picnic table, was all hers now. Not a quarter share, or even half. *All* of it. She would miss Eddie Farris, sure—but not too much. Not as much as she would enjoy the cash.

The only things remaining to be done were to wipe her shotgun free of prints, put it into the lifeless hands of Red McLain, wipe down the door handle on her side of the Camry, take the spare tire out of the trunk of the Ford, stow the money in the empty tire well and under some old blankets she kept in the trunk, weigh down the two empty duffel bags with rocks and throw them into the lake, change into her other outfit, and beat feet out of here. Traveling alone at night in a different car and different clothes and a scarf tied around her hair, she'd be home free. Next stop, Mexico.

And then she heard the buzz. A vibrating cell phone, very loud now only because it was so quiet here beside the water after all the shooting. At first she hesitated—but only for a second. Whoever the call was for, or from, it might be something she needed to know about. Knowledge was power, or so Farris had always said. It took three buzzes before she located the phone in the front pocket of Wiley's jeans.

Holding her breath and trying to avoid any of the blood, she fished it out of his pocket, pressed the green button, and held it to her ear.

"Wiley," a voice said, "this is the chief. Don't say anything, just listen. We're on the dirt road and heading your way, all your Fed buddies and my men and a couple of state cops, too. You should see our headlights any minute now, through the trees. When you do, try to ease away from the group, and keep that orange cap on your head so if there's a gunfight our guys'll know who not to shoot. And by the way—good work!"

Long after the call disconnected, Twelve stood there holding the cell phone in one hand and the shotgun in the other. Finally her trembling fingers dropped the phone on the ground, and a second later she felt her knees go weak. She sagged, and sat down heavily in the grass. Her head started spinning.

So Mark Wiley had been a traitor. An undercover cop, probably FBI. No wonder he could shoot so well. He'd fooled them all.

She'd been right about one thing, though: it was over.

Behind her, Twelve heard what sounded like laughter. At first she paid it no mind; she knew she was alone here, and her nerves were stretched tight as a drum. But then it happened again. She twisted around to see a fat crow cawing at her from a fencepost at the edge of the woods. In a fit of rage, she raised the shotgun and almost fired at him, still sitting down. The crow flew away.

She could see the lights now, and hear the roar of the approaching cars. She dropped the shotgun, and fast. Struggling to her feet and raising her hands over her head in the blinding yellow wash of the headlights, Twelve was reminded miserably of what she'd said to Eddie Farris in the bar this afternoon, about her name. She decided her mother must've either lied to her or mistaken the time of her birth. As it turned out, she was more Wednesday's child than Thursday's. She had to be.

She'd gone as far as she was going.

I've never been fond of the saying, "You can't go home again." Of course you can, and of course it can never be the same. So it seems like a silly thing to put in words, or worse, to be so well-quoted. On the other hand, when Nat and Carl go home, they probably should have listened to Mr. Wolfe...

THE DEED
Laura Oles

My first instinct as I stood in front of my childhood home was to burn it down.

I had been out of my car for a few minutes and I could feel the sweat on my scalp beneath my ponytail. I reached up and wiped my brow with the back of my hand. No one should willingly visit South Texas in July. *Like fried hell,* a friend once told me. As much as I loved my home state, I despised the summers. They tested me in ways only another local would understand.

Kingsville is a town of mixed fortunes, close to Corpus Christi and the Gulf Coast but also near the brutal brush lands of South Texas. Not blessed with island breezes but only steamy, rolling air disrupting dry grass and low bushes as it travels across the grounds. The town's claim to fame has always been the King Ranch. The King Ranch is low-key famous here. The enterprise—and it is an enterprise—covers more land than the entire state of Rhode Island. Romantic visions of Santa Gertrudis cattle being rustled by skilled vaqueros aside, my reality growing up here was quite different.

As wonderful as the Wild Horse Desert is for many, my favorite memory of the town was seeing it in my rearview mirror.

Yet here I was, back in the one place I vowed never to return. I remained a good distance from the house, the lot surviving solo on a vast field without another structure in sight. No cattle, few trees. Twenty acres of isolation. Just the way my father liked it.

It's lonely out here, I'd say to him.

I hated this house. And now it's the only thing of value I own.

I stared at the building, straining to summon even a single good memory. The house stood defiant, battered from years of neglect and the harsh glare of the land's relentless summers. It was a single-story ranch with weathered blue paint and traces of white trim. The right side of the stairs showcased a sagging wooden railing, large jagged splinters dangling like icicle lights but without the festive sentiment. Remnants of a mesh screen whispered in the corners of the doorframe. The windows, hazy with an opaque grime, offered no hint as to what was inside. The roof drooped. The place was probably worth more flat.

I stared at the porch and thought of my mother. She spent much of her time there after her shifts at the Cypress Café. I would sit with her after she had finished mowing the front yard, so proud of that riding mower she'd bought at a town auction. *Practically stole it,* she boasted. As I entered my teenage years, almost a decade after she left, I often wondered if she missed that veranda more than she missed us.

The sound of a diesel truck interrupted my thoughts. The engine's violent rumbling demanded my attention long before the vehicle was close enough for me to recognize the driver. He thundered up the dusty road, raising high a trail of gritty debris. He parked behind my Tahoe, glancing at me but avoiding eye contact, before stubbing out his cigarette. Smoke separated around the door as he swung it open.

"Checking out your lottery ticket?" Carl's eyes found mine, the lines on his face deeper, more pronounced since I'd last seen him. Twenty years ago. Nicotine and the Texas sun had left their marks. His dark hair was longer now but the accusation in my big brother's eyes was just as I remembered. Some things never change.

"Funny. Somehow I don't feel like a winner."

Carl turned his head and spit on the ground. "You know, he just gave this place to you because he was pissed at me."

"I can't imagine Jim being angry at you for anything, perfect son that you were." I kept his accusing stare and raised him some sarcasm. He didn't intimidate me anymore, not like when we'd been kids and he'd held our father's favor. He seemed smaller than I remembered, his stance more rounded, his ability to take up space reduced. Life had landed a few blows. I had the one thing he wanted and we both knew it.

"So, what happened?"

"If I tell you, will you give me the deed?"

"Hell, no," I said, enjoying the rare experience of having the upper hand in our relationship. It was new territory and I was a bit drunk from the rush.

Was this what it had been like for him during our childhood?

"This place isn't worth much," I said. "I mean, it's not like we're in the middle of San Francisco. The house is probably a total demo, so it's down to the land." I signaled to the roof. "Look at it. Bet it leaks inside."

Carl reached inside his shirt pocket and pulled out a pack of cigarettes. He held it out after pulling a single stick from the package. I shook my head, tempted, but refusing to fail in front of him. "I quit."

He shrugged and then smiled at me after lighting his Marlboro. *Asshole.*

"You going inside?"

"Not sure yet," I said, my eyes focused on the house. I didn't want to go in alone but I damned sure wasn't about to admit it. I didn't want to return to that loneliness. He and I both knew he could sense my fear.

"I'll go with you if you want." *Bastard.* "Wonder what it

looks like now. It's been a while."

"When's the last time you were here?" I was curious now, about his relationship with our father and what had caused it to sour. Maybe letting him inside would loosen him up about the things I really wanted to know.

"Ten years. More, maybe." He pulled a long drag from his cigarette and stubbed it out with his Justins, the dust kicking up as he moved his foot from side to side. I envied him that moment. I missed smoking.

"Really? That long?" His answer surprised me. I had left this family behind as soon as I could hold down a full-time job and cover my own rent. In my mind, I had left them a tight unit, a family of two, the women long gone.

He extended his arm out to direct me ahead. I walked up the dusty path to the porch, careful with each step up as I made it to the front door. Carl waited for me to reach the top before putting any weight on the bottom stair. He didn't trust the structure, either.

I pulled the key from my pocket, two copies affixed to a simple metal ring with the address written on a paper tab. The lock refused to turn. I leaned in with a shove and played with the key. After some jiggling, the lock gave way. I waited a beat, turned to look at Carl for I wasn't sure what—encouragement?— and pushed open the door.

The inside smelled of rot and neglect. A mixture of stale food and warm sour air filled the space. I swung the door open and closed in an effort to move some newer air through the place. Then I went to a nearby window.

"Was he really living like this?" I asked as I struggled to un-stick the window frame.

"I guess so. No family here to clean up except us, so…"

"I'm not cleaning this," I replied, perhaps with too much venom in my voice. "I did enough of that as a kid."

To say Jim had let the place go was like saying the Pope leaned towards religion. Still sparsely furnished, I stepped ahead into the living room, Carl following behind. Jim's favorite couch was flanked by yellowing stacks of newspapers, magazines and other assorted papers. The wood paneling was in poor shape, chipped and sagging, and the other couches and chairs were ripped with stains across the dark green fabrics. All of it needed to be tossed out. I walked past the mess and checked out the kitchen. There was a stack of dishes and plastic cups piled in the sink, a few flies buzzing around, the only real sign of life. The beige counters were littered with items ranging from needle nose pliers and hammers to a box of random cables so old as to be considered useless. I decided against opening the fridge. No good could come of that.

I moved towards the dining room and saw that the space had been claimed for storing yet more useless crap. The wood table I remembered was still in the center, with two chairs on each side, the floral fabric faded from the sun streaming through one window. Piles of boxes filled with everything from crockpots to auto parts lined the walls. One thing in the room brought a small smile to my face.

"I remember when Dad let me pick out that wallpaper," I said, pointing to the diamond-patterned surface decorating the far wall. The stacks of boxes covered most of it now, and papers were piled so high that the pattern barely peeked from the corners.

Carl walked over to examine my childhood decision-making prowess.

"That was the summer I was at baseball camp," Carl said. "Got back and Mom was gone." I studied his face and realized how much our mother leaving had hurt him, too. Being six years older, he must have remembered more about her than I did, and growing up, I'd resented him for it.

"Yeah," I said, gesturing to the peeling paper, "I guess her leaving lit a fire under him. He decided we needed to redo the dining room. Had Larry over here helping him with some construction stuff, and he took me to Corpus to pick it out. Said I could choose whatever I wanted. Even stopped at Dairy Queen on the way home."

"Larry died a few years ago," Carl said. "Heart attack. Probably too much chicken fried steak. Heard about it when I was in town. He was really the only friend Dad still had."

I stood for a few moments, basking in the memory of that day. I didn't want to remember him fondly but maybe leaving me this house had involved more than simply spiting his son. Maybe it was his way of apologizing to me.

Carl walked through to the back bedrooms. I considered following him but let him be. I didn't want to go any further. If the living room and dining room were any indication, I'd seen enough. The place was a disaster. Now that I'd seen the inside, I knew the lot would be worth more without the house on it.

"Bedrooms are horrible, too," Carl said, returning from the back, his gaze moving from the kitchen to the living room and back again. "Couldn't get him to get rid of anything. We used to fight about it. All this worthless crap."

"On his way to full blown hoarding." I tried to reconcile what I observed with what I remembered growing up. Even after my mother had gone, the place had at least still been clean. I then realized it was because cleaning had become my job. There'd been no one to fill the position once I left.

"Didn't Jim have any other friends?" I asked.

"He hated that you called him that, you know." Carl's expression softened for the first time since he'd arrived. I tried to feel sympathy but couldn't muster it.

"He didn't act like a dad, so why would I call him that?" I could feel my jaw tightening and reminded myself to take a breath. "You were his favorite. I was the maid."

"I think you looked too much like Mom," Carl said, his candor surprising. "You really were the spitting image. Drove him nuts."

I shrugged. "Well, none of matters now."

Carl signaled to the front door. "C'mon, Nat, let's get out of here. How about we hit Cypress Café for dinner? Old times' sake?"

I nodded, following him out the door and closing it behind me. Maybe I should give him the house, I thought. Then I scolded myself for being too soft.

The Cypress Café had experienced a facelift since my last visit two decades ago. A wooden plaque with current typography and clean lines had replaced the faded metal sign I remembered. Located between Herschel's Barber Shop and Henry's Pharmacy in a restored brick building downtown, the café was doing steady business as we approached the glass door. I wondered if there was anyone left that ever talked about my mom.

We walked in and the cold artificial air blasted us in the face. I welcomed it. We chose a booth towards the back.

"Can you imagine Mom working here?" I asked, once the waitress had left us to consider our order. I couldn't reconcile my memories of her and this place. "It's so different now. Nothing like I remember."

"The leftovers she'd bring home were my favorite dinners," Carl said.

I nodded. She always thought the cook had a thing for her. Just another rumor for the list."

"New owners took over six years ago," Carl said, looking over his shoulder to survey the restaurant. "I like it. Still a diner, but updated, you know?"

We sat making small talk until our food arrived. It was surprising how civil we could be over Cokes and barely shared memories. My BLT covered most of the plate, with a healthy serving of French fries threatening to spill over the side. Carl's chicken fried steak and mashed potatoes looked delicious but also reminded me of Larry and his heart attack.

"So," I said, between bites of my sandwich. "What happened?"

Carl shoveled a healthy portion of chicken fried steak in his mouth and chewed. He took his time before answering. "There was a period that I wanted to try to find Mom and we had some huge fights about it. He said she left us and I didn't need to go looking for answers I'd never get. I kept pushing him and finally he said he was going to give you the house just to piss me off."

He took a sip from his water glass. "It worked." He shrugged. "Besides, Mom's parents died when she was little and she was an only child, so who was I going to ask?"

"Tell me what you heard about Mom leaving," I said. I looked down at my plate and played with the napkin in my lap, avoiding eye contact. "I was only eight, and all I heard were rumors and what Jim said."

Carl leaned back in his seat crossed his arms. "Why should I answer your questions now? You took off and never looked back. You left me to handle Dad alone."

I'd gotten too comfortable with him, thinking our relationship may have healed a bit during this single day together. His comment was the match that lit my anger. I threw my napkin on the table. "You were always his favorite, Carl!" I glanced around and realized I had the attention of half the patrons in the place. I lowered my voice and leaned closer to the table. "Would you have stayed if he had treated you the way he treated me?"

"I know it was tough but you did the same thing Mom did. She left and that was it. No looking back. She was gone, and then you were gone."

I pushed my plate to the side of the table. "Maybe Mom's leaving taught me that I could start over, too. Maybe she got tired of juggling an alcoholic husband and two kids. She got a fresh start, no matter how much it hurt us. I realized I could do the same thing. So I did. And I didn't owe Jim an explanation then, and I don't owe you one now."

I stood up to leave. It was foolish to think that the death of our father could tighten our bond. Carl looked up at me and gestured for me to sit back down. My first impulse was to leave, to berate myself for ever coming back here, let alone for agreeing to meet Carl at the house. But I returned to my seat and reached for my water glass. I could still feel dust in the back of my throat.

This town.

He said, "I don't know much more than you do. They were fighting a lot. Mom would come home after her shift here and give him a hard time about sitting on the couch and drinking beer all night. She wouldn't hand over her tips because he'd just spend it at the liquor store."

I remembered the arguing but not many of the details. I'd hide in my room. The walls were thin but at least the voices were muffled. Lots of yelling and breaking of dishes. I wondered if there were some things I didn't see, being young and avoiding their rows.

"There were rumors going around that she left to be with some other guy. Dad even said that but I never believed him," Carl said, finishing the last of his steak. "Kids at school would say stuff sometimes, but you know, I tuned it out. Got used to acting like I didn't hear what they were saying."

"You were pretty lousy to me when I was a kid," I replied, my eyes now meeting his. "It was so hard without Mom there, and you and Dad were like buddies. I was alone."

Carl leaned in. "I know, Nat. I was fourteen. I took it out on you."

I reached toward him and tapped on the table.

"I have an idea and it's cheaper than therapy. You want in?"

Carl raised an eyebrow. "I'm listening."

The next day, I drove up to the house and found Carl had beaten me there. He stood leaning against his old diesel, smoking a cigarette, legs crossed, his boots making an X in the dirt.

"You got the tools?" I called from the window of my Tahoe. "I brought sledgehammers, gloves and some plastic bags."

Carl reached inside his truck and pulled out a metal toolbox. I recognized it immediately, and he took note. "He gave it to me a long time ago."

I nodded towards the house. "Not like he was fixing things around here anyway."

For the first time, I looked forward to going inside the house. It was time to put some ghosts to bed. For good. I refused to be haunted any longer.

"You sure about this?" Carl asked. "You won't change your mind later? Maybe the house is worth something still."

I shook my head, confident in my decision. "Even if it were, it would have to be brought to the studs." I carried my tools to the front door. "I'm sure. Let's do this."

Once inside, we made quick work of opening all the windows to circulate the stale air. Carl went back to his truck and returned with goggles and a box of trash bags. I handed him a set of work gloves, and we decided to split spaces. He would handle the kitchen because the cabinets were going to be tough. I chose the dining room. It seemed like the right place for me to start.

Carl swung his sledgehammer with force, making quick work of the kitchen counter. I moved an entire row of boxes to the side, clearing the way for my diamond-patterned wallpaper to be released from its misery. Sweat dripped off my brow and down my back, and I took a break to stick my head out an open window. The fresh air helped my resolve.

"Okay," I called. "Say goodbye to the dining room!"

I took the sledge over my head and swung it toward the wall. It was heavier than I expected and I didn't do more than poke a neat little hole between two of the diamond shapes. Carl observed my novice technique and came over.

"Put it in your left hand first," he instructed, "and then swing it more like a baseball bat. Maybe that would be easier for you."

I gestured toward the wall for him to take a swing but he declined.

"Nope. This one is all you."

I nodded and took his advice, finding it easier to swing at an angle. I made contact with the wall and created a bigger hole. I thought of all the years of loneliness in the house, of being isolated and misunderstood. I swung again. A section of the wall pushed back and I reached over and pulled the wallpaper and drywall towards me. I kept swinging, and the circle widened, a large section collapsing inward. I reached over to pull the piece out and stopped cold.

"What is that?" I asked Carl as I leaned in. White plastic peeked out from the hole I had created, but it was clear there was more hidden behind the wall.

"Workers leave trash all the time inside walls," Carl explained. "Old cans, papers, whatever." He gestured for me to stand back. "Let me take a swing on this side."

He struck the surface with force and punched a new hole, pulling down and toward the floor with the hammer. An even bigger section of the came apart. Carl and I both dropped our tools and worked on pulling the ruined pieces back. Sections of the diamond-patterned paper scattered on the floor like leaves. With one more pull, I opened a large gap and found a piece of tan fabric. I picked it up and immediately recognized it.

I held it in my hands, stretched out for Carl's examination.

An apron.

From the Cypress Café.

I held it, the wrinkled fabric of the front pockets showing a single piece of paper inside. I kept the apron in one hand and pulled out the paper with the other. I could never forget that handwriting.

I'm so sorry, Marie. I didn't mean it.

I looked at Carl as I considered what might be behind the wall. Heat enveloped me my heart beat loud in my ears, my face going flush. My legs gave way and I reached for Carl. He grabbed my arm and we hit the floor together. We hugged each other tight, the first time we'd done that since we'd been kids.

"Ms. Tillman?" Sheriff Martinez stood over me as I sat on the front porch, my head between my knees. Lightheadedness would come and go. I moved my head slowly upward, shading my eyes against the sun with my hand.

"Is it true?" I asked.

He scratched the top of his ear. An enormous Stetson covered his head. "We may need a DNA test to be sure but we don't know who else it could be in there." He knelt down next to me and placed his hand on my shoulder gently. "I'm really sorry you had to come back to find…this."

I waved my hand upward and returned my head to my knees to catch my breath. "Is Carl still inside?"

"Yes," he replied. "Should I send him out?"

I nodded and Sheriff Martinez went inside. Carl came and sat down and put his arm around me. I tucked the apron on the floor between my legs, unwilling to relinquish it just yet, even though the crime scene tech had asked for it a half hour ago. I had something of my mother's and I refused to let it go.

"I don't understand." I wiped my hair off my forehead, sticky from sweat, and used my shirt to dab the salt from my eye. "How could he?"

Carl put his hand to his lips. "I don't know, Nat. Things got pretty heated sometimes but I can't believe he'd…" He left the sentence unfinished and I couldn't do it for him.

"All those years we'd thought she left us, and she's been right here." The idea that my mother's body had remained hidden behind the wallpaper I had chosen as a child turned my stomach. I took long breaths to slow the spinning of my world.

"She didn't leave us, Nat," Carl said, offering comfort.

I hugged him tighter. "Now I wish she had."

Carl and I moved away from the house and stood by his truck as Sheriff Martinez and the other officers continued their work inside. Numbness had taken over.

I wondered what my dad's intention had been when he'd left me the house instead of Carl. He'd been trying to tell me something.

* * *

I knew I would never again step inside that place.

Sheriff Martinez came down the stairs towards us. "We'd like to take your statement soon if you're feeling up to it."

I nodded. "I think I can do that." I glanced at Carl. He remained leaning on his truck, smoking a cigarette, watching the activity coming in and out of the house.

"Let me know if there's anything I can do for either of you."

"Maybe there is," I said. I looked to Carl to get his attention. "Do you think the fire department would want the house?"

"For what?" the sheriff asked as he looked at Carl with an *Is she doing okay?* look in his eyes.

"They can burn it to the ground if they want," I told him. "For practice. I hear they do that sometimes. We were going to demo it anyway."

"When we're done here, if you still want to donate it, I'll let them know."

"I'm sure," I said. "If you don't do it, we will."

Carl nodded in agreement. "She's right. The house can't stay standing."

The sheriff went back to his men, leaving Carl and I to stand on the sidelines. I had no idea what to do now. Everything I thought I knew was wrong.

I rested my head on my big brother's shoulder and cried.

Pay very close attention to the start of Josh's story where he tells you what to expect. And then sit back and enjoy the ride. It's the getting there that's all the fun...

WHEN YOU SUE, YOU BEGIN WITH *DO, RAY, ME*

Josh Pachter

Let's start at the very beginning,
A very good place to start:
When you read, you begin with A, B, C;
When you sue, you begin with Do, Ray, Me...

Do is Dorothea Kensington-Warburton, the younger daughter of Jasper and Amanda Kensington, originally of Chippewa Falls, Wisconsin. Jasper was one of the first people in America to amass a fortune selling bottled designer spring water to the suckers born every minute. In 1954, when Little DoDo was three and her older sister Juliana was five, he moved the family south to Texas. They bought a gorgeous eight-bedroom Frank Lloyd Wright home in Piney Point Village, an upscale residential community in West Houston. Amanda went to her reward in 1984, and Jasper joined her in death two years later. For reasons unexplained and unfair yet legally unchallengeable, a quarter of the estate went to Dorothea and three-quarters plus the house to Juliana. Do by then was married to Frank Warburton of the

189

Bunker Hill Warburtons. Frank had family money of his own, and they built a lovely home in a gated community in Frostwood. It didn't hold a candle to Juliana's mansion, but most Americans would have considered it palatial. Frostwood is eighteen miles from Piney Point as the crow flies. A little over half an hour by car, whether you take the Sam Houston or loop north and east and south on the 610 to avoid the toll.

Ray is Raymond Warburton, Do and Frank's only offspring. He survived the elite Kinkaid School from pre-K all the way through the twelfth grade. His parents gave him a generous graduation present: a cherry red 1965 Ford Mustang convertible with a 164-horsepower 260-cubic-inch V8 engine, lovingly restored to pristine condition. Do and Frank then immediately announced their intention to get a divorce, on the grounds that they simply no longer much *liked* each other. This time, Do got to keep the house. Ray spent an undistinguished two years at Rice, majoring in philosophy and minoring in partying. As a rising junior, he transferred to the Wharton School of Finance and Commerce at the University of Pennsylvania. He barely managed to graduate, earning a BA in economics—exactly like, though three decades later than, President Donald J. Trump.

Me is me, Andrew George Kalamakis. I was born in Clear Lake, about halfway between the NASA Space Center and the Baybrook Mall. My parents ran the best damn Greek bakery you ever smelled. I lettered in track—stepping over hurdles, which turned out to be a valuable (if metaphoric) skill in my adult life—at Clear Lake High. (Go, Falcons!) Completed my formal education with a BA in Communication Studies at the University of Houston. Went on to earn a JD from the South Texas College of Law. Began my legal career as a summer intern at Leidig, Hitchcock, Stelle. Passed the bar and worked my way up to associate, and am now a named partner at Leidig, Hitchcock, Stelle and Kalamakis.

Introductions complete, I'm here today to tell you about the dumbest case I have handled in my legal career.

Cautionary note: if you're looking for a juicy murder, an artful art theft, a daring drug bust, a captivating kidnapping, you should probably flip ahead a couple of pages to the next story in this book. Yes, it's a crime I'm about to describe for you, but not the sort of thing you're probably expecting. This is a tale, I warn you from the jump, of a more subtle malfeasance, a crime more of the heart than of the statute books. The good news is that almost everyone involved—*almost* everyone—will live happily ever after when the final curtain falls. To use the vernacular of the crime fiction community, this is more a cozy than a *noir*. So keep your peepers peeled for doilies and cups of tea, rather than, say, mean streets, PIs and *femmes fatale*.

Enough already. Let's cut to the chase, shall we?

At the time these events occurred, Do Kensington-Warburton was sixty-seven years old. Ray was thirty-two and a supposedly confirmed bachelor. I was forty-one, happily married, with a son in community college at HCC's main campus and a daughter about to graduate from high school and head off to the University of Michigan. (Go, Blue!) My firm represented both Mrs. Kensington-Warburton *and* Juliana Kensington, who'd retaken her maiden name after her own divorce. As the junior partner, I handled pretty much all of Do's lesser legal affairs personally.

What set things in motion was Ray meeting Falila Ansari. Fa—I swear I'm not making this up, that's what everyone called her—was a very pretty and extremely brainy young computer programmer.

Her parents emigrated from the island emirate of Bahrain to Texas when she was an infant in diapers. Ray and Fa met on one of those online dating services, you know what I mean? They scoped out each other's profiles and liked what they saw, exchanged increasingly flirtatious messages for a week or so, then met face to face at Antidote in Woodland Heights. This obligatory coffee date wound up lasting three and a half hours, segued into margaritas and mariscos at Hugo's and finished after midnight with the two of them head over heels in love.

Fa was twenty-six, a few years younger than Ray, but they didn't give a damn about the age difference. Falila's parents—though Muslim—were pretty thoroughly westernized and had no objection to their daughter hooking up with a non-Arab. The fact that Ray came from family money didn't make them any more receptive to his wooing of their daughter, but it certainly didn't count against him.

Four months later, Ray and Fa announced their engagement. Fa's parents offered to pay for the wedding, of course. Fact was, though, they owned and operated a 7-Eleven franchise in Rolling Fork, which is not exactly on the wrong side of the tracks though not anywhere near the same socio-economic league as Frostwood. So when Do offered, in a way that came off as sweet and motherly and not at all dickish, to spring for the sort of affair her pride and joy Ray and his lovely intended deserved, the Ansaris gratefully agreed.

When things began to go off the rails was when Juliana Kensington stepped in and did what older sisters from privileged backgrounds often do: she rolled up her *crepe de chine* sleeves and took control of the preparations, turning what originally would have been a simple but charming ceremony into the sort of bridezilla affair WE TV would have died to turn into a six-week miniseries.

Even the invitations Juliana ordered were spectacular. They were thermographically printed on ecru shimmer paper bordered with gold glimmer, tucked inside a laser-cut paper doily—I told you there would be doilies—and secured with antique white satin ribbons, accompanied by ecru shimmer reception cards, response cards and envelopes. I've kept one as a souvenir and—trust me on this—they were *gorgeous*.

Juliana herself was childless, and she went at Ray and Fa's wedding with a vengeance. She booked the Couples' Choice Award-winning Agave Estates out in Katy for the ceremony and reception. She spared no expense, hiring A Fare Extraordinaire for the catering and Bella Dia Floral for the flowers. She managed to snag the almost impossible to get Tomás Ramos for the photography and videography. And she arranged for Drywater, the best damn cover band in the Lone Star State, to provide the music.

Where Fa finally put her foot down was with the guest list. With a regal flourish, Aunt Juliana presented the happy couple with a twelve-page, single-spaced Excel spreadsheet. There were forty numbered lines to a page, four hundred and eighty spaces in all, neatly typed in a curlicued script font. Names, mailing and email addresses, phone numbers. There was even a column for notes, which seemed mostly to consist of the identification of long-standing grudges that would prevent Mrs. A from sitting at the same table as Mr. B, and so on.

On page one were listed Ray and Fa and Do and Juliana, of course, plus thirty-six assorted Kensingtons and Warburtons. Fa had never met most of them, and some Ray himself had never heard of. A few more cousins and great-aunts straggled over onto page two. Then came a page and a half of Juliana's society friends, followed by an endless procession of A-listers Aunt Jules wanted to impress.

On page eight, Fa looked up with a stricken expression on her face.

"What about my family?" she said, and Ray overlapped her with, "What about our friends?"

Juliana smiled beatifically and held up her hands in a benediction. "*Nil desperandum*, children," she beamed. "I've left plenty of room for them."

"Plenty of room" turned out to mean the last thirty spaces on page twelve. When they saw that, Ray tossed the pile of papers onto his aunt's Henkel Harris ball and claw foot mahogany coffee table. "Thirty spaces, Aunt Juliana? You're inviting hundreds of people we don't even know and only allowing thirty spaces total for Fa's relatives and our friends?"

Juliana frowned, not comprehending the problem. "Well, Agave can only accommodate five hundred, Raymond, and, *honestly*, I've pared my list down to the *bone*. I simply can't offend any of my dear friends by leaving them out. That would be unthinkable."

Fa's beautiful chocolate-brown eyes flashed with fire. "It was very nice of you to offer to put on the wedding for us, Juliana, but this is not acceptable. I have no intention of telling *my* friends they can't come to my wedding because my husband's aunt needs to invite the entire social register." She turned to Ray and took his right hand in both of hers. "Let's just go back to Plan A, honey. We'll let my parents do the best they can, and invite the people *we* want to share our special day with."

Aunt Juliana coughed delicately into a D. Porthault lace handkerchief embroidered with her initials. "I'm afraid that's quite impossible, dear," she said. "I've already ordered the invitations and put down payments on the venue, the caterers, the florist, the photographer, the band. Just wait until you see the menu, darling, you'll—"

"You've already picked out the menu?" Fa bristled, outraged. "Without asking *us* what *we* want to serve our guests? Ray, this is ridiculous. I'm sorry to offend your aunt, but this is not how I'm going to get married. Come on, let's go."

She got to her feet, still holding onto Ray's hand, and looked down at him expectantly.

And Ray, after much hemming and hawing—which was ironic, because Gayle Hunnicutt, the second wife of actor David Hemmings, was on page six of Aunt Juliana's list, and Jayne Wilde, the first wife of theoretical physicist Stephen Hawking, was on page ten—let her down.

He looked up at Fa, the love of the last six months of his life. He looked over at Aunt Juliana, who had been overriding his mother and making his important decisions for him for most of his life. Then he caved like a glass-jawed boxer, caved a cave any spelunker would have been thrilled to explore.

"I-I-" he said, and Fa knew at once that the next word he said would be the word "can't."

When push came to shove, her fiancée had turned out to be a cad, a coward, a wimp, a mama's boy...or, in this case, an auntie's boy.

She ripped off her diamond engagement ring, with its center stone weighing in at almost one and a half carats, surrounded by six additional gems that collectively added another three-quarters to the total. (It was a gaudy concoction many a bride would have killed for. Frankly, though, she found it ostentatious and not at all to her taste. Of course she'd oohed and aahed appropriately when Ray had gotten down to one knee in her parents' living room and presented it to her. But it was—there's no other word for it—*fugly*.) Biting back an expletive, she flung it at Juliana, whom she realized at that moment was the person who had surely picked it out and paid for it.

Fa flounced out of the drawing room and out of Juliana's Prairie style castle. She fully expected Ray to chase after her, but he didn't. After five minutes of furiously tapping her foot on the circular driveway's perfect asphalt, she called an Uber and had the driver whisk her out of Piney Point Village and out of Ray Warburton's life.

As her nephew sat there in hopeless befuddlement, Juliana worked her way through denial to anger. Before half an hour passed, she sent him on his way and was on the phone to Charlie Leidig, the senior partner in Leidig, Hitchcock, Stelle and Kalamakis. Charlie in turn sent me to calm the old termagant down.

But Juliana Kensington was not to be calmed. How *dare* that little snip of a colored girl go against her wishes? After she'd swallowed her all-too-natural prejudices and welcomed her into the family? After all she'd *done* for her?

She was not about to let the ungrateful wretch get away with it. Juliana demanded I draw up a breach of promise lawsuit and file it instanter. It took me the better part of the rest of the morning to convince her that not only would this be a waste of time and resources, it would be in really bad taste.

Next she wanted to sue the company that had printed the wedding invitations for a full refund, and follow with the florist, caterer, photographer, band, and the Agave Estates for the return of the assorted down payments. I was eventually able to get her to see that it didn't make sense to go through the trouble and expense of filing a flurry of lawsuits until she'd first requested her money back and given the various vendors a fair opportunity to comply.

Meanwhile, two weeks after Fa broke off their engagement and stormed out of Chez Juliana, Ray drove to Rolling Fork and begged her to forgive him for being such a pathetic wuss. Fa—who had been miserable ever since the break-up—mussed his hair and hugged him. "There, there," she whispered.

A month after that, they got married, after all.

Falila was stunning in a gown with long lace sleeves and a detachable train. Her mother had hand-sewn it from a Butterick pattern she'd bought for sixteen dollars on Etsy, using white charmeuse silk she'd allowed Do to pay for. Ray wore an off-the-rack black Kenneth Cole suit he'd found marked down to a hundred and ninety-nine dollars at the Men's Wearhouse. Fa's uncle Mahmoud, who owned a jewelry stall in the Bab el-Bahrain souk in the center of Manama and wasn't well enough to travel from the Middle East to Texas for the occasion, DHLed them a pair of matching gold wedding rings. Their names and the date were hand-etched in Arabic and English characters around the inside of each band.

They held the ceremony under a canopy dripping with wisteria in Do's lovely Frostwood back yard. The reception was at the VFW, two doors down from the Ansaris' 7-Eleven. Except for Uncle Mahmoud, most of Fa's family was there—including a contingent of aunts and uncles and cousins who'd flown in from Bahrain and found the Texas heat comfortingly familiar. Several dozen of the happy couple's friends and coworkers were there. Do was, too, of course. And Frank, Ray's father, who came from Palm Springs with his current wife, his third or fourth, a trophy blonde not much older than Falila.

Juliana, perhaps unsurprisingly, was not invited.

Actually, nobody had been invited in the sense of getting a fancy invitation in the mail, RSVPing and all that. Mostly Ray and Fa just told the people they wanted to be there, either face to face or by email or text, and the people they'd asked showed up. Unheard-of, by Juliana's standards—a wedding without invitations—but Ray and Fa were young and in love. They believed in simplicity, not tradition, so they did it their way.

And their way was perfectly fine, thank you very much. Everyone agreed it was a storybook wedding, a beautiful start to Ray and Fa's life together.

As things turned out, everyone but the printer had been perfectly willing to return Juliana's deposits, less their standard contractually stipulated cancellation fees. She was one of the local elite, after all, and someday there might be another opportunity to work for her. Why burn bridges there was no need to burn? By the time I had that all sorted out, Juliana's ruffled feathers had settled. The fees were reasonable and unavoidable she agreed, and she withdrew her demand for full repayment.

But the printer refused to refund any part of the cost of the invitations, seeing as how they had actually gone ahead and printed them.

As I said before, I have saved one, and it is truly a masterpiece of the art. "Juliana Kensington requests the honor of your presence," it says, in a flowing font that stands out beautifully against the ecru background, "at the nuptials of her nephew, Raymond Bennett Warburton, and Fallila Shazia Ansari, daughter of Ishtiaq and Basma Ansari." And so on. Those invitations cost twenty-three dollars apiece, I came to find out, what with all the shimmer and glimmer and laser cutting and doilies. Ten-thousand-three-hundred and fifty dollars plus Texas sales tax for the four-hundred and fifty of them Aunt Jules had ordered—and Falila's name had been misspelled.

Juliana's next brilliant idea was to sue Fa and her parents for the cost of the invitations as well as the various cancellation fees. She backed off about the fees when I broke it to her the firm couldn't represent her in such a matter, since doing so would constitute a conflict of interest. But she got on the phone to Charlie Leidig, demanding we at the very least sue the printer.

"You ordered the damn invitations, Jules," Charlie barked, "and they fulfilled the order."

"But they spelled the wretched girl's *name* wrong," Juliana wailed. "I can't be expected to pay for their mistake."

Charlie told her to put me on the line and told me to handle it. I filed the paperwork for a suit and we actually went to court where the printer's attorney smugly produced the original order sheet for the invitations—which contained the incorrect spelling of Falila's name in Juliana's own handwriting. So Auntie Jules got nothing...and had to pay the printer's legal expenses and the court costs to boot.

I came out of the whole thing pretty well, myself. Billed the firm for thirty-four hours and socked away a tidy little sum.

All of this happened four years ago. Ray and Fa remain together, happy as a pair of songbirds. Little Amia is almost three now. Samir is nine months old and has his first tooth coming in.

I assume that those of you who are reading this account have been more or less patiently waiting to find out who gets murdered, and who figures it out, and whodunit. This is, after all, a collection of crime and mystery fiction. You have every right to expect gunshots in the night, ATF agents breaking up a ring of fentanyl smugglers, the kidnapping of Mayor Sylvester Turner's daughter Ashley Paige and her daring rescue from the clutches of her captors, a gang of masterminds heisting Renoir's "Girl Reading" from the Museum of Fine Arts, perhaps a modern-day reincarnation of Bonnie and Clyde knocking over the JPMorgan Chase Bank. (Located, I am Texas-proud to say, in the eponymous JPMorgan Chase Tower, the eighteenth tallest building in the United States and the number-one tallest pentagonal building in the world).

But I'm afraid I am going to have to disappoint you. There are no murders in this story. No stolen French impressionists. No drug busts or kidnappings or bank heists. The only crime at issue here was Ray Warburton's aunt's attempt to Juliana ten-thousand bucks out of a printer who'd only done exactly what she'd instructed him to do—which resulted in a court case lasting all of twenty minutes before the judge dismissed it.

Not much of an ending, I recognize. I hope all y'all won't feel too terribly cheated. But it's all I got, seeing as how it *is* how the story ended.

I warned you it was a dumb case, remember? And I'm a duly constituted officer of the court, so would I lie?

It means "bad luck." There's your spoiler, but it sounds better in Spanish. Not that it works out any better for the (mostly) wonderful people in the story...

MALA SUERTE
Debra Lattanzi Shutika

Maria Elena watched David move through the maternity ward taking long strides, his white sneakers squeaking on the ceramic tile floors.

She didn't quite trust him, although she couldn't articulate why. He was a competent nurse. His uniform was starched and brilliant white. And the mothers seemed to like him. He wasn't handsome but had an impish smile and an easy way with babies which was unusual for men. American men. He held the nursery newborns like a mother. But misfortune seemed to follow those in his care.

David had been raised in Mexico by his adoptive mother. The day that Maria Elena interviewed him, he said he had worked with midwives in Mexico. That was why he wanted to work in a St. Philomena's Hospital for Women and Children. He said becoming a midwife was his calling.

David's first days in the hospital were impressive although the other nurses were slow to warm up.

"A male nurse?" her daughter Erika asked when Maria Elena told her she had hired him. "Did he flunk out of med school?'

"Erika, it's 1986. Surely there must have been men in your nursing class."

"No one who would want to work at St. Philomena's."

* * *

"This is a women's hospital," Nadia complained one afternoon in Maria Elena'a office. Nadia was the head nurse on the maternity ward. "It's unseemly to have a man washing women after childbirth. I can't believe the husbands don't raise a stink."

As St. Philomena's chief of nursing, Maria Elena listened to all the staff complaints but she wasn't worried about David's contact with the new mothers' nether regions. Like all hospitals, St. Philomena's had doctors who examined women and delivered babies; they were men—what of it? But she understood Nadia's complaint, echoed by nearly every other nurse who walked the corridors of St. Philomena's, a hospital staffed by women to care for women and their children. Women ran the hospital, attended the laboring women for hours, and the male doctors showed up for the deliveries and cutting of the umbilical cords. The nurses ran this enterprise and had for decades. It was the last hospital of its kind in in Laredo, probably in all of Texas. Until David arrived.

Maria Elena watched David and his ease with the patients. One afternoon he brought a new mother a bouquet of flowers from her family, singing "*bebé te ama, mami.*" The new mothers adored his attention and the expert way David managed the infants.

Maria Elena was pleased, even if some of the nurses were not.

On Saturday afternoon Maria Elena scrubbed her uniforms by hand in a galvanized tub on the patio in her walled garden. She shook out the laundry and hung it on a line on her roof she heard her daughter, Erika, calling to her as she unlocked the patio gate. "*Mami, estas?*"

"Up here, *hija*. Just hanging the laundry."

Erika emerged through a curtain of bougainvillea that Maria had allowed to overrun the patio. She had plaited her hair in a thick black rope, and she wore pink scrubs. Erika had been named the head nurse in the newborn nursery at St. Philomena's. Maria Elena disapproved of the scrubs, preferring starched whites, but she said nothing. Times were changing.

"How was your shift?"

"That's why I'm here. A baby died this afternoon."

"Why didn't you call me?" Maria Elena glared at her daughter. "I'm to be notified anytime a patient expires."

"It just happened, *Mami*. David found the baby dead in his bassinet and called the code. Thank God the pediatrician was still in the house. Dr. Pedraza led the resuscitation, but it was too late."

Newborns, even those who appeared perfectly normal at birth, sometimes died. Maria Elena knew this. Maria Elena had been a twenty-two-year-old graduate nurse the first time she turned over a beautiful baby girl, just eight hours old, and saw her blue lips. She'd hollered, "I need a doctor," and was scolded by an older nurse who thought she was being dramatic. "This baby isn't breathing," Maria Elena had screamed and everyone in the nursery sprang into action, but the baby could not be saved.

Less than an hour later Maria Elena entered the hospital in a starched white dress, stockings and freshly polished shoes, her thick black hair knotted under her nurse's cap. She headed straight for the newborn nursery. She found the grieving mother, a young Mexican woman who had no English, trembling in a corner of the nursery cradling her lost baby.

"Nadia, has anyone called that mother's family?" There was a dangerous edge in Maria Elena's voice.

"Her parents are in Mexico. They're taking the bus to the border today."

"Her husband?" Maria Elena snapped.

"He left for a job in San Antonio two weeks ago. We haven't been able to reach him."

"Well, send a nurse aide to sit with her, for heaven's sake. Where is David?"

"He's in the station doing paperwork." Nadia's sidelong glance said, *I warned you about him.*

David sat in a private office off the main nurse's station. It was a designated smoking area, and David smashed the butt of his cigarette into an overflowing ashtray as Maria Elena entered. She grabbed the filthy bowl and emptied it into the trash then took a paper towel and wiped down the counter. "This place is disgusting," she said.

"The custodians skip this room on the weekends," David said. Maria Elena saw his eyes were red and swollen.

"I'll take care of it," Maria Elena said. "Tell me what happened."

"Sofia Rodriguez's baby was born at 7:48 a.m., preterm labor, but it was a normal spontaneous vaginal delivery. Her water broke about 6:00 a.m. The baby was thirty-three weeks' gestation. Mom is twenty-two years old, this is her first baby. No prenatal care. The father's away on a job."

"Did the baby have respiratory distress?" Maria Elena knew this was a common problem with premature birth.

"None," David said. "But he was having trouble maintaining his body temperature. We wrapped him in warm blankets and kept an eye on him."

"Leave the incident report on my desk. I'll make sure Dr. Pedraza arranges for a post-mortem."

David nodded and went back to work on his report. She heard him tapping his pen nervously against the formica counter as she walked back to the nurse's station. The young receptionist stood when Maria Elena entered. Would you please page Dr. Pedraza?" she asked. The girl nodded and picked up the phone to call his answering service.

In her office, Maria Elena pulled out the file of incident reports for the last six months. Most of the reports were medication errors, given either too early or too late. In one case, a nurse had infused intravenous potassium chloride in a 50cc IV bag instead of 100cc—a potentially fatal mistake that thankfully had no consequences.

There had been three infant deaths in the six months before the baby expired this morning.

All had been in David's care.

Maria Elena organized the reports and made a request for the deceased patients' charts. Then she carefully read each of David's reports, taking notes. Nearly an hour had passed when Dr. Pedraza knocked on her door.

"Ernesto, please sit down. What happened this morning?"

"It was a precipitous delivery. The baby was crowning when she walked into the hospital. He seemed fine when I examined him after delivery. Except for his temperature regulation he appeared to be a normal baby."

"Did you notice anything unusual during the resuscitation?"

"We worked on him for nearly an hour, then it was clear he was gone. There was some blood on the bassinet blankets, but I assume he expelled blood after delivery,"

"That's far from normal."

"But not unheard of," Dr. Pedraza added quickly. "Maria Elena, I know what the nurses are saying, but we need to be careful not to rush to judgement."

"What are the nurses saying?"

He sighed. "I've spoken out of turn. I shouldn't have mentioned it."

"Ernesto, if the nurses are being hasty, I need to know."

Pedraza shifted his weight and look away. "Erika and Nadia were talking about the male nurse as the nursery's grim reaper."

Maria Elena's face reddened. "That's completely unprofessional."

"People often say things they later regret in times of crisis. This is a sad day for all of us, especially the young mother. We should revisit this after the post-mortem," Dr. Pedraza said.

On Monday, Maria Elena's desk was piled high with a stack of patient charts newly retrieved from Medical Records. She sifted through each file, the final stories of people who had come to her hospital for care. After hours of scrutiny, she'd found nothing that suggested the babies should not have survived their hospital stays. This was a quandary.

Maria Elena did rounds through the hospital three times a day: first thing in the morning, late afternoon, and in the early evening before she left for home. She prided herself in the way she managed her staff and served as the steward of the historic building. The original structure of St. Philomena's—a Spanish colonial mission built in 1872—now served as the façade of the modern hospital that was added in 1960. Her daughter, Erika, had been the first baby born in the new hospital.

At the window of the newborn nursery, Maria Elena admired David's ease with feeding, burping and changing the diapers of the infants. In a far corner she saw Erika in her pink scrubs helping a new mother as she struggled to nurse her squirmy newborn. Erika appeared calm and confident and after a few failed attempts, the baby latched on and suckled her mother's breast. The young mother melted into the rocker as the stress of the moment evaporated.

Maria Elena hoped that Erika would one day take her place managing St. Philomena's. She also knew that the building would one day become obsolete, not during her career but perhaps in Erika's. She hoped that the hospital trustees would maintain this building. So many Laredeños had started their lives here.

When she entered the maternity ward, Nadia was updating the nursing assignments for the day. "Good morning, Nadia. How is Sofia Rodriguez this morning?"

"Physically, she's fine. Her mother arrived last night. We moved her to a private room on the G-Y-N unit." There would be no new mothers there, nor would she be subjected to the sound of crying babies.

"Has the post-mortem report come back?"

"Just the macro—no abnormalities were detected," Nadia said. She stood erect and straight-faced. "And there's—" She stopped herself.

Maria Elena raised her eyebrows. "Yes?"

"We'll know more when the lab results are here."

"I'm aware. What were you going to say?"

Nadia struggled over whether to speak. "It's just, this was the fourth baby to die in his care this year."

"I'm aware of that, too." Maria Elena said.

"I'm only worried about the liability for the hospital, our reputation."

"That is my concern to worry about, not yours."

Maria Elena walked away, knowing that Nadia was more concerned about David's male presence than she was the gossip or any legal culpability.

But Nadia was correct, a small hospital like St. Philomena's thrived by maintaining a reputation as a trusted place where women from all walks of life could come to have their babies. Sofia Rodriguez was undocumented but wealthy women from Laredo came to this hospital to have their children as well. Rich or poor, all patients received the same expert care.

Maria Elena found Sofia Rodriguez tucked away in a far corner of the gynecology ward. She grabbed her chart from the nurse's station, then knocked on her door. Inside a small voice said, "*Passe.*"

Sofia was sitting in a chair overlooking the courtyard of the main building. "*Buenos dias, Señora Rodriguez.* My name is Maria Elena Perez. As the head of nursing at St. Philomena's. "I wish to tell you I am very sorry about the loss of your son."

Sofia's hazel eyes filled and tears washed over her round face. According to the chart, Sofia was twenty-two years old, but she appeared more a frightened child.

"*No entiendo,*" Sofia said. "Why would God let this happen?" She wiped her nose and her eyes widened, panicked. "The baby needs to be baptized."

Maria Elena flipped through the chart. "*Ya se ha hecho.*" She had seen to it already and handed Sofia a baptismal certificate signed by Erika.

"*Gracias.*" Sofia drew a tissue from the box on her bedside and dabbed her eyes.

"Señora Rodriguez, I'm here to offer my condolences, but also to see if there is anything I can do for you? Has your family been able to contact your husband?"

"We spoke last night. He has a good job in San Antonio. He told me to go back to Mexico with my mother."

"When you're discharged, the nurses will set up your medical appointments. Here is my card. Please call me if you have questions or if you need anything."

Sofia reached out and took the offering, then nodded. She turned to look out the window as Maria Elena left the room.

Back in her office, Maria Elena reviewed her notes about St. Philomena's deceased patients, two women and four infants, all in the last six months. The babies' deaths had all been ruled sudden infant death syndrome cases which meant the causes of death were unknown. The two woman's cases were more complicated. One had died of post-partum hemorrhage. She'd had a normal spontaneous vaginal delivery at forty-one weeks. Her post-mortem had revealed retained placenta—a common cause hemorrhage. The other had died of a pulmonary embolism, another regular cause of maternal mortality. She concluded that these were very sad yet eminently explainable deaths. The infant tragedies were open to debate.

Maria Elena started her final rounds of the day and she always preferred to visit the newborn nursery last. Normally it was the happiest place in the hospital. First she let herself into Erika's office at the back of the nursery and sat in front of the large one-way mirror that provided Maria Elena a bird's eye view.

One by one, the nurses wheeled the infants back to the nursery for shift change. The nurse's aides wheeled in several bassinets and began changing diapers and placing new bottles and nipples in each cradle. David entered a few minutes later holding a baby. Maria Elena watched him expertly change the baby's diaper and swaddle it in a fresh blanket like a little burrito, then lay the child on her belly as per hospital protocol.

Next Erika entered carrying a clipboard. She walked through the nursery, confirming that every baby had a fresh diaper and all the bassinets were well stocked with blankets, diapers, and formula for the incoming shift. When she came to David's charges, she noticed his had not yet been resupplied and she called him over. Although Maria Elena couldn't hear what they said, it was clear there was a disagreement. David stormed away to the supply room.

Maria Elena stood to leave the office but saw something that gave her pause. Erika started to refill one of the bassinets with diapers and formula and then she placed a small blanket beneath the baby's face. Not a cloth diaper—all the nurses lined the cribs with extra padding for potential spit-ups—but a soft blanket that could easily block a baby's breathing.

The shift change started and a team of fresh nurses entered the nursery for report. Erika called them to the assignment board to divvy patients as David returned laden with diapers, blankets and formula and set to work stocking his bassinets.

Maria Elena left the office and washed her hands, then walked to the bassinet where she'd watched Erika and turned the infant over. The baby's face was pink and warm, but Maria Elena removed the blanket and tossed it in the dirty linen hamper. This was a rookie mistake. Maria Elena was disappointed. She would speak to Erika about this tomorrow.

The next morning, Maria Elena heard someone calling her name as she passed through the hospital lobby. It was Nadia. "Can I speak with you?"

"Of course."

Maria Elena motioned for Nadia to follow her into the administrative offices. They sat facing each other across Maria Elena's desk, stacked with piles of paper and files.

"The final post-mortem report came back on Baby Boy Rodriguez," Nadia started. "It was ruled a SIDS death, but the pathologist noted dried blood in the baby's airway. It was his own blood."

"From the delivery?" Maria Elena asked.

"Possibly. The pathologist's report mentioned an unconfirmed trauma that may have occurred during delivery." Nadia sat perched on the edge of her chair.

Maria Elena felt the small muscles in her neck tighten. "Something else?"

"There is a rumor that David is *mala suerte*. It's mainly the older nurses and aides, but there is talk—"

"Bad luck! I certainly hope you're doing your best to stifle such talk?" Maria Elena said, raising her voice, eyes blazing. "I don't abide with *chismes*."

"I'm not a gossip, but I hear it." Nadia's posture turned erect. "I thought you'd want to know."

Maria Elena steadied herself. "I'm sorry, Nadia. I'm very frustrated. David is a good nurse."

"Then how do you explain these deaths? You have to see he doesn't belong here. This is a women's hospital."

"Nadia, you're holding on to an antiquated idea."

"I know it's a new time and yes, I'm old fashioned. But I also know that we haven't lost four babies in one year in the entire twenty years I've worked here. Something isn't right."

Maria Elena checked her watch. "It's time for shift change. You better get up to your ward."

Later that afternoon, Maria Elena typed up a report about the SIDS cases at the request of Dr. Pedraza. "Four SIDS deaths in such a short period of time at one hospital is troubling," he had said. "I'm afraid that the Texas Board of Medicine will initiate an inquiry. It's best that St. Philomena's be prepared."

Above the clacking keys, Maria Elena heard the intercom buzz "Code Blue, Newborn Nursery." She jumped from her desk, frantic, and ran through the corridors. When she arrived, the blinds to the nursery were pulled. Inside, she encountered buzzing activity as Dr. Pedraza and the entire nursery staff worked to resuscitate yet another infant. Maria Elena held her breath as she watched the small heart monitor. She breathed a deep sigh when she saw the electronic trace of his heartbeat blip across the screen along with a steady *beep-beep-beep*.

"*Gracias a Dios*," the nurses all murmured.

Erika walked over to Maria Elena and pulled her aside. "He was one of David's," she whispered.

"I'll wait in your office," Maria Elena said. As she walked toward the door, she heard Erika speaking to David in a calm, a soothing voice. "If you're not up to this, I can do the paperwork for you."

David sniffed and said, "No. No, I'll do it." His voice was coarse with emotion.

Maria Elena paced in Erika's office for what seemed like many hours. She leafed through a copy of the *Journal of Perinatal and Neonatal Nursing* she found sitting on the desk then noticed Erika had brought her small cedar treasure chest to the office. Maria Elena smiled—she had a similar box, a gift of the Lane Cedar Chest company to all the girls who graduated from Laredo's high schools. She ran her hand over the buffed surface then started to open it so she could inhale the sweet scent of the fragrant wood.

"Nurse Perez?" Maria Elena looked up and saw David's crumpled visage.

"Have a seat, David." She motioned to the empty chair.

"I—don't know what happened," David said. "That baby was fine." He reached across the desk and grabbed a tissue and blew his nose.

"David, I've always been pleased with your work, as have

our patients." David nodded as he dabbed his eyes. Someone knocked at the door.

"Yes?"

Erika walked in. "David, we're transferring the baby to the medical center. Dr. Pedraza heard a heart murmur. He suspects a defect. That's probably why the baby's heart stopped today." She walked in and stood beside him, gently placing her hand on his shoulder. David nodded without consolation.

"I have to finish my nurse's notes before the transfer," David said. He stood to leave. Erika walked out with him.

Maria Elena sat motionless for a moment, then absently ran her hand over the cedar box and opened it. She stopped short when she saw what was inside: four tiny patient identification bracelets.

Every infant born in St. Philomena's was banded with two ID bracelets at birth. Each displayed the same patient number as the infant's mother, one for the right wrist and another for the left ankle. If a child were to die, the hospital protocol was to give both of them to the mother. Her heart racing, Maria Elena pulled one bracelet out of the box and read the name: *Rodriguez, Baby Boy*. She shuffled through the others, each bearing the name of another of the three infants who had died.

She dropped the last bracelet and snapped the lid shut. Maria Elena stood up and took a deep breath, smoothing her crisp, white uniform in small, rapid movements. Her heart was racing.

"Oh *Mami*, what a day."

Maria Elena turned to see her daughter at the door. "Indeed."

"You look pale. Are you feeling alright?"

She nodded at the one-way window to the nursery. "That was upsetting."

"But the baby survived, thank heavens," Erika said.

"Y-yes. I'm so relieved."

Erika's smile was warm, but it made Maria Elena's hair stand on end.

"*Hija*—" Maria Elena said. "I found—"

Erika tilted her head. She was such a good listener. Such a good nurse.

"Yes, *Mami*?"

"Nadia tells me the nurses think St. Philomena's is plagued with *mala suerte*."

Erika nodded. "I've heard the rumors."

"And?"

Erika stared at her mother, then said, "*Caras vemos, corazones no sabemos.*" *Appearances can be deceiving.*

Maria Elena looked out on the nursery. "It's my responsibility to ensure our patients are safe."

"That's a responsibility we all share, *Mami*."

Maria Elena looked at her daughter, willing her to meet her eye. "Erika, I'm not sure those infants died of natural causes."

"But they did die of natural consequences," Erika said.

"I-I don't understand."

"David is careless. He's witty and charms the new mothers, but he doesn't watch over the infants as he should. Newborns can't move their heads if something blocks their breathing."

"You left a blanket in a bassinet yesterday. I moved it."

"Exactly. A good nurse knows so much of what we do is surveillance—watching over our patients, especially those most vulnerable. Any good nurse, in fact, every other nurse in this hospital, would have found those infants before they were gone." She met her mother's eyes with a cold determination. "Good nurses know there is no real luck. Only good care."

"Erika-Y-you did that? With all of them?"

"Mother, you don't expect me to tell you something like that."

"If you thought he was careless, why didn't you come to me?" Maria Elena asked. Tears were filling her eyes. "Why did you work so hard to protect him?"

"You know I have to report this," Maria Elena said.

Erika shook her head. "There's nothing to report. But David needs to go."

"N-no. That's not your decision."

"David needs to go."

Through the window they could see even now a new baby being admitted into the nursery. "I need to get back to work."

Maria Elena's knees weakened and she eased herself into the chair and buried her face in her hands. She had dedicated her life to taking care of others at St. Philomena's. Erika was following in her footsteps. She was going to take over when Maria Elena's career was over.

Caras vemos, corazones no sabemos. We see the face, but we know not the heart.

How could she have missed this?

Maria Elena looked out to the nursery and watched closely Erika weighing, measuring and diapering the newborn infant. She saw the darkness that had enveloped her hospital, and she realized that only she could stop it. Her hands shaking, she picked up the phone and dialed.

"Hello, this is Maria Elena Perez. I'd like to start termination paperwork for David Wallace."

Lower class, upper class, bullets—what could go wrong? Don't watch the news, it'll be on again tomorrow. Ken's story is much more entertaining...

THE DEATH OF AN ASS
Kenneth Wishnia

Champion Jack Thompson stomped on the brakes seconds before his paint-spattered pickup truck hit the first red light off the interstate and rattled to a halt.

Whoa, didn't see that coming, he thought as an old white lady in a boxy Chrysler puttered by blasting Christian country music for the hard of hearing. She glared at him with her witchy green eyes, seeing right through his deep blue ball cap and flannel shirt to the dark brown skin beneath.

He reminded himself to slow down, running his fingers over the stiff leather cover of a worn family Bible on the passenger seat, dog-eared to a passage in Jeremiah delivering a stern warning that *anyone who stiffs his workers will suffer the death of an ass.*

He arm-wrestled the stick shift into first gear, and the truck lurched onto Route 67 as soon as the light changed. He wanted to floor it—wanted to rev it up and crash through the front windows of the Brinkman Building doing 120 mph—but he had to keep it under control or risk spending the next thirty days in the county jail.

Palming the wheel with his left hand, he placed his free hand on the Bible and said a quick prayer for the success of his mission. He didn't want to tangle with the suits in Accounts Payable, the bowtie wearing bozos who were always shoving forms at him through a slot in a barred window. All he wanted was his damn money.

A procession of olive drab pickup trucks hauling day laborers to the tomato fields pulled into traffic from the pothole-scarred side roads, each vehicle depositing a fresh layer of mud and grit on his windshield. When his wiper blades cleared it away, Thompson found himself staring at the hind end of a monster GMC six-wheeler adorned with a full-size Confederate flag flapping in the breeze, an array of red and white MAGA stickers, and a fully functional gun rack.

Maybe he should have called ahead.

His big hands grew cold and tingly as the muddy side roads gave way to tree-lined suburban streets, making it hard to grip the steering wheel, and his stomach lurched sideways when he hit a pothole crossing the town line into the county seat.

Traffic slowed near the center of town, stopping for a long light at the intersection of Jackson and Lee. Out the passenger window, he caught a glimpse of the statue of the first Grand Wizard of the KKK on a rearing stallion dominating a small public park formally christened in the colonel's name.

Out the driver side window, an electric blue Nissan Juke pulled to a halt, a crew of three young dudes talking and gesturing excitedly, filling the air with the defiant rap lyrics emanating from their speakers.

Ooh, man. Wouldn't it be sweet to hit the Megaball jackpot and tool around in one of those candy canes instead of this paint-and-rust-eaten carryall?

He looked their way and nodded in approval, his woolly gray head bopping to the beat, but the young men failed to acknowledge him.

An elderly woman with a wispy boll of pale blue hair chose the precise moment the light changed to green to enter the crosswalk in front of them. So he waited. The young dudes in the Juke waited, too, then left a layer of rubber on the blacktop, peeling out the second she passed by.

Thompson eased up on the clutch and the gears scraped, the shift knob shuddering violently in his hand like a mean-ass rattlesnake.

"Come on, baby, work with me," he said, sweet talking the gears into cooperating before they caught and launched the pickup into the intersection. He was wrangling the shift into second when the funk-drenched wah-wah guitar intro to "Papa Was a Rolling Stone" filled the cab. He fumbled around for his cell phone, keeping a sharp eye out for any more blue-haired senior citizens with a death wish.

"Jack? It's Jacob Rubinstein. Got a minute?"

"Not really," Thompson replied.

"What's all that background noise? Are you driving right now?"

"You made any progress on my case?"

He passed the local bank, its Depression-era façade adorned with soaring tableaus of god-like laborers, the deeply etched lines of their stern profiles partly obscured by the array of security cameras hanging off the topmost cornice like a colony of Mexican bats waiting for sundown.

Security cameras. He hadn't thought of those.

"This is a really bad idea," Rubinstein said.

"What's a bad idea?" Thompson said, turning off Lee and pulling up in front of an empty storefront with a LOST OUR LEASE—EVERYTHING MUST GO! sign taped to the fingerprint-smeared window.

"I can't have you driving while talking on a cell phone. Is there somewhere you can pull over?"

"I'm pulling over right now," Thompson said, ramming the shift into first and fishing around in his toolbox for the big flathead screwdriver. "So–any progress?"

"Jack, I told you a hundred times we don't have the manpower to investigate every claim—"

"This ain't about a *claim*, Mr. Rubinstein. Those crooks owe me *three thousand dollars* for three weeks' work I did on that new Malwart's on Highway 51," he said, dropping to the ground and creeping around to the rear bumper.

"Malwart's is the parent company. Your claim is against the subcontractor, Massey-Blankenship."

"I know the damn subcontractor's name," Thompson said, gripping the cell phone so tightly his fist nearly crushed the device. He suppressed the urge to smash the thing on the cement sidewalk, maybe stomp on it a couple of times for good measure. But he kept calm, the phone in his left hand and the screwdriver in his right, as he sank to his knees. With trembling fingers, he guided the tip of the screwdriver into the rusty slot in the top right corner screw and began removing the rear license plate. In case they had security cameras where he was going.

"Then you know the agency laid off two-thirds of our staff," Rubinstein said. "We can barely manage basic oversight, much less launch a full-scale investigation into every claim of wage theft. There are more than a thousand cases of wage theft in Shelby County alone."

"Then you better get started on them," Thompson groused, keeping his voice low. "I'm being evicted! I'm getting thrown out of my own home, you get me? They already cut off the gas! Where am I supposed to go?"

"I thought you were working out a deal with your landlord."

"I was, till he said no."

"It's worse over in Clay County. With the latest round of budget cuts, they just scrapped the agency's whole enforcement division."

"How about the state agency?"

"Don't ask."

"So what am I supposed to do?" Thompson said, aligning the screwdriver with the slot in the top left screw.

"I can send you a list of lawyers who specialize in wage and hour claims—"

"Like some hotshot lawyer's gonna give a shit about me and a lousy three grand."

The license plate slipped from his fingers and clattered to the blacktop with a *clang*.

"What am I supposed to do?" he responded, scooping up the dented metal plate. He got to his feet and tossed it into the cab, breathing heavily into the silent phone.

Finally, Rubinstein made a sensible suggestion:

"Just sit tight, okay, Jack? Don't do anything stupid."

Thompson pulled into the employee lot and parked in the shadow of the featureless concrete slab that served as the rear wall of the Brinkman Building. His stomach felt hot and jumpy, like a bag of microwave popcorn bursting with high-carb projectiles. He clutched the Bible to his chest as he scuttled past the window slits carved into the building's concrete ribcage as if the payroll department's strategy involved hiring a team of Saxon longbow-men to defend the company from hordes of barbarian invaders.

"Looking for someone in particular?" said the receptionist, whose battleship gray metal desk served as the first line of defense against the invaders. Quite a responsibility for a lady with a fluffy pink cloud of hair crowning her tiny head and a plain gold cross dangling from her neck. The nameplate on the desk said "Doris Dupree" with the kind of authority usually reserved for heavy bronze plaques listing the names of the dead on Civil War battlefields and monuments.

"Uh, yeah, I'm here to see Mr. Blankenship—"

"Do you have an appointment?" said Doris, her cold blue eyes evaluating Thompson's wealth and standing through a pair of black-framed cat-eyeglasses. "Mr. Blankenship won't see any-one without an appointment."

"I tried calling, but you folks never answer the phone—"

"You need to make an appointment. No exceptions."

"How can I make an appointment if y'all never answer the phone?"

"I can check his calendar for you right now, Mister—?"

"Thompson. Jack Thompson."

He held the leather-bound Bible at his side, his index finger pressed between its pages marking the passage from Jeremiah, itching for the chance to cut loose and get biblical on their asses.

"Mr. Blankenship has an opening next Thursday at three-thirty—"

"I can't wait till next Thursday—"

"Well, you'll just have to be patient, Mr. Thompson—"

"You know employer non-payment is a crime in this state?" he said, flipping the Bible open to chapter twenty-two of Jeremiah.

She stared at him, her ice blue eyes clashing with the swirl of strawberry frozen yogurt on top of her head.

A muffled sound come through the closed door behind Doris— something like the soft slap of a self-satisfied man closing the lid on a solid cedar humidor full of luxury cigars.

Thompson shoved the Bible under his arm and plowed past Doris before she could fling her body between him and the door to her boss's office.

Bobby Blankenship looked up from the contraband Cuban Cohiba he was lighting with a butane torch, his normally bright pink jowls flushing a deep, smoky red.

Look at this guy, Thompson thought. "Man, all you need is a brandy snifter."

The boss's burst of *What the hell is this* indignation overpowered the secretary's *I'm sorry Mr. Blankenship but he wouldn't listen* excuses.

"So what's the problem with paying me?" Thompson said. "There aren't any old ladies or blind people you could rob?"

"What in the hell you talking about, son?"

"Don't cheat your workers. That's a goddamn commandment," Thompson said, opening the Bible and filling his lungs like a fire-and-brimstone preacher of old.

"He who makes his fellow man work without pay and does not give him wages," Thompson proclaimed, *"shall have the burial of an ass, dragged out and left lying outside the gates of Jerusalem."*

Now that's some old-school justice.

"That supposed to be some kind of prophecy?" said Blankenship.

Thompson shook his head. "Word of God."

Blankenship resumed lighting his cigar and took a few leisurely puffs.

"Can I see that?" said Blankenship, nodding toward the Bible.

Thompson held the holy scripture under the boss's nose, stabbing the chapter's opening verse with a paint-flecked finger:

"Thus says the Lord."

"Well, how 'bout that."

"I'm here to collect the money you owe me."

"Must be a bookkeeping error," said Blankenship, blowing smoke at the prophet's words. "Leave your name and contact info with Doris and somebody'll look into it."

"I ain't leaving without my money."

Blankenship took a long drag on the Cohiba to hide his amusement.

"I worked a string of eighteen-hour days for your company," Thompson said. "I ain't leaving till I get my money, or I'm gonna lose my home, my truck, my phone service—"

"Do you want me to call someone, Mr. Blankenship?"

"That won't be necessary, Doris."

"Go ahead and call the cops," Thompson dared them. "Then we can show the world how it's standard operating procedure for you people to screw your workers—"

"I'll have Doris cut you a check right now," Blankenship offered. "Would that be all right?"

Thompson didn't move.

Blankenship fiddled with his cigar, tapped the ash into a tray much sooner than he should have.

"Look, uh, Mr. Thompson, I can tell when a guy doesn't know if he can put his trust—"

"That'd be fine," Thompson said.

"But I've got an important meeting to get to, so—"

"I said a check is fine, Mr. Blankenship. Sir."

Blankenship froze mid-word, trails of silky gray smoke curling upward from the tip of his Cohiba.

The boss signaled the okay to his secretary who scurried back to her desk, her low-heeled pumps going *clickety-clack* like a perky adding machine. Thompson gave the boss a quick nod, acknowledging their deal, and followed her out.

Doris worked speedily and efficiently, selecting the blank paper forms and aligning them with the tabs, calibrating the settings on the vintage piece of office equipment, and exchanging bland pleasantries with the boss as he smoothed the lapels on his granite gray sport jacket on his way to the parking lot.

Doris slammed the check writing machine's lever down hard, like an executioner's ax. She carefully folded, refolded and ripped through the perforations, waited for the special blue-and-red ink to dry, then handed the check to Thompson.

His eyes had grown weary but the numbers jolted them wide open: $250.00.

"Two hundred and fifty dollars? You owe me *three thousand.*"

Thompson was out the door before Doris had a chance to hand him any more lies. The boss was at his reserved parking spot, taking out the keys to his white Mercedes SL500 Roadster.

The wind kicked up, sending dust flying. By the time Thompson blinked the grit from his eyes, Blankenship had shifted position, standing with his legs apart, the tails of his sport jacket flapping in the breeze.

"What the hell is this?" Thompson said, holding the ridiculous check high and striding forward like an offensive lineman for the Tar Heels taking the field.

"Hold it right there, jackass," Blankenship growled, pulling a gleaming semi-automatic pistol from the folds of his jacket and pointing it dead center at Thompson's chest.

Thompson slowed and held his hands up, but kept moving forward.

"Don't threaten me, boy," said Blankenship, pivoting and firing three warning shots into the rear door panel and cargo bed of Thompson's pickup.

Thompson lunged and got his hands around the warm barrel of the pistol, grappling for control. Blankenship resisted, pulling the trigger several times, making lots of noise and smoke and raining hot brass shells on them like chunks of flaming brimstone as he emptied the magazine into the dried mud at the edge of the parking lot.

When Blankenship discharged the final round, the slide flew back with a heavy *clack*, reducing the deadly weapon to a less deadly assemblage of metal.

Thompson broke his hold and ran to his truck. He jumped in, turned the ignition, yanked it into reverse and pulled out of the spot, jammed it into first and took off, flying past Doris as she stood in the doorway with her hand frozen to her chest in horror.

When the dust settled, her boss said to her calmly: "Doris, call the police."

"Yes, Mr. Blankenship."

Thompson drove in a half-blind vortex of rage and confusion, adrenaline pumping, fear sweat nearly making him carsick. It was bad enough that rich SOB had to wave a loaded pistol in his face but you didn't shoot up a man's truck unless he was screwing your wife and the whole town knew about it. As if Blankenship hadn't done enough to him already. Those shots could have hit anyone if it weren't for him. And God only knew what he would do for the rest of his money now.

He put more than a dozen blocks between him and the gun-crazy madness at the Brinkman Building before he stole a glance at the passenger seat and saw the burnt streak—the undeniable sign that a bullet had grazed the leather cover of the family Bible, that the trusty old volume had deflected a round that may well have been headed for his heart. Before he had a chance to clear his head and think things through, he figured he should at least stop at the bank to deposit the lousy $250 check before the boss got a chance to change his mind and stop it. Or worse.

He was standing in line, filling out a deposit slip, when he heard the sirens.

His body slammed to the ground.

Hands jerked behind his back.

Cuffs on, hard.

Witnesses say they saw him struggling with Blankenship and heard the gun go off several times.

The suspect claims they were arguing over a check.

Check? What check? We didn't find any check.

Let me tell you what we *did* find:

We got his prints on the barrel of the weapon.

We got deliberate removal of the vehicle's rear license plate.

We got bullet holes in the flatbed and rear door panel.

We got gunshot residue on the suspect's shirt.

Correction: *particles consistent with gunshot residue.*

We recovered a weapon at the scene. The suspect's prints are all over it.

Then there's the witness's statement:

I distinctly heard him threaten Mr. Blankenship.

What exactly did he say?

He said, *I'm going to bury your ass.*

Thank you, ma'am, you've been very helpful.

Why are we washing the truck? The forensic team hasn't even gone through the vehicle yet.

Why bother? We've got enough for a conviction.

On what charge?

Aggravated assault. Unlawful discharge of weapon.

I hear they're considering charges of attempted murder.

Yeah, don't worry, we'll think of something.

We always do.

ABOUT THE EDITOR

RICK OLLERMAN has written four novels and is the author of a collection of essays on writing topics as well as paperback original era authors and their works. A second collection is forthcoming. He edits *Down & Out: The Magazine*, and his most recent anthology, dedicated to the memory of 2014 MWA Raven Award winner Gary Shulze, *Blood Work*, was released at Bouchercon 2018. He is working on an anthology honoring the late Bill Crider and among other projects, his next novel, *No Bad Days*, is on its way soon.

ABOUT THE CONTRIBUTORS

Award-winning ex-journalist **CAROLE NELSON DOUGLAS** has authored fifty contemporary and historical mystery/suspense novels. She is the first woman to write a Sherlock Holmes spin-off series and the first author to use a female protagonist. In the *New York Times* Notable Book of the Year, *Good Night, Mr. Holmes*, she reinvented Holmes frenemy Irene Adler as a detective. Going doubly noir, she cast real stray black cat, Midnight Louie, PI, as an intermittent narrator shepherding four pro-am human detectives through thirty-three mysteries. Her books have made national and genre bestseller lists, including *USA Today*. Her writing blends strong women (men too), genres, social issues, satire, and substance. The Café Noir series debut, *Absinthe Without Leave*, is her 63rd novel.

JOHN M. FLOYD's short stories have appeared in *Alfred Hitchcock Mystery Magazine*, *Ellery Queen Mystery Magazine*, *The Strand Magazine*, *The Saturday Evening Post*, *Mississippi Noir*, two editions of *The Best American Mystery Stories*, and many other publications. A former Air Force captain and IBM systems engineer, John is also an Edgar nominee, a three-time Derringer Award winner, a three-time Pushcart Prize nominee, and a recipient of the Edward D. Hoch Memorial Golden Derringer Award for lifetime achievement. His seventh book, *The Barrens*, was published in late 2018. John and his wife Carolyn live in Mississippi.

DANA HAYNES is the award-winning author of eight mysteries and thrillers from Blackstone Publishing, St. Martin's Press/ Minotaur and Bantam Books. He is a newspaper journalist and former political speechwriter. His latest, *St. Nicholas Salvage & Wrecking*, made its debut in 2019 and is the first thriller starring Michael Finnigan and Katalin Fiero. The sequel is planned for 2020. Dana lives in Portland, Oregon, with his novelist wife, Katy King. Find out more at DanaHaynesMystery.com.

THOMAS LUKA was a prosecutor in Miami, Dade County, Florida, during the rise of Eastern European Organized Crime in the late 1990s and early 2000s, with first-hand experience with oligarchs, bratva, Vors, and former Soviet military officers working the shadows between criminals, secret agents, and mercenaries. His novels are fiction, but carefully researched for authenticity and accuracy. Thomas has been writing short stories and novels since childhood.

MICHAEL ALLAN MALLORY is the co-author of two novels featuring mystery's first zoologist sleuth. Lavender "Snake" Jones first appeared in *Death Roll* and returned in *Killer Instinct*, which *Mysterical-E* called "a tale that will enchant you." Michael's short fiction has appeared in numerous publications. He often can be found lurking at SnakeJones.com.

ANGELA CRIDER NEARY is an attorney by day and writer by night. She was inspired to write the first book in her cat detective mystery series, *Li'l Tom and the Case of the Parrots Desaparecidos*, by Telegraph Hill in San Francisco. Her second book, *Li'l Tom and the Case of the New Year Dragon* is now available. Angela has also published short stories in *Ellery Queen Mystery Magazine (January/February 2018)* and *Nine Deadly Lives: An Anthology of Feline Fiction*. Angela lives in California wine country with her husband and their extremely spoiled cat.

LAURA OLES' debut mystery, *Daughters of Bad Men*, was an Agatha Award nominee, a Claymore Award finalist and a Killer Nashville Readers' Choice nominee. She is also a Writers' League of Texas Award Finalist. Her short stories have appeared in several anthologies, including *Murder on Wheels*, which won the Silver Falchion Award in 2016. Before turning to crime fiction, Laura spent two decades as a photo industry journalist covering technology and trends. She lives in the Texas Hill Country with her family. LauraOles.com.

JOSH PACHTER is an author, translator, and editor. His short stories and translations appear regularly in *Ellery Queen's Mystery Magazine* and many other periodicals and anthologies. He is the editor of *The Misadventures of Nero Wolfe* and *The Man Who Read Mysteries* and the co-editor of *Amsterdam Noir* and *The Misadventures of Ellery Queen*. He has been a finalist for the Edgar, Derringer, and Silver Falchion awards. You can find him online at JoshPachter.com.

JOHN SHEPPHIRD is a Shamus Award-winning author, two-time Anthony Award finalist and writer/director of television films. Novels include *Bottom Feeders* and three novellas that complete *The Shill Trilogy*. His short fiction has appeared in *Alfred Hitchcock Mystery Magazine*, *Down & Out: The Magazine* and *44 Caliber Funk: Tales of Crime, Soul & Payback*. He has created both a private eye and police procedural series for the flash-fiction App *Hooked* with over 100 million users worldwide. As director, titles include *Chupacabra Terror*, *Jersey Shore Shark Attack,* and *Teenage Bonnie and Klepto Clyde.*

DEBRA LATTANZI SHUTIKA is a professor at George Mason University. She is author of *Beyond the Borderlands* (University of California Press). Her fiction has appeared in the 2018 Bouchercon anthology and in *Abundant Grace: Fiction by D.C. Area Women.*

JULIE TOLLEFSON landed her first paying writing gig just out of high school, investigating such hard-hitting stories as "Do blondes really have more fun?" and "Does father know best?" for her hometown newspaper. Her short fiction has appeared in *Alfred Hitchcock Mystery Magazine* and several anthologies, most recently *Life is Short* and *Then You Die: Mystery Writers of America Presents First Encounters with Murder.* Julie grew up in the sand hills of Southwest Kansas and now resides in the northeast corner of the state with her family. Find her online at JulieTollefson.com.

TIM P. WALKER ekes out a living in the streets of Baltimore as a legal researcher. When he's not being told he looks like Quentin Tarantino by the bartender for the six thousandth time, he's cranking out the kind of short, sharp shocks that can be found in such illustrious publications as the late, great *Baltimore City Paper*; *Out of the Gutter*; *Pulp Modern*; the NoirCon anthology, *Atomic Noir*; and the newly launched *Rock and a Hard Place.*

ROBB WHITE lives in Northeastern Ohio. Many of his stories and novels feature private investigator Thomas Haftmann: *Haftmann's Rules, Saraband for a Runaway, Nocturne for Madness,* and *Doggerel for Dead Whores. Thomas Haftmann, Private Eye* is a collection of 15 stories. Raimo Jarvi is featured in *Northtown Eclipse.* His latest is *Dead Cat Bounce.* In 2019, he was nominated for a Derringer for "God's Own Avenger" and "Inside Man" was selected for inclusion in *Best American Mystery Stories 2019*. TomHaftmann.wixsite.com/RobbTWhite

KENNETH WISHNIA's novels have been nominated for the Edgar, Anthony, and Macavity Awards, and have made "best of the year" lists at *Booklist, Library Journal*, the *Jewish Press*, and the *Washington Post*. His novel, *The Fifth Servant*, won a literary award in Italy. So he's got to get translated into Italian to win an award? Get with it, America! Sheesh! Oh, yeah—he recently edited the Anthony Award-nominated anthology, *Jewish Noir*, and his novel, *Blood Lake*, a crime novel set in Ecuador, was recently translated into Spanish as *Lago de Sangre*. So there. KennethWishnia.com

MARK WISNIEWSKI's third novel, *Watch Me Go*, was praised by Daniel Woodrell, Lou Berney, Dan Chaon, Salman Rushdie, *The Wall Street Journal*, and the *Los Angeles Review of Books*. More than 100 short stories of his have appeared in venues such as *The Sun, Glimmer Train, The Missouri Review, The Southern Review, The Georgia Review, and Virginia Quarterly Review*; have won a Pushcart Prize; and been chosen to appear in *Best American Short Stories*. He's designed and taught fiction courses for the UC-Berkeley Extension and City University of New York. MarkWisniewski.net

On the following pages are a few
more great titles from the
Down & Out Books publishing family.

For a complete list of books and to
sign up for our newsletter,
go to DownAndOutBooks.com.

Skunk Train
Joe Clifford

Down & Out Books
December 2019
978-1-64396-055-5

Starting in the Humboldt wilds and ending on the Skid Row of Los Angeles, *Skunk Train* follows two teenagers, who stumble upon stolen drug money, with drug dealers, dirty cops, and the Mexican mob on their heels.

On a mission to find his father, Kyle heads to San Francisco, where he meets Lizzie Decker, a wealthy high school senior, whose father has just been arrested for embezzlement. Together, Kyle and Lizzie join forces, but are soon pursued by Jimmy, the two dirty cops, and the Mexican cartel, as a third detective closes in, attempting to tie loose threads and solve the Skunk Train murders.

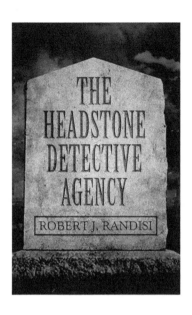

The Headstone Detective Agency
A Johnny Headston Mystery
Robert J. Randisi

Down & Out Books
September 2019
978-1-64396-032-6

Johnny Headston runs the Headstone Detective Agency, at 50 trying to recapture his glory days as a successful private detective, before it was all taken away by one bad decision.

Now he has it back, and is trying to get started again. His first case is a missing persons case, a wealthy woman whose husband just seems to have vanished from his Wall Street stockbroker job. Headston finds the man, who is now living under very odd circumstances, but the missing persons case quickly turns to murder.

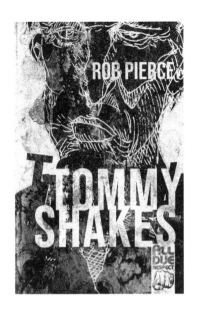

Tommy Shakes
Rob Pierce

All Due Respect, an imprint of
Down & Out Books
September 2019
978-1-64396-034-0

Tommy Shakes is a career criminal, and not a very good one. He earned his name as a heroin addict. He's in a marriage he wants to salvage. He convinces himself that his wife will stay with him if he can bring home enough money. She tells him that won't do it, but Tommy gets a crack at a big heist and decides to pull the job.

The job is ripping off a popular restaurant that runs an illegal sports book in back. A lot of money gets paid out on football Sundays; the plan is to pull the robbery on Saturday night. What can go wrong?

40 Nickels
A Carnegie Fitch Mystery Fiasco
R. Daniel Lester

Shotgun Honey, an imprint of
Down & Out Books
September 2019
978-1-948235-16-7

Carnegie Fitch can be called a lot of things. Ambitious is not one of them.

Months after escaping death in the circus ring at the hands of the Dead Clowns and the feet of a stampeding elephant, he is no longer a half-assed private eye with an office and no license, but instead a half-assed tow truck driver without either. Still, he daydreams about landing that BIG CASE.

Well, careful what you wish for, Fitch.

CPSIA information can be obtained
at www.ICGtesting.com
Printed in the USA
JSHW021628081019
1856JS00002B/6